DARK POOLS

Brian Terry

ABOUT THE AUTHOR...

Dr Brian Terry spent the first sixteen years of his career in the City as a senior executive in two major US investment banks and a UK venture capital company, after which he has had a twenty-five year career as a management consultant to innumerable companies around the world. Brian holds a PhD in Finance from Warwick Business School, UK, and, in his early days as an academic, has lectured and published extensively. He brings to this debut novel an intimate understanding of the major financial centres of London, New York and Hong Kong; the key players, policy makers and institutions involved; and the nuances of the carefully selected locations where the book takes place. *Dark Pools*, while fictional, is an authoritative, well researched, entirely plausible story, drawn from real events happening today. It reflects the political aspirations of China and the ease with which financial markets could be manipulated by super computers to bring about the economic downfall of America.

DARK POOLS

Hēi'àn Chi 黑池交易

BRIAN TERRY

Matador
9 Priory Business Park,
Wistow Road, Kibworth Beauchamp,
Leicestershire. LE8 0RX
Tel: 0116 279 2299
Email: books@troubador.co.uk
Web: www.troubador.co.uk/matador
Twitter: @matadorbooks

ISBN 978 1785890 697

British Library Cataloguing in Publication Data.
A catalogue record for this book is available from the British Library.

Printed and bound in the UK by TJ International, Padstow, Cornwall
Typeset in 11pt Aldine401 BT by Troubador Publishing Ltd, Leicester, UK

Matador is an imprint of Troubador Publishing Ltd

To my Children and Grandchildren, for the joy they bring.

ACKNOWLEDGEMENTS

My sincere appreciation and gratitude goes to the following list of dear friends and colleagues who were kind enough to read and comment on the manuscript as it took shape: Mary, Lucy, Desiree, Beth, Ian, John, James, Mike, Alasdair, Philip, Martin, Steve and Alex. Thank you all for your encouragement and continuous support during the process, it was much needed.

Front and rear cover with kind permission from Paul Bowen, PaulBowen@AirToAir.com.

Inside portrait photo: Peter Searight, TheRemarkableStudio.com

LIST OF PRINCIPAL CHARACTERS

Sir John d'Abo	Chairman of d'Abo Merchant Bank
Anne-Sophie Moreau	Private Secretary to Sir John d'Abo
Lady Isobel d'Abo	Wife of Sir John
Rt. Hon. Charles Sheer	Chancellor of the Exchequer
Alasdair Tims	Board Director at d'Abo Merchant Bank
Sebastian Fortes	Senior Banker at d'Abo Merchant Bank
George	Sir John's driver
Rosalind	Sir John's cook
Lewis Moyns	Vice Chairman of the Federal Reserve
Amanda Price	PPS to the Chancellor
Mackenzie Gore ('Mac')	MI6 & GCHQ
Alison Fletcher	Chairman of the Federal Reserve
Colonel James Sanford	USAF, European Head of SAC
Captain Lynette ('Lyn') Andrews	Special Forces Group (A), US Army
Dwight Mason	Co-Chairman SQT
Bill Burns	Co-Chairman SQT
Dr. Alexander Cadbury	Head of Quantum Trading, SQT
Cyrus Jian ("CJ")	Pro-Democracy Movement, HK
Bain	MI6, London
Reed	CIA Asian-Desk, HK
Sapphire	Companion of CJ
Vice Admiral Farley	C-in-C US 7th Fleet, USS Washington
Mr Seng	Central Bank of Singapore
Chang Jin-soo	Managing Director Daesong Bank
Rt. Hon. Christopher Compton	The U.K. Prime Minister
R. J. O. Chessington IV	The U.S. President
Liú-Sūn	The Chinese President

CONTENTS

CHAPTER ONE

Guangzhou, China, D-22

Deep within the bowels of a nondescript, grey, crumbling industrial building – whose only distinguishing feature was an unbelievably large satellite dish on the roof – the phone burst loudly into life, startling everyone in the room and causing them to instantaneously stop working at their computers.

The phone rarely rang and when it did so they all knew it could only mean one thing: a new assignment. They carried out their duties with exceptional diligence from the dimly-lit basement, slept in shifts one floor above, ate sparsely on food delivered daily by an external catering company, never drank or socialised and were under strict instructions to only refer to each other by their internet tag names.

The four-man team comprised a specialist cell dedicated to industrial espionage and the state-sponsored dissemination of whatever untruths their masters demanded of them. They were young, exceptionally gifted computer programmers, plucked from the very best universities and promised a lifetime of self-indulgent pampering once they had concluded their endeavours. In return, they had to dedicate themselves to whatever tasks were thrown at them, day and night, without question and with total obedience.

Their new instructions were concise, although the leader of the cell immediately appreciated that their execution would be very complicated indeed. They were to conceive of a way to infiltrate

1

the American banking system and, when ordered, be capable of bombarding it with millions of messages, all in the space of a split-fraction of a second. Given the gravity and urgency of the task, they were to be granted unprecedented, indeed limitless, access to the very latest computer the country had developed. Its usual deployment, engaged in deeply complex weather-forecasting, would be put on hold for a few weeks.

If nothing else, this was a massive vote of confidence in their cell. They all felt deeply honoured. Unquestionably, this was a big step up from their usual fare of causing mayhem in the commercial world and they were all very excited and intrigued.

Time was very limited however, so two additional 'very senior personnel' from the computer laboratories at Sun Yat-sen University in Guangzhou were to be drafted into the cell, with specialist knowledge of the banking software systems used by the major US banks. They would be with them by the end of the day and bring further details of 'the plan', its timetable, and new computer hardware to link them with Milky-Way 2, the world's fastest, most powerful, computer. No stone was to be left unturned.

The caller made it abundantly clear that failure would not be countenanced; this was to be their last project together, after which they would disperse and be helped to blend back into normal society and given houses, cars and even a wife, should they wish. The State would look after their every need, providing they accomplished this one task.

The group was instructed to drop everything they were engaged in and concentrate on this single event. They should rest until the new people arrived, then be prepared to work around the clock until they were one-hundred-percent-sure they could achieve the goals set for them. Then, and only then, could they relax.

The new members of the team arrived surreptitiously in the dead of night, with two large trucks and a mountain of equipment to unload and install. It was their intention to use the cover of darkness to set up the new kit and be ready for operations by dawn. Unbeknownst to them however, someone had seen them. He, too, had a phone. Little did the observer realise when he made the call to his controller in Hong Kong, to report the highly unusual nocturnal goings-on, that he too was being watched. In only a few days' time, he would lose his life for the cause he held dear: democracy and free elections.

That was a week ago and, in the intervening period, the newly enlarged cell had accomplished a great deal together. They were, thankfully, gelling well and making exceptional progress. Their familiarity with the US banking system and considerable inside knowledge of Wall Street had enabled the new team to construct a detailed computer model capable of fulfilling their masters' demands.

There was an intense debate about whether they should test it against their own central bank, or possibly against one of the country's smaller banks, but it was decided that a full scale test risked disclosure, so it was to be an all-or-nothing attack. Till then, they would just increase the daily – highly clandestine – interrogation of the target bank's computer systems in New York and London and, as instructed, replicate the procedures a thousand times until they were flawless. They shared a nagging doubt, however, that a thousand times was nowhere near enough for such a momentous event.

Satisfied with their efforts, the cell reported back to their handlers that they were now ready. They would be on schedule, as requested, for 0930 hours and one millionth of a second Eastern Daylight Time in New York on Monday, 22nd August. Given the 12-hour time difference, this meant they would be called into action at 2130 hours China Standard Time, on the 22nd.

Until then, they would wait, exercise patience and run computer simulation after simulation. Glory and clean sheets beckoned.

* * *

The immensely powerful Standing Committee of the Politburo had within its ranks a group of seven belligerent and increasingly bellicose men. Once more they had all secretly gathered, late at night, deep within the labyrinth of the Great Hall of the People in Beijing. After months of planning and scheming, they were about to make a momentous, possible brilliant, possibly utterly catastrophic, decision.

Truculent and pugnacious to a man, the group was hell-bent upon an imperialistic expansion to rival any before experienced in their country's long and turbulent history. To conceal their plans from the President it was unanimously concluded that they would proceed without the normal protocol of passing the subject matter in hand through the full Central Committee machinery: such was their desire for the utmost secrecy in their actions.

The level of contempt around the table for their country's leader and their fellow Politburo members was palpable; confidence in their preparations undoubted; to a man they knew this was not the time for doubt. Now was their moment, a new epoch beckoned.

The pieces on the chess board were at last to be moved from defence to attack. China would once again dominate the globe.

"So, gentlemen, we are in full agreement. We proceed as planned on the 22nd."

CHAPTER TWO

Whitehall, London, D-21

Anne-Sophie put her head around the Chairman's door:

"The Chancellor's Office has just called, Sir John. Can you make a meeting at the Treasury this evening at eight? In attendance will be the Chancellor, Amanda Price his PPS, the Vice Chairman of the Federal Reserve and, although I didn't really understand it, they said some man from 'Six'?"

John glanced up from the papers on his desk and for a moment was captivated once again by Anne-Sophie's incredible beauty and effortless *chic*…what film had the phrase, 'A body like mortal sin', he pondered? Well, that's what I am staring at.

He had been remarkably fortunate to have recently found a new and incredibly competent PA, especially after his previous secretary had been injured in a car crash only a few weeks ago. Anne-Sophie's unsolicited CV had landed on his desk – as if by divine providence – days later, enquiring if there were any vacancies as she would be re-locating to London for the next year.

Parisian-French, effortlessly sophisticated, multi-lingual, impeccably dressed, magnificent references and utterly, utterly desirable; how can anyone accomplish so much and still not be thirty he silently reflected.

"What on Earth is it all about this time, Anne-Sophie? Did they give you any clues? Could you kindly let Charlie know that I will be there. As the Permanent Secretary appears not to be joining us, just double check if it's Chatham House Rules please and should I come alone? Oh and tell George I'll probably need him and the car until midnight; and tell cook I'll pop back for a quick bite to eat before the meeting."

John d'Abo had just turned fifty-six, slim, greying slightly at the temples, always impeccably dressed in Savile Row suits and Hermes ties. He was regarded by those who knew him as the epitome of a 'proper-chap': an unimpeachable family tree, schooled at Radley and Cambridge, a pillar of the old-monied establishment and a member of all the right London clubs, (none of this Bullingdon nonsense, he would remind anyone who wished to know). Most importantly, he was someone who was on first name terms with just about every mover and shaker who was worth knowing in the City, Wall Street and Hong Kong. But much more than that, he was utterly trusted, both in the very inner circles of government and on Capitol Hill, for the tireless work he had undertaken behind the scenes during the 2008 banking crash, for which he received a knighthood, ostensibly for charitable 'good works'.

Following a meteoric and, seemingly, effortless career in the d'Abo family's merchant bank, which had made him even wealthier and astonishingly powerful, he was also gaining increasing international visibility and political clout. He was the personal advisor of choice on some of the largest and most complex mergers and acquisitions in town and in recent years had been gently persuaded to take on various 'below the radar' roles advising the PM and Charles Sheer, the Chancellor, on matters financial. Naturally, he had been at the same school and university as both of them; albeit in a more senior class. No need for the Cabinet Office to do 'due diligence' on d'Abo; he was, and always had been, part of the charmed circle of the great and the good.

He did, however, like many members of the landed

gentry, have a wandering, but regrettably unfulfilled, eye for the ladies; and although he was ostensibly happily married to Lady Isobel, the once vivacious daughter of Viscount North, over the years they had drifted apart. They now lived two parallel but apparently disjointed lives: she on their vast Buckinghamshire estate expanding the arboretum without her husband's constant interference, while simultaneously dedicating considerable time to developing her already outstanding skills in dressage. Her only regret: the lack of children in their lives. He, meanwhile, languished in their South Audley Street penthouse fulfilling, in her eyes, his only vice: making yet more money.

"It will be a confidential, off the record, briefing on some flap or other apparently", she said later, via the intercom, "and the Chancellor has passed on a note saying, 'don't bring that bloody tedious oaf, Alasdair' but you're welcome to bring someone who is security-cleared. He would prefer, and I quote, 'that young chap who worked with you on the bank rescue. He could turn out to be useful'."

"Excellent! Let Sebastian know I'll pick him up from the office at 7.30."

'His' merchant bank was, by modern day standards, a complete minnow, but the senior directors had unrivalled experience and a well-deserved reputation for creativity, integrity and, above all else, complete discretion. The term 'bank' was, of course, a complete misnomer, as the idea of them actually lending any money was considered almost vulgar and best left to the Americans. Founded just ten years after Rothschild in 1820, they specialised in intellectual capital: their stock in trade, brilliant ideas. All they were interested in was the size of their simply unconscionable fees: don't even cross their elegant front step without your banker's draft for five million!

The organisation comprised of only sixty people and had some outstanding up-and-coming, hand-picked stars as junior staff. However, Alasdair, one of the bank's senior directors and Charlie Sheer simply did not get along, following some bust-up or other in the past involving a 'shared' girlfriend, which, being gentlemen, was never discussed again.

The bank's offices were located, nameplate-less naturally, in a discrete corner of Berkeley Square, walking distance from John's flat: although he never, ever, walked anywhere. George, the chauffeur, butler, dogsbody and laughably even, his bodyguard, was now approaching retirement, but had been with him and the family for years. The failure to fire him was his only sentimental action in a lifetime of utter ruthlessness in business matters. George did, however, know how to drive the Arnage with consummate ease through London's horrendous traffic.

"Anne-Sophie, tell George 'five minutes' and can you close the shop down, please? I'm going to nip home shortly and change. There is no need to stay late, but there is a Stock Exchange document here on the oil takeover which requires filing and a copy sending to what's his name in Dubai. Then email me my Middle-Eastern travel schedule for later this week."

The four-bedroom apartment was sumptuous, yet comfortable and filled with magnificent works of art brought over from the estate where they had been meticulously accumulated by past generations of d'Abos. John, by contrast, spent most of his life in extremely swish hotels across the globe so it was, in reality, a multi-million pound crash pad, in use probably on only forty-or-so nights a year. But, for him, it was a place to 'kick off the Church's' and relax, while listening to Puccini.

Rosalind, his brilliant and tireless chef, was a delightful, if somewhat rotund, lady of around thirty five: pleasant enough and unfailingly polite, if at times a little too Eliza Doolittle for his social standing.

"Could you prepare something quick Ros? I have to leave in about twenty minutes."

"I can rustle up a chicken Caesar salad, if that's OK with you, Sir?"

Sebastian always enjoyed the opulence of the Bentley and although his car of choice was a Maserati, they hadn't as yet installed a cocktail cabinet in one. There was something about the Bentley's serenity that put you in the right frame of mind for a meeting he thought, as they discreetly entered Horse Guards Road; something indefinable that instilled an inherent sense of superiority. You had won the negotiation before you had even started the discussions. Yet, on this occasion, neither Sir John, nor Seb, knew what to expect as they walked up the steps of the Treasury.

Although John regarded Sebastian as his protégé, he felt there were one or two rough edges that still required to be smoothed out before he made it to the bank's board, possibly in a year or two. But, hey, he was young, mid-thirties, with black wavy hair that was slightly too unkempt from his point of view. He had, however, been thoroughly blooded under his tutelage in the banking crash and had an air of supreme confidence about him. At the moment, he very successfully ran one of the international corporate finance teams, but more importantly he was the bank's most computer-literate member of staff.

"I'm not having, or wearing, a bloody name badge! If you don't know who I am then don't invite me", snarled d'Abo at the poor chap at the reception desk. Luckily the Chancellor's Parliamentary Private Secretary, Amanda Price, was there to greet them, waive the tedious formalities and usher them into the office where the others were already having a drink and chatting.

"Usual Oban whisky, John? And for you Sebastian?"

"G&T, please, Chancellor".

"Jolly good. Let's sit over here and I'll introduce you to everyone."

The Chancellor's office was the epitome of faded elegance and well-worn sofas. The pictures on display were a roll-call of past incumbents, framed, seemingly forever, on the panelled walls. It was exceptionally unusual for Charles to serve drinks, but on this occasion he felt it appropriate, given the gravity of the situation that was about to unfold.

"Firstly, it goes without saying that tonight's meeting is totally off-the-record, no notes, and classified at Prime Minister and POTUS level: so, as you can probably guess, what is about to be divulged is extremely sensitive. One whiff of this in the market and there will be absolute hell to pay. The events in 2008 will seem like a rounding error. You probably know my utterly indispensable PPS, Amanda and, John, I'm sure you've previously met Lewis from the Federal Reserve?"

John nodded at them both, with his usual consummate ease and grace. He knew Lewis well after working together on untangling the unmitigated mess that was the swaps book at Lehman Brothers. They had grown to respect each other's very distinct style of operating. Lewis was quintessentially Texan, softly spoken with impeccable manners and irreproachable integrity. He had risen slowly, but consistently, through the innumerable ranks at the Fed and had accumulated unrivalled experience: a good man to have in a crisis, John thought, if indeed this was a crisis and not politician-speak for a little local difficulty.

The Chancellor continued, "You won't have met Mackenzie Gore, I doubt. He's presently attached to the Cyber Assessment Centre at GCHQ, but is on secondment from his base at MI6 while we try and sort out this mess. Mac, if you would be so kind."

Mackenzie Gore was most definitely not from the James Bond department, but was uncomfortably thin, professorial in appearance and gait, somewhat dishevelled, with an ill-fitting suit and disproportionately large glasses, which he polished

10

incessantly; as if somehow this would improve his vision of the world and its miscreants. 'Mac', as he preferred to be called, was regarded as one of the world's leading experts in, as he often put it, 'the never ending dodgy goings-on in the banking world'.

"Thank you, Chancellor. I would like to commence my remarks by thanking Mr. Moyns, who came in overnight from the Fed, for the incredible co-operation that has been forthcoming from his colleagues over the past few days, as this matter has begun to unfold in the utmost secrecy. My role in this endeavour is to assist all at this meeting in the technological aspects of 'Our Problem', if I can put it in those terms, working in very close conjunction with the usual agencies, to wit: the CIA, my colleagues in Cheltenham and those by the Thames. In a nutshell, gentlemen and Miss Price, the dollar is potentially under co-ordinated attack, presently in a very discrete, almost undetectable, way, but potentially in an exceptionally destructive 'cascade-into-oblivion' way that could – not to put too fine a point on it – bring the world economies to a shuddering halt. As I speak, we are struggling to get to the bottom of 'who and why', but I will give you my 'first-cut' suppositions shortly. In *simpliciter*, we have very recently detected what we believe is a new way to 'short-sell', and then, by implication, if followed through to its logical conclusion, destroy the dollar."

"By way of background and clarification, you may recall George Soros nearly brought down the UK economy when he shorted sterling in the 1992 Black Wednesday crisis, which came very close indeed to breaking the Bank of England. That was – by comparison to today's matter – a very simple operation in the Foreign Exchange, or FX, markets, completed with speed and making him a mere $10 billion one-way bet. What we are prospectively looking at here is off-the-chart: trillions!"

He gazed, almost blankly, towards a portrait of Asquith hanging on the panelled wall just over the shoulder of the current incumbent of the Chancellor's office and continued, "You may not really be too familiar with another comparatively recent phenomenon in the stock market, namely the concept of the 'Dark Pool'. In these so called pools, shares are bought and sold outside the gaze of the normal market channels – almost as if in total secrecy, under the counter, until the Exchange and the companies involved finally get wind of it – by which time vast profits have been made by a very lucky few. This presently unregulated market is causing the authorities in America considerable trouble, because it unfairly disadvantages those market participants who are outside this merry little club. The techniques of Dark Pools would now appear to have been cleverly replicated in the currency markets, to potentially devastating effect."

"If I may just add a point, Mac?" interrupted Lewis.

Lewis Moyns was the Fed's *de facto* head of banking supervision. The whole sorry mess had landed on his desk less than a week ago, much to the embarrassment and almost shame of his colleagues because they had completely missed it, when someone from GCHQ cyber-crimes monitoring unit dropped the bombshell. To say he was not best pleased would be an understatement, as he was just about to go on holiday with his new trophy wife.

"I cannot stress enough how this needs to be contained and very quickly indeed. Even the major money centre banks in New York, where this is being surreptitiously trialled by parties unknown, have not grasped the enormity of it, but they will. Being the people they are, they will unquestionably try to see if they, too, can make a quick buck out of it. My boss, Alison Fletcher, is meeting with the big three New York banks over the weekend at the Jackson Hole Economic Policy Symposium, which hopefully will not attract undue suspicion."

"Well put, Lewis. To continue: our first line of enquiry is based on our natural mistrust of the Chinese on the world financial stage and their desire to elevate the status of the renminbi, with the unit of currency more colloquially being referred to as the Yuan, to become the world's new reserve currency in place of the dollar. Of course, we all appreciate it's a contradictory position to take, as they hold about $1.3 trillion of US treasuries, which could be rendered worthless if the dollar went to hell in a hand-basket. The boys back at the Fed are therefore wrestling with the question: to China – is this sequence of events a price worth paying to ensure their currency dominates world trade?"

"And the Dark Pools you referred to earlier, Mac, if I may call you Mac?" enquired Sebastian. "How do they relate to the issue at hand?"

Removing his glasses for the third time, dreamily polishing them and staring into space, as if momentarily distracted by the question, he wanted to say that it could, of course, be his other theory, but decided to keep that quiet for the moment and continued:

"Well, Dark Pools are used to buy and sell shares off the market radar. By definition, such transactions are opaque to the general market participant and potentially lack all transparency to our regulators, but they have been around since the 1980s in some form or other and we feel we now have a grip on them. Even though they may well now account for about 50% of all trades on the New York Stock Exchange, we feel confident that we can eliminate the practice, by consensus, eventually. The problem has, however, got worse over the years, as so-called High Frequency Trading computer systems have been able to manipulate the trades, with even more destabilising consequences, so we may have little choice to eventually regulate the problem away."

"And what has this got to do with China?" Amanda interjected.

"Well, Miss Price, some very odd things have been taking place in the dollar market over the past month. As I said,

13

nothing massively dramatic as yet. 'Perturbations', we might call it. However, the key technique used by Dark Pool operators is to interrogate what lies behind a specific pool of shares being bought or sold by a so-called market maker. This is done by sending discrete electronic messages to try and establish if someone is buying or selling; in what volume and at what price: then to make an educated mathematical guess from the feedback they receive, about which way to play the information. If they get it right, they make a fortune. The key is speed: can they execute the deal before anyone else?"

Lewis interjected: "At the Fed, we suspect that this practice has now moved into the FX market and, as you well know, Ma'am, Uncle Sam will not tolerate any such threat to the Green Back. Period! But Citibank, JPMorgan-Chase and Bank of America will definitely smell something fishy sooner or later in their dollar clearing departments, which will need containing, indeed forcibly suppressing if necessary, well away from the eyes and ears of the press."

With a quickening of tone in his voice, Mac continued: "The external interrogation process of these pools takes the form of a neat little trick called 'pinging', where a request is sent, ostensibly to make enquiries about a possible purchase or sale and the counter-party's computer 'pings' back a tiny snippet of data, thereby revealing its hand. If you are familiar with the card game of poker, it's the equivalent of a 'Tic'. No humans involved, note. From that point on, the mathematical algorithms kick in and the bad-guys try and squeeze the other sucker for all they can. Las Vegas on Wall Street, you may say."

He reached for his glass of water and reflected to himself that computers would be the death of us all one of these days.

"The really curious thing is that, in the past twenty or so days, GCHQ has been monitoring these tell-tale pings, but, in the foreign exchange market for the first time. Their volume is growing at a quickening pace; however, as yet, no transactions have actually been executed, so we are lacking real fingerprints, so to speak, which will identify the miscreants. It looks, for-all-the-world, like a precursor to an all-out attack on the dollar, especially as the pings apparently emanate – disturbingly – from mainland China. My chums at Langley have been poring over the data and have identified other 'ping' locations, would you believe, in Iraq, Syria and God help us, North Korea. Perhaps you could just embellish a little on this, Lewis?"

In his usual languid, melodic drawl, Lewis resumed as if he didn't have a care in the world, (nothing could be further from the truth, however).

"Thus far, we have detected only about 100 confirmed inbound pings, which in due course we should be able to give a more precise locational fix on; especially if they continue using the same source and server. Whether it is just some young-buck, techie-bastards trying their luck, we don't, as yet, know. However, given the simply incredible amount and diversity of state-sponsored cyber spying we now encounter on a daily basis, we cannot dismiss the strongly held viewpoint within my headquarters that it's the Chinese in cahoots with goodness knows whom. Our worst-case worry is that it's ISIL, the new Islamic militants, hell-bent on some apocalyptic mission that may now have turned its attention, bizarrely, to the foreign exchange markets. We know they are awash with oil revenues, which they may be putting to other more cunning uses. Given their truly destructive ambitions and what would appear to be an alarming and growing network of supporters around the world, we are giving this the very highest priority."

Sir John sipped at his whisky and interjected, "So why are we here, Charlie?"

"John, my dear friend, the problem is twofold: on the one hand we can use GCHQ's and the CIA's highly-sophisticated techniques to trace the inbound communications. Personally, I have no doubt they will get to the source or sources very quickly, but as you well know, they are very slippery eels indeed which can relocate effortlessly across borders. I hate bloody computers as well you know. The second and far more intractable problem is the pools themselves. We urgently need to know who has set them up, where the hell they are, and indeed, are they the real threat we currently perceive them to be, or just some Wall Street wide-boys on the make?"

The Chancellor got up from the sofa to stretch his legs before continuing.

"John, that's why I have asked you and Sebastian over tonight. You are the very best team in the country to get to the bottom of these damn pools. We need you to drop everything and do a lot of ferreting-out with your banker chums across the globe."

"Very interesting indeed Charlie, but how do you suggest we go about this and what's in it for us?"

"John you're so predictable in matters of money! Thank goodness you're more subtle in other cerebral subjects! You know full well that this is a *pro bono* request on behalf of Her Majesty's Government. We can't afford to have such a large fee running through the Treasury's books. Tony Blair's bloody Freedom of Information Act will catch us in the end. But I'll tell you what: take my well intentioned advice and quickly pass responsibility for the oil takeover you're currently working on to your chum, Alasdair. It's going to fail spectacularly, because we simply won't give it our approval. The bloody Business Secretary keeps bleating on about security of energy supply, blah, blah, blah! You'll need to drop it very soon or find yourself a fall-guy in about a month's time. That's why I know your desk will be miraculously clear, as of this evening and you will be free to assist HMG. But, as a *quid pro quo* for your efforts in this endeavour, I'll throw in a very senior role for your bank when we conclude the privatisation of the Royal Bank of Scotland next year. I've no doubt you'll make a killing in the grey market

16

in the shares before the float, which should more than make up for your efforts helping us! I'm sure the Fed will also think of ways to sweeten the deal stateside; don't you agree Lewis?"

"Sure do Chancellor. I'll discuss it with the Chairman later this evening."

Charles Sheer smiled and with a nod to his PPS added, "Amanda here will act as liaison, so, please direct all priority communications for me, via her, should I not be available. Mac will issue you both with scrambler cell phones. Lewis would like you to visit the States tomorrow and has organised a plane for you, leaving at noon. Meanwhile, I'm now planning also to go to Jackson tomorrow to meet Chairman Fletcher and the heads of a couple of the New York banks possibly under threat. We can meet in New York, in, say, three or so days' time, to discuss progress. All agreed?"

John could feel his blood pressure rising and his *sang-froid* momentarily disappeared. "You're really going to veto the oil merger, Charlie. Jesus; and I thought we were friends! I need to think about this very carefully! My bank's reputation is at stake here. This really is a *fait accompli,* Charlie, I take it? No wiggle room?"

"None whatsoever, John. So, is team d'Abo on board? Admittedly it could all get very messy, but it will be reputation-enhancing John! Something to add to the family crest and all that!"

Taking a long gulp from his whisky John spluttered, "That's six months work up in smoke, Charlie. And, if I pass this to Alasdair and it goes tits-up, it will finish him in the City."

"Couldn't happen to a nicer chap", the Chancellor intervened. "A dish served cold and all that."

John turned to his colleague and enquired, "I'm assuming this is all OK with you Seb?"

"Wouldn't miss something like this for the world, Sir John," responded Seb excitedly.

"OK Charlie, we're in. But, I need a minimum of six weeks before the merger talks get anywhere near collapsing. My board will want written confirmation of our role in the privatisation, shall we say within two weeks? And, to sweeten the deal, I would like a fast-tracked banking licence in the States, please, Lewis. Plus, if you can throw in some US Government work, so much the better."

Charlie responded, "That's all do-able from my end, and I presume you have no objections, Lewis?"

"I'm reasonably confident I can deliver that Chancellor. Sir John has not put a foot wrong as far as my guys are concerned. His track record within the Fed is impeccable. Some of us even like him."

As the meeting came to an end and while a final refilling of the glasses occurred, John took Lewis to one side, "Out of curiosity, I think I know pretty well how one of these pools works in the stock market world. However, how could such a thing take place in the FX world, where you guys watch each and every dollar, no matter where on earth it comes from, or goes to?"

Lewis, who was enjoying his third Jack Daniel's whiskey immensely, took a mouthful of cashew nuts and continued, "In a sense that's both the problem and the solution John. We've become supremely over-confident about our ability to control the dollar, but imagine if you could build up an unseen short or long position in the market, of enormous proportions and only observable in the aggregate to the perpetrators. Then, just wait for the right moment, press the computer button and the market collapses in on itself within milliseconds, as all the holders of dollars get severely burned. I don't need to tell you that any 'fiat' currency, which by definition is not backed by gold, relies entirely upon the confidence of the markets. If that goes, so does the currency. Added to which, if you concoct a political crisis at the same time, provide some credible terrorist danger to the United States and, say China merely threatens to switch out of the dollar; then you really do have a very potent cocktail of problems indeed. That's why we need you to subtly dig into the deeper recesses here, because we are all presuming that, whoever is behind this, China being top of our guess-list, we have to cover all our bases, as it may not be 'the usual suspects'! So I'll wish you and Sebastian a goodnight. I have to go and report to the States. See you both at RAF Mildenhall tomorrow, at noon sharp, please, where we will have a jet waiting for you."

The meeting drew to a close just as Big Ben struck nine-thirty. Charles Sheer summed up the evening's discussion with a simple statement, "I don't know whether we have a tiger by the tail here, but time may well be of the essence. I thank you all in advance for the work you are about to embark on. Let's keep very closely in touch."

Sir John got into the car first. "George, can you drop me at White's for, say, an hour or so, I need to think a few matters over. Then take Seb home to his apartment. St George's Wharf, I seem to recall, Seb?"

"Not a problem, sir. I'll be outside your club at eleven-thirty."

Deep within one corner of the smoking room, John ordered an Armagnac and pondered what he had just heard. Grabbing a pad of paper he started to scribble a few very private notes which he would get Anne-Sophie to type up tomorrow. His first thought was how to untangle the oil deal without engendering 'massive-egg-on-corporate-face'? Perhaps he could pass the deal over to ICBC, one of China's largest banks with whom they were developing a growing relationship, claiming his bank had found itself with an irresolvable conflict of interest. As a result, d'Abos simply had to make arrangements for another institution to step into the breach. Besides which, China may well have use for the oil reserves themselves, so there is a fig leaf of plausibility to the story. He decided that he would send an instruction to Alasdair tomorrow and see if he could pursue that line of thought.

The deal may come back to haunt them, but given the evening's revelations it might be suitably ironic and, in any event, for d'Abos, it was a two-way winning bet. First, he enhances his friendship with ICBC if tonight's problem is a flash-in-the-pan and government-to-government diplomacy could somehow resolve the British concerns over oil security; and, secondly, if it's all true, then his bank has given the Chinese a hospital pass, for which he will be able to gain bragging rights subsequently. The more intractable problem was – where to start with these damn pools? And, he pondered, I really ought to ensure we are not long-the-dollar, but I'll have to be very circumspect in the bank with that information. Perhaps I'll just let all these thoughts wander around the brain while I sleep and discuss it with Seb tomorrow on the flight over?

Later that evening, with his mind still buzzing uncontrollably with how best to play the news he had received earlier to maximum financial advantage, John simply could not get to sleep. As he rolled around in bed, his thoughts gradually and inexorably turned to more enjoyable matters as he wondered, guiltily, if it was too late to get Anne-Sophie to come along on the trip to the States, under some pretext or other and perhaps get to know her and her indescribably long legs, a little better.

CHAPTER THREE

New York & Greenwich, Connecticut, D-20

RAF Mildenhall, in rural Suffolk, is one of the United States Air Force facilities which is often used in covert operations and, to the casual observer, appears as decidedly sinister and menacing. However, on this occasion, when George gracefully turned the Bentley into the airport security cordon, Colonel Sanford was there to greet them personally. As the newly-appointed head of Strategic Air Command, Europe, Sanford, soon to be General Sanford, was a formidable figure, festooned with medals and possessing the cold empty eyes of someone just emerging from the dark recesses of an undercover operation deep behind enemy lines. He would, frequently and with evident relish, cajole his men into incredible deeds of daring-do with SAC's legendary motto: 'Peace is our Profession, War is our Hobby'. He was, finally, but regrettably, moving from 'field operations', where he excelled, to the dreaded 'desk job', where senior command had told him his experience would be invaluable.

The cap under his arm was instantly reset on the almost bald head, a snap of a salute made and a welcoming handshake proffered.

"Welcome to Mildenhall, Sir John. My name is Sanford. Just to let you know that Mr Moyns is already aboard. If you would just follow my sergeant's jeep we will have you airborne within ten minutes."

The Falcon 7X was as sleek a corporate jet as money could

buy. At US$60 million a pop this was a serious executive toy, but, on this occasion, its ownership belonged, not to some industrial magnate or other, but to 'the Company', as the CIA was often referred to. Although, needless to say, it's true ownership was totally untraceable and decidedly off-balance sheet: it was in fact held in one of the impenetrable budgets which Congress allocated yearly to the secret services.

"Hi guys", said Lewis, as he put down some briefing papers, which he had received overnight from his office, on the desk. "Great, isn't she? All yours for the duration apparently, according to the Director! He would like her back in one piece, but just let the guys up front know where and when you want to travel and they will be delighted to oblige. Drink, anyone?"

He motioned John and Seb to sit down in the opulent seats opposite.

"Lynette here is ostensibly in charge of the cabin staff, but don't be fooled gentlemen! She's a fully-fledged Captain in the 7th Special Forces Group, Airborne Division and could kill you with one flash of that pretty little smile", he winked at her, "Ain't that just so Lynette?"

"If you say so, Sir. Happy to be at your disposal on our flight to New York, Sir."

"Sanford thought that you may need some very discreet military support as this matter moves forward. Seb, you may have to work on loosening up Lynette here; she needs a little more time on Civvy-Street, I think. Could you be so kind, Lynette and tell the boys at the sharp end that we are ready to depart? We're flying into Teterboro Airport, New Jersey, so as not to arouse suspicion and I've booked you rooms at the Carlyle for the week, which from memory, you prefer."

Over a languid and decidedly liquid lunch together, ostensibly served by Lyn, (they were now more-or-less on first name terms, although she was at pains to tell them that if they must drop the 'Captain' formalities that her rank deserved – and she would demand under normal circumstances – then she much preferred Lyn to Lynette), they bandied around who they should meet with and in what order. By the time they landed, Alison Fletcher would already have had meetings with the big banks to discuss what, if anything they knew, so there would be an update waiting for them on their arrival. John conjectured out loud, "What if the bankers knew nothing?"

What then should his team do first? Alison had initiated discussions on the banking side, but board directors in major banks, let alone chairmen, rarely know anything within their organisation at the micro-level. Why should they? It could take ages to get a sensible reply.

John broke away from his thoughts, "Perhaps we can go up to Connecticut and check out a few of the bigger hedge funds. Would that be OK with you, Lewis? If anything devious is going on, these gentlemen will surely have a finger in the pie somehow."

Lewis moved the fruit bowl and took a sip of his coffee, "Goodwood Capital Partners may be the place to start, John. I know the top guys there well and we could concoct some story about your new banking licence, new deals you have in the pipeline they may wish to assist with, *et cetera*, and we can quietly slip the real purpose of the visit into the conversation over lunch" replied Lewis. "Oh, and we should also visit Saturn Quantum Trading to get some insight into what's new in computer-generated trading."

"Excellent suggestions, Lewis, especially SQT. Can you make the arrangements? I think we also ought to visit Jackson Hole, if time permits. I've lost track of when the conference finishes. Can you check that as well, please?"

The Falcon came smoothly and effortlessly to rest on runway One Nineteen and they slowly taxied to the private-jet terminal. Out of the window they could see the magnificent Manhattan skyline, glistening in the distance. Disembarkation took all of two minutes and they were off into the city in some unfeasibly large limo, driven by a rather large chap named 'Tag', apparently – another service provided by 'the Company'. They were also accompanied by Lyn, who had now changed into a demure blue suit and white shirt, so as to be utterly indistinguishable from a million others in and around Mid Town or the Wall Street district. Except, of course, she had a rather menacing, fully-primed, 9mm Glock 27 beneath her jacket.

Seb cast an approving, even lustful, eye over Lyn and reflected, 'She is quite some lady, but I wouldn't like to mess with her on a dark night'.

The drive to the Carlyle, located on the Upper East Side, was the usual snarl of traffic, honking horns and steam emanating from the street vents, compounding the heat of a late summer afternoon. It is the hotel of choice for the more traditional, even old-fashioned guest, if for no other reason than it is comparatively small and very well-located. Everyone there, from the bell-hop upwards, seems to know your name within five minutes of arriving. Needless to say, John had stayed there many times before and was very well known indeed.

"Welcome once again, Sir John." The deputy manager at the concierge's desk lowered his head to look at the computer screen, "We have four suites reserved for you and your colleagues. Let me see: Mr Lewis Moyns, Mr Sebastian Fortes and Miss Lynette Andrews and you will be staying for a week, I gather. Is that correct, Sir?"

"Absolutely", said John before addressing the group and decisively telling them, "I'm going to spend a quiet night thinking, so I'll meet you all at breakfast, say, 7.30am. Then we can make arrangements to visit Westport." They all nodded perfunctorily and strolled casually to the elevators and their rooms.

Lewis turned to John and, speaking to no one in particular,

said, "I'm just popping into the office for a 'SitRep' and see whether the chairman has made any progress."

Taking advantage of John and Lewis' movement away from the desk, Seb took Lyn gently by the arm and cheekily asked, "Would you care to have a nightcap or stroll before we turn in Lyn; say at The Top of the Rock?"

To his delight and amazement she said "Yes Seb, but only on the basis that you understand that I don't want you wandering the streets of the Big Apple alone! Let's meet downstairs in twenty minutes."

Given it was a beautiful, balmy evening, Seb slipped into his favourite chinos and polo shirt and headed to the lobby. What he saw took his breath away! Lyn truly was an all-American beauty out of uniform: five-feet-four, short blonde hair in a bob, incredibly toned body and legs, wearing a royal blue pencil skirt and closely-matching silk shirt. Her skirt stopped three or so inches above the knee and her shirt was just sufficiently unbuttoned to reveal a modest amount of perfectly tanned cleavage. The phrase 'pocket rocket' would not leave his head for hours.

"My God, Lyn, you look absolutely tremendous. Let's grab a cab."

"Not so fast, Seb! Security procedures dictate absolutely no walking, taxis, cabs, horse drawn carriages, or anything remotely similar. Tag is on call 24 hours a day and is already outside with the limo. Oh and for the avoidance of doubt and, please note, the categoric abandonment of English chivalry, I exit the hotel first. Any sign of trouble move straight back inside, please."

The two-mile drive from the hotel to the Rockefeller Centre took them down Fifth Avenue, running parallel to Central Park and lasted all of ten minutes – with not a bad guy in sight thought Sebastian. The conversation was light-hearted but inconsequential.

At the entrance, Seb suddenly realised that you needed

tickets to get to the top of the building and, given what a glorious evening it was, the queue was stupendous. Lyn simply produced two tickets from her small purse and, as if by magic, they were whisked onto the next elevator! 'How the hell did she arrange that in twenty minutes', he wondered. The views were, of course, breathtaking with a million no, ten million, lights twinkling from every building up and down Manhattan. He wanted to prick himself to see if it was all a dream, with this simply stunning girl at his side. Bliss!

As they gazed in awe at the views, Seb continued, "I suppose I should give you a quick *résumé* of my life's story Lyn as we may well be working very closely together for quite a few weeks if all this proceeds further. Where to start? I'm thirty-four, single, have two brothers and am half Spanish, half English. My father came to the UK about twenty years ago and, prior to retirement was a Professor of Spanish Literature at King's College, London. My mother still works as a director at the Royal Shakespeare Company, specialising in highbrow drama. I've been a banker at d'Abos from the day I left university, where I read English and Spanish, obviously. I live in central London with an apartment overlooking the Thames. Oh and they tell me I don't have too many bad habits!"

"Well, being Texan, Spanish goes with the territory. That's possibly why Colonel Sanford and Mr Moyns allocated your case to me", replied Lyn. "As for me, well, I'm twenty-eight, been in the army for ten years, the last few in Special Forces, mostly single. I just relish the daily challenge of being exceptionally fit. I was born and raised on a farm just outside Fort Worth, love horses naturally; was engrossed in ballet as a young girl and, unsurprisingly, wished my daddy had a few oil wells, but alas no, just the ranch."

"I think we are going to get along famously, Lyn. Let's go to the bar and have a drink before turning in."

They went just around the corner of the Rockefeller complex

to 48; a suitably discerning, upmarket bar to adjourn to at that time of the evening and known to Seb from a previous visit a year or so ago. "Sensational cocktails here, Lyn," as they settled snugly into a banquette, perhaps a little too closely for what was not even a first date, where a definite bolt of electricity flashed between them as their hands briefly touched. "Two Manhattans please, and if you've got it, use Noah's Mill Bourbon; my friend swears by it."

Lyn passed a very approving look directly towards him; one of those looks which says: great choice for a Brit. "I gather we are going to Connecticut tomorrow for lunch", she continued. "The plane is available; it's too far to drive there and back comfortably and it gives us more flexibility. Lewis hasn't called me yet, but I'm assuming we will leave the hotel around ten thirty."

"Good, then we have a few hours to kill! They do great nibbles here, the mini Cuban sandwiches are highly recommended! Let's get a couple."

The waiter quickly brought a small selection over, placed them neatly in front of them and silently left. As Seb gestured to Lyn to try one, his arm accidentally knocked his napkin off the table. Bending downwards, his hand descended unthinkingly to the floor to pick it up, when he inadvertently placed it for a fleeting moment on her upper thigh and was jolted backwards in total surprise.

"What on earth is that?" he exclaimed, "Surely it's not…"

"Small arms protection, Seb, the inner leg is the best place to keep it warm when you have a small purse."

In open-mouthed amazement, he moved his hand down to feel it once more. To his delight, it was not taken away. Lyn looked at him and smiled with such openness, he was convinced she was allowing him to linger there longer than was strictly necessary. She leaned closer to him and whispered, "Move your hand one inch higher and something may explode."

"I think it already has," he replied, red faced and decidedly flushed.

"If it weren't for your green-brown eyes and beautiful hair, I think I may have no option but to kill you with my bare hands, Seb. Strictly against regiment rules to allow anyone to fiddle with your pistol! But you'll appreciate I can't easily take it off at the moment. I can see already you may be quite a handful", she smirked.

"I'll have to buy you a bigger purse", he spluttered, before taking a long swig of his drink.

On the way back to the hotel, the ice well and truly broken by now, Lyn's phone rang. It was Lewis who asked to speak to Sebastian.

"I've just spoken to Alison after her meeting with the guys at Jackson. She said they had no idea about any of this – which is hardly surprising frankly – but they will all make internal enquiries tomorrow and get back to her. So I don't think it will help any if John were to go down there, unless something new turns up. You can probably unearth more here."

Over breakfast they concluded that SQT might prove to be the more valuable meeting, but Goodwood Capital was an excellent place to start. The schedule was phoned through to the plane by Lyn and would take the team to Westport for lunch and Greenwich for dinner.

Goodwood ran a simply enormous fund, with over US$80 billion under management and, by definition, had financial fingers in virtually every pie there was, almost anywhere in the world. Lewis knew the senior partners well. Lunch was perfunctory and business-like, but frankly and regrettably not much information was obtained and they all left somewhat dejected.

"Maybe we will have better luck this afternoon at SQT", said Lewis as they headed back to the jet to fly the short distance to Greenwich. "Shall we stay overnight? I could book us rooms at the Delamar, by the harbour, which you might enjoy?"

John agreed, "That probably makes sense, Lewis, just in case there is a need to move on pretty quickly tomorrow."

SQT, or 'diddly squat' as they were affectionately called by competitor and friend alike, was the misnomer of the century, given that the two senior partners were now billionaires many times over, thanks to their top secret pursuit of Quantum Computing. This enabled SQT to develop much more sophisticated procedures, or algorithms, to manage the funds under their control, thereby ensuring they topped the league tables every year for the world's best performing hedge fund. These techniques were also being developed simultaneously at Langley and the National Security Agency, in an endeavour to use computing power to unlock the most complex encrypted files – which the spooks encountered on a daily basis. If they could be electronically unlocked, they would produce untold riches and knowledge for the espionage community. Members of SQT's highly-regarded technical team were, therefore, strongly encouraged by the US government to develop Quantum Computing, providing they scrupulously shared information and any breakthroughs they uncovered. As a result, over the past three years, they all co-operated very productively with the security services and met regularly to collate new developments. Another high-level government delegation visiting the SQT offices was, therefore, almost a daily occurrence.

"Sir John, we're very pleased indeed to see you and your colleagues and thanks for making the arrangements to visit us, Lewis. I think we may have met before, in '08 or '09, possibly, in DC?" Dwight Mason opened up the meeting, while sat next to Willard (call me 'Bill') Burns in the company's boardroom. From two of the very best East Coast families, they had graduated from Yale together and started SQT in their final year. Greatness and unimaginable wealth clearly beckoned from day one, as they rapidly outsmarted the market on innumerable occasions and the dollar bills just kept rolling in. Bill and Dwight were inseparable friends, patriots to their very core, as the preponderance of US flags in the boardroom testified – now sitting at the very top of the pile, as co-chairmen of SQT.

"What can we do for you?" said Bill and Dwight, almost simultaneously.

"Could you kindly drag Alex from the depth of his dark burrow, please, Bill? He may be able to unravel a mystery for us?" Lewis, from his position within the higher strata of the Fed, knew the incredibly brilliant Dr. Alexander Cadbury extremely well. Their work together on the so-called 'Flash Crash of May 2010' SEC Enquiry – when 'high frequency liquidity providers' withdrew simultaneously from the US stock market resulting in a 1,000 point drop in just 30 minutes – which, when published, was to start a furious debate on Wall Street. Their joint report, while controversial, focused the spotlight on the simply staggering power of today's super computers; the so-called trading technologists who ran them; and, critically, their almost desperately conceived 'Race to Zero' – the holy grail of being able to conduct a trade to 'buy-or-sell' a share in a nano-second, literally one billionth of a second.

Giving him his customary bear-hug, Lewis exclaimed, "Alex, you son-of-a-gun, great to see you! Guess what, we could be up the proverbial shit-creek again without a god-damn paddle!"

"That's what I like about you Lewis, you old cowboy, a spade is always a fucking shovel in your part of Texas. What's hit the fan this time?"

Lewis stood up to introduce Alex to everyone. "Sir John d'Abo here is over from England at the express invitation of the US Government. It's a matter of vital national security, so I'd be very grateful if you could extend him your full courtesy and usual perceptive wisdom. Any leakage of information from this room and Captain Andrews here will come by real soon and kill you all with her bare hands, won't you, honey?"

Lyn smiled and added, "I'm sure Dr Cadbury and his distinguished colleagues are more than well aware of the need for complete confidentiality and secrecy, Sir."

Lewis continued, "Sir John is heading the small team assembled here to get to the bottom of a breaking development in the foreign exchange markets. It is an almost parallel process to the Dark Pools found within securities trading, but on this occasion it's being directed straight at the heart of the dollar by forces and parties unknown. Our colleagues across the pond at British Intelligence have detected a series of so-called 'pings' into the trading floors of a couple of the money centre banks in New York. It was pure fluke to have spotted it, as a result of tracking some hoodlums from ISIS in northern Syria. Now that they have fully focused the guys at GCHQ on the issue, they have started to see a small but growing pattern emerge. Highly discreet computer interrogation, out of the blue, by a single ping of, say, Citibank's dollar position; but no execution of a buy-sell trade, so the bank itself has not been alerted to it as yet. This interrogation is spreading to the other banks and may well, and I do stress 'may well', be a precursor to a coordinated assault. So, in a nutshell, we are here Alex to see if you have come across this, what your views and those of Bill and Dwight might be and whether you can help us figure out what is going on." He paused, somewhat theatrically, "Before it's too late!"

"If you can pass over the relevant data Lewis I'm sure my two bosses here will let me spend some time looking through it", said Alex, while gulping down yet another double espresso.

"Fine by us, eh Bill? If those commie bastards in Moscow think they can mess with us, then...."

"Our information suggests it's the Chinese", interjected John, "but I will get our technical chap, Mackenzie Gore, to send you anything and everything they have. Chairman

Fletcher and the UK Chancellor are meeting again later today, or possibly tomorrow, at Jackson, so we may have more to say in due course. Meanwhile, any theories, ideas, conjectures?"

"It's times like these that I wish I hadn't been forced to give up my beloved pipe", reflected Alex, "always helps the concentration no end. I'd be delighted and intrigued to look into this further Sir John. Are we working to a deadline?"

"My instructions are that this is what I believe you chaps call a 'clear and present danger'; or in my terms, our feet may be getting awfully close to the fire."

"Don't you just love the wonderful example of English understatement Dwight? Our nuts are in the wringer and their feet are hot!" Everyone simultaneously laughed, which broke the tension somewhat.

"We probably need a day or two to peruse the data before we have a considered opinion," noted Bill, "but if you guys are staying over tonight, maybe we can buy you dinner, Sir John? I've still got a couple of bucks left on the credit card to spend before Armageddon?"

"That would be excellent. We intend to stay at the Delamar. Shall we book a private dining room for say 7.30? Come casual. It will give us more time to chew this over in a relaxed atmosphere." They all nodded politely and the meeting languidly broke up into little groups enabling everyone to properly introduce themselves before the team left for the car.

Lewis, who, by now, was reluctantly beginning to take on the role of head concierge to the party, proceeded to cancel the Carlyle and make all the arrangements during the ride back to enable them to effortlessly check in at the new hotel. Meanwhile Lyn phoned goodness-knows-whom, to ensure their rooms were swept, secure and the guest-list checked.

"OK, guys", Lewis interjected, "we have a table booked at the private dining room of the L'Escale Restaurant for drinks at 7.00, dinner at 7.30. See you all anon. Seb, can you get in touch with Mac to send over the data files to Alex; and John, could you see if you can raise Charles to establish if he has arrived in the States yet? Meanwhile I'm going to speak to Langley and see what's new."

The palatial dining room overlooked the simply stunning Greenwich harbour. The sun was by now low on the horizon, glistening off the sea and the door open just enough to let in the evening breeze. In the distance the evocative sound of the clanking of the halyards against the masts and the hustle and bustle usually associated with busy harbours. No one outside seemed to have a care in the world. Little did they appreciate what was brewing on the financial horizon!

Bill and Dwight arrived together in classic country club attire, to be greeted by Lyn, looking immaculate in a long, off-the-shoulder white dress, very little make-up and just a hint of pale pink lipstick. Alex joined them five minutes later, with a sheaf of papers under his arm, directly ahead of John and Sebastian. Immediately they all began a very animated conversation over cocktails.

Lewis was the last to arrive, looking decidedly rattled.

CHAPTER FOUR

Greenwich, Connecticut, D-19

"I've just come off the phone with Alison", remarked Lewis in a somewhat staccato tone, "Charles has arrived and they have already concluded a quick, initial meeting with the big three banks. From what I've just been told, I fear we may have a perfect storm brewing here."

Silence fell across the room. "In just over two weeks' time, or to be more precise, on Monday, August 22nd, there would appear to be a confluence of events in the foreign exchange swap markets which has been overlooked. Central banks in several countries, notably Brazil, Japan and Singapore have to simultaneously roll-over many billions of dollars of forward currency swaps and derivative contracts on the same day. Normally this would be a formality for all concerned and easily coped with in the markets, with replacement swaps being put in place. However, there is going to be an exceptional, indeed extraordinary, volume of activity taking place on the 22nd which the markets may have difficulty dealing with in one day. Alison and Charles estimate the number at around half-a-trillion dollars, involving over 200,000 swap contracts, which may lead to a systems failure somewhere in the chain. Just suppose all the test pings we are getting are building up to coincide with this timetable; and indeed exploit it by creating an unprecedented level of disruption in the markets. It could trigger a meltdown similar, as you will recall, Alex, to the Flash-Crash, only a thousand times worse."

"Hell's teeth," spluttered John, "unwinding the swaps book at Lehman's was an unmitigated bloody nightmare which took years. Even though the eventual losses were not great, because the book was more or less in balance, the disruption it caused was simply incredible. If your supposition is correct, Lewis, we do indeed have a potentially serious problem on our hands; and the roll-overs on the 22nd could be the ideal cover to mount a covert attack on the dollar. Presumably, though, the Fed can start making contingency plans for the possible market disorder?"

"It's already being looked at," replied Lewis, "but it reinforces the need to act with all possible speed to get to the bottom of who, and what, is behind the pings. We may only have a matter of days. The Chancellor has arrived and asked if you could join him in Jackson ASAP to have a 'confab', whatever that is. Alex, can I ask you to dig a little deeper into who might have a computer system capable of a massive, coordinated assault on the FX markets. There can't be that many super computers around. Also, can you put yourself in their shoes and see if you can come up with an idea of how they might undertake such an attack? Ask yourself the simple question: how would you do it?"

Alex put his bundle of documents on the table, which was set for dinner, and said, "It can only be the Chinese, Lewis; it must be them, after all no one else has access to that level of processing power. The word in Silicon Valley is that China's Tianhe-2 supercomputer, or as we say in the trade "Milky-Way 2", has now hit 50 petaFLOPS a second."

Simultaneously, John and Lewis furrowed their respective brows, while silently thinking, 'What in God's name are you talking about'? "Sorry guys, let me rephrase that! Technical jargon for it goes really and I do mean, really, very fast. Warp speed. They ostensibly say it's being developed for weather-forecasting and climate research, but it would take no time at all to switch its output to bombard the FX market with zillions of sell-orders. It's a stupendous machine. We're all very jealous."

With a semblance of colour returning to his initially ashen face, Lewis was now in full flow, firing instructions at all concerned. "With your permission John, can I task Sebastian with a trip to Hong Kong? We need someone nearer the centre of gravity if this does blow up. Take Lyn. We'll make arrangements for John to be suitably accompanied while he's in the States. And Dwight, Bill, could I kindly ask you to think about ways the Fed may be able to mitigate the effects of the upcoming roll-overs? Can we pre-empt them in some way? Is there anything we can do in advance to lessen their impact?"

Everyone nodded in agreement at their allocated tasks. They sat down to dine, although no one seemed to have much of an appetite. Sebastian enquired of Lewis, "Shouldn't I go to Shanghai or Beijing? I'm sure I could be more effective there?"

"Don't think that will be necessary at this stage Seb; but you may possibly find yourself there later, depending upon events. I also took another call from the boys in the CIA earlier this afternoon, who have been putting their collective wit and wisdom to the problem. They have a line they would like you to follow with an embedded contact of theirs from the pro-democracy campaign in Hong Kong. I'll brief you tomorrow, when I get another update from them. If you don't mind, they would like you to leave around noon?"

Lyn and Seb were, by now, sat very close to each other, engaging in animated discussion about the upcoming trip, while everyone else was engrossed in conversation with their immediate neighbour. Lyn was mentally running through a check-list of critical security items for their trip to Hong Kong, a place she had never been to before. Her bailiwick was the Middle East, where she had been involved in endless fire-fights with the insurgents over the years. Meanwhile, Seb's mind was buzzing with an unexpected opportunity to get to know Lyn much, much better.

"Great that we are teamed up together!" He smiled directly into her iridescent blue eyes, somewhat too lustfully, "Did I hear Lewis correctly; that I'm under CIA orders to, what was the phrase he used, 'take you'? Very thoughtful of them!"

She leaned over to get even closer to him, the intoxicating smell of Coco Noir drifting upwards from the drops she had dabbed on her cleavage earlier. Pheromones raging, she very, very discretely handed over her spare room key to him. "It would be against my sworn oath of allegiance to the Commander in Chief to defy the CIA, Seb. One hour only, then back you go. I want to make sure you can still walk in the morning," she winked, provocatively.

Dinner drew to a close, with Alex, who was almost nocturnal on such occasions when he was asked to think deeply about a problem, saying he had to go back to the office and quietly meditate until inspiration hit him. John, meanwhile, stayed with the others on the balcony for one last glass of the Wolffer Merlot, the much sought-after and highly-regarded 2000 vintage produced nearby, before calling it a night; allowing Seb and Lyn to discreetly depart, unseen, for the lift. "See you in five minutes" he whispered in her ear, while ever-so-gently biting it.

Lyn slammed her door shut behind Seb, pinning him against it, gripping his hair with both hands while kissing him ferociously. "Undo my dress!" she said insistently, as if there were no time to lose. Gulping for air, he grabbed the zip and, with one practised movement, tugged it downwards to the small of her back. The purple lingerie was an utter explosion of femininity as his eyes and then his hands devoured her taut frame, causing an incredible surge of animal lust to rush through both their bodies in response. His eyes, like her nipples, were out on stalks. Within sixty seconds they were naked, clothing scattered to all parts of the room. At her express insistence, they rushed, pell-mell, to the shower, without a word being uttered. The powerful jets scattered water and steam across their intertwined bodies as they made love against the glass with such ferocity he could hardly breathe. He had never had such a shattering climax in his life.

She grabbed two large bath towels, wrapped one around herself and draped the other tightly around his neck, and pulled him forcibly towards the bed. "My God" whispered Sebastian breathlessly, "you are insatiable, deliciously and utterly insatiable", as she literally flung him onto the bed and straddled him.

"This is what you get for trying it on with a Texan girl Seb. If you survive tonight, next time I'll wear my spurs!"

"Does this pain in my chest mean I love you Lyn darling, or that I'm in imminent danger of a heart attack?" he spluttered, through a very wide smile. He rolled her over onto her back, passionately kissing her breasts, shoulders and neck. "Time I took control of the situation Captain-fantastic", as he moved to lock her arm firmly above her head, her blonde hair glistening against the pillowcase, with no resistance being offered to his powerful grip. "Now for some good old Shakespearian, the beast with two backs!"

Twenty frenetic minutes later they separated momentarily, exhausted. Then, like magnets, they were immediately intertwined once more, intimately staring at each other, like new lovers do; no one else in the world mattered, no one else existed. The only thing they needed at that moment was to be as physically close to each other as possible.

"You really do like to be in command, Lyn; I like that in a lady. I've never, ever, seen such a fabulous body: strength and delicacy blended to utter perfection."

He started to kiss her once more on her perfectly flat and taut stomach, as he moved his tongue lower, "Special Forces Airborne Group's delicious landing strip, here I come."

"You haven't enquired where my gun is Seb", as she moaned uncontrollably. "It's under the pillow and if you have not gone to your room in five minutes, I may well have to whip it out and shoot you."

"Five minutes it is Captain…incoming."

★ ★ ★

Dawn broke on a delightful midsummer's day; all could very easily be well with the world thought Seb, as he dressed, grateful that no one would see the indentations in his back where Lyn's fingernails had been. Breakfast of scrambled eggs, crispy Canadian bacon and freshly squeezed orange juice was eagerly consumed on the terrace by both Lyn and Seb at 7am sharp. Contented smiles beamed across their respective faces as they chatted aimlessly with each other, awaiting John and Lewis to join them at the table.

"Glad we are all here, I've had quite a flow of messages overnight", said Lewis. "Firstly, Mac and his team at GCHQ have identified many, many more pings in the last twenty-four hours and think they are confident enough to have established a locational fix on them by the end of the day. Langley is on the case as well. Getting a fix, however, doesn't tell us who is doing this and to what end. We still need more detective work on our side. I hope that John and I can make some progress on this when we visit Jackson later today. Alex also called to let me know that his team will start to write some computer code today to try and replicate whatever it is the bad guys are up to and reverse engineer it."

Seb added, "Well, we are ready for the flight at noon, if that is still the plan?"

"Indeed", replied Lewis, "there will be a briefing paper available by the time you depart. In essence, its Langley's view that, if China is behind this, then maybe, and I stress just maybe, we could thwart them from the inside via the pro-democracy movement's contacts within the country. It goes without saying that the US and, indeed, the UK Governments want Hong Kong to remain a free, essentially capitalist bastion and buffer against Chinese imperialism – but the whole region is a powder keg. We've also noticed in the last few days – which may be coincidental – that they are once more building up a significant military and naval presence in the South China Sea, in an attempt to annex the Spratly Islands. You will recall this is the dispute for the oil and gas rights between China on the one hand and the Philippines, Malaysia, Brunei, Vietnam and Taiwan on the other; it's all getting very tricky and could explode at any moment into a major regional conflict. From what I have seen of the first draft of the briefing you are going to get later Seb, the CIA's view is that a destabilisation of the currency markets could be just the cover for them to attempt to forcibly take control of this part of the world. You'll appreciate their actions are entirely in contradiction with the laws governing the continental shelf, which give a country rights to 200 miles from its shores. China is 1,400 miles away, so their aggressive posturing is entirely illegal; not that they give a damn."

"The only news I have to add is directed more towards Sebastian really," said John, "and its small beer to be honest. It's an update from Alasdair in London. Overnight, the Chinese bank, ICBC, has agreed to take over the oil merger financing from us. He said they acted as if they knew about our decision to pass it over to them already, which is curious. No negotiation, no bartering, just, where do we sign. Very out of character! They normally pontificate for weeks before making a definitive pronouncement. Maybe we ought to check our security processes again, Lewis. I just wonder if we have a leak somewhere."

"That's a never-ending concern John. The other item, worthy of a bizarre footnote", he continued, while the others busied themselves with coffee, "relates to traffic coming in from ISIS. I gather they may very well have got their hands on half a dozen Airbus 320s which, would you God-damn believe it, have – and I quote – 'gone missing from Libya'. Stolen from Tripoli International Airport by the terrorist group Libyan Dawn! What the hell is the world coming to? Apparently, so Colonel Sanford tells me, we are now on Defcon 2, in preparation against a repeat of 9/11."

"Must be time for a cup of green tea all round then Lewis....kept the Empire functioning for decades in a crisis," quipped Seb, far too light-heartedly he realised, judging by the expressions on people's faces. "My apologies everyone, I assure you my mind is focussed on Hong Kong and marching to the sound of gunfire", even though in reality it was to something, someone, far closer to hand.

"So, John, you and I depart for the delights of Wyoming at 2.00 this afternoon, with Seb and Lyn leaving for Asia at noon. Time differences are going to make communication problematical between us, but the indomitable Amanda Price, and her colleagues at the Treasury in London, tell me she is available night and day to forward messages and assist in any way she can be of help. Please use her as a secure link between all parties."

With that, breakfast broke up and everyone went to their respective rooms to pack and prepare for the journey ahead.

CHAPTER FIVE

Jackson Hole, Wyoming, D-18

On the Gulfstream G550 down to Jackson Hole, Lewis and John sat for a long time in silence, reading notes from their respective organisations and governments, while sipping the occasional glass of champagne. Anne-Sophie had called, but simply left a message asking if John could call her back when convenient. After a couple of hours of concentration on other matters, he unfortunately had forgotten all about returning the call.

These CIA boys certainly know how to live, thought John. If this were reversed, Lewis would be freezing his nuts off in the back of a Hercules transporter. Given the number of banking 'road trips' he had been on, criss-crossing the world in the past twenty years with his clients, he had come to appreciate how effortless it was to move around the States – in considerable style, it must be admitted – from one regional airport to the next. Try doing this into Heathrow on a busy Friday night!

Although you occasionally got something worthwhile out of these grand symposiums, John found them tedious in the extreme: a never ending flow of central bankers, policy makers, economists, academics, finance ministers, G7 leaders, even the odd Vice Chairman of the Federal Reserve. Precious few laughs, not a deal to be had, or a buck to be made, anywhere. Just what was the point of these gatherings for someone whose sole interest was 'doing deal'?

Given his acknowledged position in the rarefied world of international finance, John had been on the guest list since the early 1990s, going every couple of years or so, giving the odd speech, pressing the flesh. Although because of other commitments he hadn't been for the past five years, this time it would be different – not the usual self-inflicted fiscal or interest-rate emergency to pontificate on, but, yet again, another possibly catastrophic banking crisis. The unfolding events put him in his element, where he excelled, where he mattered! The adrenaline was beginning to rise: the passions stirring again, just like the old days.

"The note I have here from the UK Treasury, Lewis, suggests that the Chinese are indeed up to something. Amanda Price has learned from her counter-parties in Hong Kong that various rallies and demonstrations currently being planned to disrupt the Central Business District are going to be seriously crushed by Beijing. Mercilessly, it says here! The dates, ominously, are set for the second and third weeks of August. No leniency is going to be shown. Riot police are already being surreptitiously drafted in from the mainland. She reckons it could be a major showdown and the perfect pretext to seriously disrupt the financial markets; which such an event would precipitate anyway. I'm not sure if Seb has been copied on this, but just in case can we see he receives it, please?"

"Not a problem John. Pass it over here and I'll have it sent to their plane immediately: where's Lyn, when you need her?"

"It's all starting to form a pattern," Lewis pondered, out loud. "Political disruption, public disorder, sabre rattling by China's navy, something entirely devastating brewing in the financial markets. Whatever happens, someone is going to pay a massive price here and it better not be us! Who the hell is running the pools, John? It must be, can only be, the Chinese central bank. Have the guys in the Politburo decided to make one massive bet with their dollar reserves, aimed at us, but also against themselves? It's quite unfathomable. This could turn into a life or death struggle in the FX markets, assuming we are correct. Or are we just being sucked into our own conspiracy theory?"

They were on their approach to Jackson Hole Airport, when Lewis received a call from Alison Fletcher. She was a tough, no nonsense New Yorker. Every word she uttered in public was measured, precise, and never, ever, capable of misinterpretation. She was, without question, the most powerful woman at the Symposium – maybe even in the world – and took her responsibilities immensely seriously. She and Lewis made an excellent team: he was exceptionally sociable and full of Texan bonhomie; while she had a reputation for being taciturn and severe. In a crisis they complimented each other perfectly.

"Lewis, I have set up a private meeting at 5.00 tonight. Important people. Just checking you will be here?"

"Sure will, I think we land in fifteen minutes."

"Excellent! Bring John d'Abo please. I've organised you to have rooms at the Lodge."

"Hope you didn't have to throw a few of the Chinese delegation out of their quarters for us, Alison?"

"Not at all, I have a modest amount of influence here Lewis! See you shortly."

Both John and Lewis had been to Jackson many times, but its breathtaking beauty never ceased to overwhelm the emotions. The Grand Tetons mountain range was as spectacular a sight as you could witness anywhere in the world. Mount Moran glistening, snow topped, in the distance; Snake River in the foreground and just over the horizon Yellowstone National Park. You could spend a lifetime simply looking at the view and enjoying, indeed, revelling in the panorama: and if you liked skiing or fly-fishing, well this was seventh heaven. Such a tragedy that the bubble might have to burst soon!

Why do Americans 'de-plane', thought John? Whatever

happened to 'disembark'? They were soon in the terminal, which, he noted, was new since he was last here, and a big improvement. It was a shortish drive in the waiting limo, another 'Company' service, to the Jackson Lake Lodges where they were to stay for at least a couple of days.

Lewis had yet another sealed document waiting on the back seat; this time ominously marked, 'Top Secret': quite a while since I've had one of these, he thought. Opening it up, he saw it was from Colonel Sanford and was brief and to the point. He was just about to read it to John, when he decided to close the interconnecting window between the driver and themselves: you never know, he reflected.

"Sanford says the following. 'The Joint Chiefs of Staff have issued a directive from the Pentagon at 2300 hours last evening. They are increasingly convinced that August 22nd is a pivotal date. I would ask you to move with all urgency. Assuming they are correct, we are at D minus 19 today. Am flying to the Philippines tomorrow to join the SAC Asia command team aboard the Washington. Will liaise with Mr. Fortes and Captain Andrews on their arrival in Hong Kong'. End quote."

"I don't know what response is more appropriate Lewis, good grief; Jesus Christ; or as you might put it, Holy Shit!"

"Let's get checked in and go find Alison", gestured Lewis, as they exited the car and headed for their rooms in the Lodge.

The Chairman of the Federal Reserve was always the principal guest at the Jackson Symposium, ever since Chairman Volcker elevated the status of the get-together in 1982 by deigning it with his presence. Then and indeed now, the tone of the conference was frugal, austere even, most decidedly off-the-record and, ostensibly low-key. Fed officials would however frequently use the occasion to hold secret meetings to galvanise their response to whatever was the latest turmoil and corral the other heads of central banks and finance ministers to follow their lead.

Alison Fletcher was responsible for the keynote speech on the last evening's newly-introduced formal dinner, scheduled for tomorrow, which had, of late, been an opportunity to signal a change in Fed policy; or to be a rallying call to follow the lead set by the United States in whatever was today's problem. The Friday-night event was, by comparison to the casual nature of the preceding week's events, the only sumptuous and official get-together during the week. She had several draft speeches prepared by her staff and would pick the version to be used later, once she had the opportunity to gauge the mood of the delegates. On this occasion however, she was in a quandary as to which direction to go: either the standard fare, where she would discuss the Fed's new policy relating to relaxing their quantitative easing programme – slightly less of the same she would say, which was far from controversial – or to be more radical and present a review of her vision of what may be a forthcoming series of global financial and geopolitical shocks. Was this wise, or a dangerous approach which could prove incendiary? She mulled the matter over in her private rooms and wondered whether she ought to discuss it with the Oval Office, on the basis that the 'worst case scenario' may be better coming from the President himself?

There was a knock at the door and in walked John and Lewis. "Madam Chairman, a pleasure to meet you again," said John in his best, deeply resonant, 'knight of the realm' voice reserved for such occasions. "We meet in interesting times, as the Chinese are wont to say."

"Not the phrase I would have used in the circumstances Sir John, but it's nice to have you here. We have a lot to discuss, and quite a collection of people to meet. I gather that the military top-brass believe something serious is brewing. The Fed shares their view, as does your government. The Chancellor will join us in about an hour. He's presently in a meeting with EU finance ministers."

Alison gestured them to sit on the terrace overlooking the Willow Flats with the Tetons as a glorious backcloth and ordered some coffee. "To ensure we are all on the same page, if I may, I would like to share my thoughts with you both. First, I intend not to discuss any of this with the Chinese delegation; the matter is still conjectural and highly contentious. I do, however, feel I can raise the worry we have regarding the August 22nd swap roll-overs with the countries concerned, but again in private. Please don't be offended, Sir John, if you are not invited to some of these meetings at this delicate stage; to do so would arouse suspicion, I feel." He nodded, sipped his coffee, and politely waved his hand to gesture as if to say, please continue I'm not in the slightest bit affronted.

"Instead, I would like formally to announce this evening that I have personally appointed you to become my Special Advisor for International Market Stability, with a very loosely defined timetable to report to the Fed's Open Market Committee in due course. In that way you have immediate credibility and access to all our organisational resources and a calling-card to enter any central bank office anywhere in the world. Charles Sheer suggested the role yesterday, which we agreed to immediately. I hope that meets with your approval?"

"That would be an honour, Madam Chairman. Perhaps you could staple the invitation to our new banking licence", John responded, more than a little tongue-in-cheek, to uproarious laughter from Lewis.

"I'm quite sure that matter is well in hand already, isn't it Lewis?" She turned her head towards him, causing Lewis to nod rather too energetically. "Good, now to the business in hand. Just so that you are aware, the Fed's technical specialists have been in communication with Dr. Cadbury from SQT, so that he is now formally in the loop and security-cleared. We, at the Fed, are now fully linked up with Langley, the FBI, the NSA and GCHQ to investigate the source of the inbound interrogation of the dollar desks at the three principal US banks.

My supposition is that the People's Bank of China, the PBOC – which acts as China's central bank – would endeavour to mount a massive 'sell' of their dollar assets, by effectively dumping their reserves into the market. If that is correct, and for the moment I am assuming they are indeed the culprits here, then I think we may be able to introduce a series of circuit-breakers into the process to stop it stone dead before they do any real damage. This is almost tantamount to an act of war, so the President will have to be informed once – and only once – we have positive evidence that we are not going crazy here."

"And the swap roll-overs; can we do anything to mitigate that, Alison, assuming I may still call you by your Christian name, given my new role within your organisation?" said John.

"Of course! Good heavens we've been through enough problems and crises together; but thank you for asking: very gallant."

'Did she just blush', thought John? Alison was not conventionally beautiful. Attractive certainly, elegant certainly, with never a hair out of place. She always reminded him of the famous quote by Francois Mitterrand of Margaret Thatcher: 'she had the eyes of Caligula and the mouth of Marilyn Monroe'. The eyes, unquestionably, he reflected; not so sure about the mouth!

She continued, "We will have an initial meeting with the delegations from Brazil and Singapore later tonight, then Japan tomorrow once I've had the opportunity to gauge the first two countries reactions. I've asked Charles to join us under the pretext that sterling may also be vulnerable under such circumstances, and we could all benefit from your government's experience of 1992, when Soros gave you such a fright. Besides which, a lot of these rogue trades may well be cleared via banks located in London. I've booked a conference room for 6.30pm."

The meeting broke up, with John going to his room to freshen up after the journey, while Lewis stayed to chat further with Alison. When John entered his room, the telephone light was flashing with a message. He pressed the relevant button to see who had called. "Hello Sir John, Anne-Sophie here again. I'm just about to leave the office, but I've just received a call from ICBC about the merger. They need reassurance on a couple of points apparently. They asked if you could call. Hope the trip is going well, we are all missing you. Don't hesitate to call me at home if you need anything."

'I wish', he thought, almost out loud! Then, 'Jesus! In all the excitement I've forgotten to call her back! I wonder what pretext I can conjure up to get her out here'?

CHAPTER SIX

Hong Kong, D-17

On the flight over to Hong Kong, Sebastian and Lyn spent the afternoon switching effortlessly between outrageous flirting and very serious discussions about the classified briefing paper they had received from the CIA.

The document ended with the summary, which Lyn read out loud: "We would therefore like you to meet with Cyrus Jian – please address him as CJ, which he prefers – a very prominent member of the pro-democracy movement and a senior banker at Morgan Stanley. He has been an asset of ours for many years and as you might expect, is very 'pro' the United States, where he studied at MIT and Cornell. His underground network of contacts on the mainland is exceptional, particularly within the Ministry of Finance and the major banks. Be especially careful, however, as we know he is under constant surveillance. It is also our belief that his life is under permanent threat. We will make all the arrangements for you to meet. If anything is going on in China, he will surely know. Tensions are escalating very quickly, so, please be assured that, at all times, you will benefit from the protective umbrella of our good selves and the British security services – both agencies in Hong Kong are fully aware of your imminent arrival."

"Oh well, that's good to know," said Sebastian, "I've never been so well-protected in my entire life!"

"Better not be flippant Seb. We are, after all, quite probably heading into the lion's den here."

The plane descended effortlessly into Ted Stevens Anchorage International Airport for a refuel stop, which provided them both with the opportunity to clear their heads and to get a breath of the cool Alaskan air from the airport terrace. As they were taxiing to the stand, the senior pilot came onto the intercom to let them know that they would be on the ground for approximately fifty minutes, and that the next leg of the flight should take around 10 hours 40 minutes, assuming no weather issues. The stewardess gave them a dinner menu to peruse and let them know that during the short stop, she would reconfigure the back cabin of the aircraft for the next leg of the journey.

They were very soon back in the air for the overnight segment of the flight and thoroughly enjoying the sheer opulence of the plane and lavishness of the hospitality being shown them.

"I hope this is not the Last Supper, Lyn?" Seb commented jovially, after eating one of the finest rib-eye steaks imaginable. "You are going to absolutely adore Hong Kong. It's a magical place and in my humble opinion, far more exciting than New York. But let's hope it's not too exciting!"

Over the cheese-board and one of the most excellent Pouilly-Fumés he had ever tasted, he continued, "I gather we are staying at The Peninsula. You will not believe the views across to Hong Kong Island in the evening, especially from the ladies room! And I presume you've banned us from travelling to the hotel in one of their Rollers? Security concerns, and all that? Pity, because they generally put a bottle of champagne in the back: the very best way to get the trip off to a bang I've always found!"

"Not necessarily the words I would have chosen, Seb, but if that's what you want, I'm sure it can be arranged. Now I'm going to undress for bed. I gather we have a closed-off bedroom compartment at the back. You never know, be a good boy and you may get lucky!"

Sebastian slipped between the silk sheets, with the smile of a consummate scoundrel who had more than won the jackpot, to be greeted passionately by Lyn's welcoming arms. "Let's pray for a spot of turbulence as the evening progresses" he whispered. "I hope you are wearing your seat belt, Lyn", as his hand slid lower, "we can't have you bouncing up and down unduly now, can we?"

"I've told you before, Seb, if you don't obey my every command, I have my handcuffs ready for deployment at the first sign of trouble. In fact, to avoid any shenanigans, I may as well just place them on you right now."

"Quite the contrary, Lyn, darling. It's my turn. Our wonderful policemen have a very appropriate saying when they restrain a villain – You'd better come quietly!"

"Then, you would be wise to place your hand, gently, over my mouth, as that's the last thing I will be doing."

★ ★ ★

The business-jet centre at Chep Lap Kok airport is always exceptionally busy in the morning as a steady stream of the world's most talented businessmen and women fly in for, what seems to the outside observer, a never-ending series of meetings and transactions. Hong Kong positively fizzes, from sunrise till the middle of the night, with the raw adrenaline of commerce flowing through the very fibre of every person, in every office, on every street corner. The dollar is king; revered, fought over, even venerated! For the first-time visitor it is an intoxicating Oriental city where cultures collide; for those who frequent it a great deal, it is a mystical, unique, place to do business. Lyn, being completely new to Hong Kong, initially thought they would fly into the military base at Shek Kong Airfield, but after an embarrassing, but light-hearted discussion with the flight deck, quickly realised that it had changed hands from the RAF to the People's Liberation Army Air Force way back in 1997. The pilots prudently opted for the more conventional entry point, while she made a mental note never to make that kind of mistake again.

Their suitcases were carefully placed into the enormous boot of one of the hotel's Rolls-Royce Phantoms, always painted in the obligatory green of the company's colours. The liveried driver politely bowed and beckoned them into the very welcoming air-conditioned cool of the rear seats. She had, indeed, thoughtfully ordered the champagne, noted Sebastian with a wry smile, while he poured two glasses. The partition between them and the driver had been closed for their privacy, but it didn't stop Lyn noticing the driver looking at them intently and, on getting into his seat, immediately making a phone call. She presumed it was to alert the hotel of their arrival, but what she called her 'danger-antenna', flagged something else. 'Always trust your instincts' her Army tutors had instilled in her, a hundred times a day: they will serve you well. She put the thought to the back of her mind, for now.

The Peninsula is located in Tsim Sha Tsui, Kowloon-side, as the locals say, and is one of the finest, indeed oldest, hotels in town, having been *in situ* since 1928. There are many spectacular, much newer, hotels in Hong Kong, but none have the grandeur of 'The Pen', even with the relatively recent addition of The Tower. Lyn had reserved a stunning Harbour View suite, with two enormous bedrooms, so as to ensure they were always in close proximity, although from the moment they were first alone in Connecticut, they had hardly been out of each other's sight and reach.

Despite the opulence of their journey they still felt jet-lagged, so they decided to take a nap on arrival and make contact with their CIA liaison officer when they came to later in the day, probably, they presumed, in the early evening. Seb asked the reception desk for a wake-up call at six pm, and hung the 'do not disturb' sign on the door, although neither had regained sufficient stamina for further hanky-panky.

After showering and dressing in very lightweight clothing, Lyn decided to make contact with the States, just as the sun was setting and the lights of the skyscrapers on Hong Kong Island were beginning to blaze into the night sky. However, given the time-zone differences she failed to reach anyone, so left messages, asking for any updates to be encrypted and emailed through to her or left on Seb's secure phone.

As she was familiarising herself with the local landmarks on the hotel's map, there was a rather insistent ring from the doorbell, which Lyn moved quickly and athletically across the room to answer. As she opened the door, there, in front of her, were two very intimidating men indeed. She was just about to spring backwards to grab her gun from the coffee table immediately behind the door, when they identified themselves as part of her protection squad.

"Jesus, guys, you nearly got yourselves shot there", she said, clearly still startled, "perhaps you can call me first, next time?"

"My profuse apologies, Captain Andrews. Please forgive us. I'm Bain and this is Reed, who is a colleague from the CIA's Asian-Desk, while I'm from MI6, London. Just so that you are aware, our instructions are to take orders directly from you, while keeping surveillance at a suitably discreet distance. Is Mr. Fortes here?"

"Yes, Seb's probably still dressing. Come in, please."

Bain continued, "We gather you want to meet Reed's contact, CJ, which he is more than delighted to facilitate. He's currently off-island, Manila we gather, back tomorrow. He has made arrangements for you all to have lunch at The China Club, in The Old Bank of China Building. It's a beautiful structure, all pre-revolution art deco. We both thought, given the circumstances, there was a suitable irony in his choice. It's festooned with drawings and photos of Mao! You may have heard of it. It's Sir David Tang's place just across the harbour in Central; it will take you all of ten minutes to get there. We have arranged for a car to be here for you at eleven-thirty. Meanwhile, assuming you have recovered sufficiently from your flight here, can we show you and Mr. Fortes the town?"

"Be delighted. Seb, come and meet the muscle!" she shouted as he emerged from one of the rooms, definitely looking the part in his cream-coloured linen suit and pink shirt. "These good gentlemen are Reed and Bain, I'm sure they have Christian names, but we haven't got that far yet; probably never will. They are going to show us the very best places to have a drink in town, aren't you guys."

"Excellent!" responded Seb. "Let's all go to the Ozone Bar first. You may be fascinated to know that it's probably the highest bar in the world, Lyn, certainly in Honkers. 118th floor of the Ritz Carlton, very snazzy! You'll love it, assuming you don't suffer from vertigo, which I doubt very much?"

"Been here before I gather, Sir? Do you prefer we call you 'Sir', 'Mr. Fortes', 'Sebastian' or 'Seb'?"

"Anything you like chaps, but Seb is just fine. And yes, Hong Kong is almost a second home to me. I've been lucky enough to have been involved in quite a lot of banking work here in the past. But every time I come back it's changed, so a refresher course would be most welcome. I've still not forgiven the planning authorities for knocking down the hotel where they staged The World of Suzy Wong and replaced it with yet another marble and glass tower block called the Luk Kwok Hotel, I believe. Where's the charm in that. What is the world coming to? No wonder there is revolution in the air."

"We'll use one of the hotel's cars; it's only five minutes to the Ritz-Carlton," said Bain. "May I use your house phone to make the arrangements?" Lyn nodded and they all made their way to the lift. When they got into the Mercedes, she noticed it was the same driver who brought them from the airport, but said nothing.

The lift to the Ozone Bar was so quick it made your ears pop, but the views of Victoria Harbour and the Peak were a breathtaking compensation. The iridescent deep blue lighting of the seating area and bar made the whole ambiance exhilarating, even otherworldly. Lyn turned to Bain and said, "Can you check out our driver tonight? Don't you think it's a bit too much of a coincidence that he drove us from the airport earlier, and then he is on duty tonight? My instincts tell me he's watching us, but maybe I'm being a little over sensitive?"

"I'll get one the guys in the office onto it. Now, what would you like to drink? The cocktails and Asian tapas here are simply incredible." Bain slowly panned the room to check out their fellow guests and concluded they all looked entirely normal, if not exactly reputable. He recognised a couple of high ranking members of the Triad community, but they were here with their mistresses, so he assumed would have no interest in trouble and the resultant publicity. He relaxed.

"Does Reed ever speak?" Lyn enquired.

"Not a lot, do you Reed?" he smiled, "Taciturn chap, but great in a dog-fight!"

Over drinks, they discussed the impending street marches, scheduled for a couple of weeks hence, as part of the 'Occupy Central' movement. It was quite clear from the undercover work of both agencies, that they were anticipating a great deal of civil unrest and violent protest, which, they all agreed, was to be met with decisive force. Putting to one side any issues in the foreign exchange markets, this was all heading for a major showdown, with the pro-democracy movement hell-bent on resisting Beijing's will to impose its own choice of leaders on Hong Kong. It was going to be a stormy few weeks and to the extent that they could, it would be beneficial to have their meetings and get out quickly. Bain commented that CJ was an exceptionally gifted individual, who under different circumstances would quite probably be running the place, but "Don't be fooled by his charm, underneath it he's as ruthless as the communists he despises". Around 11pm they decided to call it a night and agreed they would meet for a full debriefing session after the lunch at The China Club.

Sebastian whispered to Lyn, "Exactly what I had in mind, although possibly of the 'silk' variety."

★ ★ ★

They arrived at the restaurant exactly as the Noonday Gun was being fired miles away at Causeway Bay, which was on the agenda to visit if they ever had a moment. What a contrast to the bar last night thought Sebastian. The decor was much like that in one of the stuffier London clubs, but exquisitely oriental and packed to the hilt with interesting *objets d'art* on every surface and wall. They were directed by the *maitre d'* to a banquette in a quiet corner of the dining room, where CJ was already sitting.

"May I introduce you to my trusted companion, Sapphire? I thought it may seem less conspicuous if we were four for lunch."

As with many people in Asia, it is often difficult to estimate their age. This is especially so for 'Gweilos', Cantonese slang for foreign devils, but Sebastian guessed he was in his late thirties, and his girlfriend, assuming that was the correct term, was a couple of years older. While CJ would not be out of place in any boardroom in the world, in his perfectly tailored suit and tie, Sapphire was wearing a simply stunning lemon-coloured Cheongsam, the traditional Chinese silk dress, with a high neckline and a slit at the side typically going all the way to the upper thigh.

"I had a longish meeting with the dynamic duo before you arrived", said CJ, "so there is no need for us to linger on the preliminaries. As you are both well aware, we are fighting for a cause that many of us who live here hold dear: the right to self-governance under the 'One Country, Two Systems' philosophy we thought we had all agreed to in 1997. However, that promise seems to have been relegated to the trash-can, along with endless others and we now face what is an overwhelmingly strong opponent, totally intent on destroying us."

"Fully understood CJ," replied Sebastian. "As you know our mission here is focused on the strange events in the foreign exchange markets that our respective agencies are monitoring. If you can assist us urgently with that, we would all be most grateful. I'm sure you don't need informing that your rally on Saturday August 20th could be just the pretext the Chinese need to mount a destructive attack on the dollar."

CJ took over the conversation, "It's been clear to me for some time now that there is a Kamikaze element in the Central Committee, with at least half a dozen senior members of the Politburo agitating for a trade war with the West. They seem hell-bent on causing trouble, no matter what the consequences. From what I gather, you would like me to make enquiries to see if they have established a technical team to undermine the US dollar; and see if I can get to the bottom of their motivation. The latter may be easier than the former. I've already instigated an RFI, sorry, request for information, from my guys in the central bank. Be warned, however, that, if they do stumble upon something big and anyone in Beijing gets a sniff that they are digging into something, then their lives are well and truly on the line. I am proceeding on the basis that your superiors will do their utmost to protect them – and indeed, me – should that be necessary?"

"You can be assured of that", said Seb, not really knowing if his reply was a true statement, or just hot air.

"Good, let's eat", responded CJ, enthusiastically slapping Seb on the back.

As lunch drew to a close, CJ was handed a note by one of the waiters, which he read with an increasingly furrowed brow. Without explaining, he abruptly got up to go. "I'll leave my business card at reception, so don't give a moment's thought to the bill. Time may be more precious than we think. I'm holding a low-key party on Lamma Island tonight; my junk leaves the Yacht Club at 6.30. I'd be delighted if you could join us. And, please, let Batman and Robin know that they are most welcome as well. Shorts and T-Shirts highly recommended; it will be very, very casual and laid-back. Just friends and a few business colleagues from the office."

CJ left the club with indecent haste, almost slamming the door behind him, leaving everyone at the table concerned and perplexed as to why.

CHAPTER SEVEN

South China Sea, D-16

The helicopter carrying Colonel James Sanford to his new temporary command hovered precariously above the pitching deck of the aircraft carrier, the USS George Washington, strategically positioned some one hundred and fifty miles due north of Sabah, off the Malaysian peninsular. The vast ocean territory that comprised the Spratly Islands lay directly ahead, although, given the early morning sea mist, visibility was decidedly poor and the swell uncomfortably heavy until you got your sea legs in a day or so.

One of the flight deck commanders saluted Sanford after the helicopter's engines were shut down and said, "Welcome aboard Colonel, I'll escort you to your quarters. Hope you had an uneventful journey, Sir? Vice Admiral Farley would appreciate your presence in the ward room at 0830 hours for a senior staff briefing."

"Good to see you again, Jim", said Farley, "I'll introduce you to everyone in more detail later over dinner this evening. Welcome on behalf of the entire crew. Let me say it's great to have the newly appointed and very distinguished head of Strategic Air Command Europe temporarily on the team. We can now also enrol you as an honorary member of the Tonkin Gulf Yacht Club, as the 7th Fleet is sometimes called by its many illustrious veterans. No doubt one of these reprobates will try and get you to sew an insignia onto your sleeve at some point. Oh and take my advice Jim, avoid the initiation ceremony at all costs!"

Farley had the navy running through his blood and that of his entire family, who had served their country with honour, stretching back years. His father and grandfather were both destroyer captains in the Second and First World Wars respectively; but over his thirty years of service, he had risen to become C-in-C of the 7th, and now commanded a truly formidable task force of over 80 ships. Although softly spoken, with impeccable manners, it would be a fool who underestimated his remarkable intellect. Everyone in the Pentagon knew that when it came to strategic warfare, there was no one more cunning or more unconventional than Farley. He had a gift, not unlike a Grand Master at chess, to out-think and out-manoeuvre anyone he encountered in the endless war games they loved to play in Virginia. He had operated in Asia for the past ten years and had engaged in endless cat and mouse games with the Chinese, whose presence was, everyone agreed, a growing danger to regional stability. However, in his mind, things were beginning to get rather precarious and increasingly unstable.

"Gentlemen, as you may be aware, back in August 2012, the Senate reacted in a measured tone to China's unilateral assertion that it intended to control a large swathe of the South China Sea – with the Spratly Islands being at its core – by declaring that this was contrary to International Law, and violated the principles of normal dispute resolution. Neither do I need to remind you of the strategic significance of this specific part of the world within the context of our remit here in Asia. The Chinese have reclassified these seas as a 'core national interest', putting them up there with Taiwan and Tibet: meaning they would be prepared to fight over it, should they deem it necessary. The technical guys reckon that there are around 20 billion tons of oil and gas reserves under the waters here, which to put it into perspective, amounts to about twice the size of the reserves held by Kuwait – and we all know what happened there. In anybody's book, that's one hell of a big prize." Farley stopped his staff briefing momentarily to take a sip of coffee.

"Oil reserves are currently being exploited around Palawan, some 500 miles north east from our current position, which now supplies around 15% of the Philippines' requirements each year. Needless to say, the government in Manila regards these reserves as inviolate: they unquestionably belong to the Philippines, who will state quite forcefully, to anyone who will listen, that they have an unfettered right to exploit them. To add to the complications we face, the Chinese are now embarked on a more covert strategy. They are surreptitiously building artificial islands all over the Spratlys, which we can only presume is a precursor to establishing permanent sites from which to exploit the hydrocarbons in the nearby areas. By inference, if this continues for any length of time at all, they will then claim territorial ownership. Our orders are to stop this development, using whatever means possible, short of a firing solution."

Using a pointer, Farley drew everyone's attention to the large regional map of the area displayed on the wall behind him. I have also identified the Scarborough Shoal here, which again is the focus of a major territorial dispute between the Philippines and China; and which marks the northern boundary of the squabble at present. As you can see, the scale of the disputed territory is simply enormous."

He continued, "There has also been an unseemly tit-for-tat in the cyber world with hackers from both the Philippines and China leaving menacing messages on government and university web sites, threatening all manner of retribution if challenged. In the context of what I am about to say, this is schoolboy stuff. The real issue – and the one on which I want you all to focus – is that 'Satellite Intel' suggests that China is moving to reposition its comparatively new aircraft carrier, the Liaoning, once again into the South China Sea. It's been in dock for a couple of months, for a major refit, but thankfully the battle group they have deployed to protect it is, by our standards, comparatively small. However, the Liaoning has recently been kitted out to carry the Shenyang J-15 and possibly the J-31 fighter aircraft. But, as you will all readily appreciate, now that we have the F-22 Raptor stealth fighter deployed on the Washington, we outgun them many, many, times over. Nevertheless, they would appear to be heading our way. Consequently I am repositioning the nuclear sub, the USS City of Corpus Christi into theatre, just as a precautionary measure."

Farley picked up his papers and finished the briefing with what, to Sanford's ears, was a rather ominous note: "Our best estimate is that they will get here around midnight on August 18th/19th, so I want you all to brief your respective teams and bring them up to full readiness. Combat manoeuvres mode; codename Intrepid Guard. Thank you gentlemen, that will be all. Dismissed."

Sanford approached Farley as the meeting broke up, "Could I have a private word, Admiral?"

"My quarters in say 15 minutes, I just need to address a couple of matters with Flight Control on the bridge. Ask the chief steward to show you where they are."

Colonel Sanford was shown into the Admiral's room by the flag officer who was located in the outer office. He could not hide his surprise at how spacious it all was, compared to his Spartan billet in Suffolk. Rumour had it that Mildenhall would close soon and the speculation was that his new command headquarters would afford him considerably more legroom. But for someone who had spent his career in the field, more often than not in very unpleasant circumstances, a comfortable office was in his mind a distraction and not something to covet.

"I'm not sure if you have been briefed on the significance of the date, Monday, 22nd August, Admiral? Part of my assignment here is to liaise with our security agencies in Hong Kong regarding the probable disruptions to the financial markets on that date. It is the Federal Reserve's belief that China will be, in some form or fashion, the perpetrator of this. I'm sure you will appreciate that financial matters are well outside my field of expertise, but there is a widespread belief in the Pentagon that the PRC is agitating on a lot of fronts simultaneously. The events unfolding here in the South China Sea may be part of a co-ordinated campaign to destabilise the dollar. Furthermore, under that umbrella, they are seeking to maximise their territorial advantage in a number of areas, including as you are well aware, the Senkaku Islands, which the Japanese are hell-bent on ensuring stay within their remit and don't fall into China's hands."

Admiral Farley rotated his pencil repeatedly around in his fingers as he thought about the likelihood that this was indeed co-ordinated; then replied from behind his desk.

"No, I haven't had any input on that specific aspect, but quite frankly there is enough going on with other events which leave me feeling very uneasy. It's like these guys are prodding at our defences everywhere. Provocations and aggressive behaviour all over this part of the world, Jim! China's growing assertiveness will have to be addressed very soon I feel. And to cap it all, we are searching day and night in the sand to try and find these damned planes that have gone missing in Libya." He raised his eyes heavenward in a gesture of despair before continuing. "Jim my dear friend, do please be seated; no protocol when we are here together. Do you want a coffee?"

"The other matter which caught my attention in your briefing was the tangential reference to internet hackers. We believe the disruptions to the financial markets, I've just mentioned, have their origins in a few rogue internet transmissions into the major New York banks from the usual suspects in the Middle East:

ISIL, Al-Shabaab, and Al-Qaeda; plus random sites in China. We strongly believe that it is all being orchestrated by Beijing. Could I ask you to alert your communications specialists to keep their eyes and ears open for any unusual transmissions which make any references whatsoever to the US dollar?"

"Not a problem Jim. I'll alert signals intelligence on board and get them to immediately link into the National Security Agency at Fort Mead. As you are probably aware Jim, the NSA normally responds to such a request by focusing the top secret ECHELON system on the problem to see if they can pick up anything unusual being bandied around the airwaves and email traffic. Let's chat further this evening and trust the guys at 'Five Eyes' to start scanning all the relevant communications channels to see if they have anything to tell us."

Although he had been on endless navy vessels in his career, Sanford always marvelled at the grandeur of the USS Washington; its unimaginable fire power; and the camaraderie of nearly 6,500 men and women on board 'Cell Block 73', as she was affectionately known. The almost constant background roar of aircraft landing and taking off was as exhilarating as ever to his senses. It had been quite some years since he flew in combat but, to Sanford, the smell of aviation fuel that permeated the carrier was as good as any fine wine; while the rhythmic throb of the turbines and endless machinery was, to his ears, utterly mesmeric. We may need all of the Washington's military capability before the mission is over, he mused.

While he was being escorted to his quarters a million thoughts in respect of his future role almost overwhelmed him. General-ship was fine, but field work was where he excelled. "I shall miss this adrenaline-rush when I'm behind my new desk", he said quietly to the marine leading the way to some much-needed sleep.

CHAPTER EIGHT

Jackson Hole, Wyoming, D-15

The Chairman of the Federal Reserve, Alison Fletcher, addressed the meeting of the central bank governors of Brazil and Singapore, with Lewis positioned to her right and John to her left. The three of them had earlier discussed a series of options that they may be able to sanction and then implement, in order to resolve the looming crisis.

"Gentlemen, we have called you here this evening to see if we can find a way to resolve a potentially explosive problem in the FX swaps markets, which is likely to occur on 22nd August. You may, or may not, be aware, that your respective countries, as well as Japan, are all scheduled to roll over a considerable quantity of currency swaps on the same day. Normally, this would not present a problem, but given the volumes involved, we want to ensure there is an orderly market on the 22nd and that the whole system doesn't freeze up, or, worse still, collapse."

There was an element of surprise, shock even, expressed by the two governors, as they too had missed the significance of three of the world's major economies all trying to renew their currency obligations on the same day. She continued, "I want to explore ideas about how we can mitigate the impact this may have?"

Almost in unison the governors nodded their agreement. The very last thing on earth they needed right now was to be unable to roll over their swap contracts and end up in some massive default.

"I can speak only for Brazil, but I'm sure my colleagues from Singapore and Japan would readily agree, we are open to any ideas you may have, Madam Chairman." The Brazilian governor took his handkerchief from his breast pocket and dabbed his forehead, on which beads of sweat were already beginning to form.

"My colleagues in Singapore are, of course, at your disposal to endeavour to resolve this matter, Madam Chairman; but I think I am correct in saying that the counterparty to a good deal of our scheduled roll-overs is China. They have been very belligerent of late across a swathe of political and economic issues and if we seek their co-operation I am pretty sure they will ask for a massive favour in return. I am very confident that my government will be most unwilling to enter into such a bargain, unless it is absolutely necessary and there is no alternative."

The governor of Singapore's central bank was regarded by everyone around the table as exceptionally astute and shrewd, having been in office for over fifteen years. He continued, "And if you think we have troubles, then I don't need to remind everyone that Japan is in a similar and, arguably, worse, position than ourselves. They have, as you English like to say, Sir John, a 'little local difficulty' with China regarding the Senkaku Islands."

"They do indeed Mr. Seng," responded d'Abo. "Who knows how they will react? But if I am any judge, they will demand a high price if they believe this situation can be played to their advantage. I have no doubt at all that when they do grasp the situation more clearly, they may well agitate for some unpalatable *quid pro quo*."

Alison Fetcher chose that moment to suggest a radical solution to their collective problems. "One potential solution to this dilemma is for the Federal Reserve to find you other counterparties to the swaps. I have a team under Sir John here, investigating whether we can get the co-operation of a couple of the major hedge funds here in the States and find a mechanism for them to replace China, temporarily or, possibly, permanently. We need to establish, quite quickly, if this would be palatable to you and your respective governments?"

John intervened, "We have in mind a structure whereby the Fed will either fund, or back stop, the obligations that these companies take onto their books via this process. The details have not been fully thought through and, to be honest, we have not put this to the hedge funds concerned, although we did meet with them over the past couple of days to discuss other interrelated issues. Before we set this hare running, we need your agreement and assistance. If you conclude that this is a viable way forward, we will make the necessary telephone calls and link up our respective teams to agree a mutually acceptable protocol."

Seng was first to respond, "The quantum of this problem is measured in many hundreds of billions of dollars Sir John. Is that sum within your calculations?"

"Yes it is," he responded instantly. "Indeed we all feel very strongly that if we fail to act, the outcome may be much more expensive in both the short and long runs for the dollar and for your respective countries. So we must act. We must act very quickly and we must all act in concert. It is our view, that we have little choice in this matter if we are to avoid a systemic failure in the foreign exchange markets."

"OK, what do you need us to do?" said the Brazilian governor, acutely conscious that his president would not countenance a further devaluation of their currency, the real, which would surely follow a failure to roll over their dollar obligations. "We don't want to end up like Venezuela."

Lewis spoke for the first time in the meeting, "With your full cooperation, firstly I would like to establish a working group between the Fed and your respective institutions and Japan, assuming they will also agree. We would assemble a technical team in New York, headed by one of our hedge fund computer wizards who would also participate in the end funding solution, plus any of your representatives you feel would assist us in this endeavour. Their initial task is to get an absolute fix, to the last dollar, on the size of the problem and then to make a comprehensive list of counterparties and those banks in New York and London who will execute the swaps. We need detailed data for every transaction involved. Once that list is produced – and we have only a matter of days to complete this – we will hopefully have concluded a procedure to resolve this matter."

The meeting concluded with an agreement to assemble at the Fed's offices at 33 Liberty Street, New York, in two days' time with all the data. John suggested to Lewis and Alison that he should also invite Mackenzie Gore to the meeting so that he could link into any UK banks that might be involved, which was immediately agreed.

A little later in the day, the group held a further meeting with the Japanese delegation who readily acquiesced to the plan, following a period of very intense, even heated, discussion within their own ranks. From their furious reaction, it was clear to all in the room that the central bank team believed they were embroiled in yet another conspiracy involving their neighbour and their determination to destabilise Japan, economically and territorially.

"This is indeed a curious turn of events Madam Chairman," said the senior representative of the group, "because – as I'm sure you recall – we have recently signed a pioneering bilateral currency swap agreement with China that allows us to hold renminbi as an alternative reserve currency. If they hold a gun to our head over this matter, it will leave us with no alternative but to retaliate and dump all the Chinese currency we hold at our central bank back onto the market. It's a comparatively small amount, a few hundred million, but politically this action could be very effective, could it not? And, if I'm not mistaken, similar agreements have been entered into with Brazil and Singapore. So between the three of us, if we act in unison, we could do considerable psychological harm in the markets if this all turns problematical."

"I'll bear that very interesting thought in mind as we work our way through this matter and thank you once again for the suggestion and your complete cooperation." With that, Alison Fletcher closed the meeting.

John retired to his room to call London and suggested to Lewis that they have a quiet nightcap in an hour or so, once he had collected his thoughts and been updated from the Chancellor's office and his bank. First call, even though it was late, was to Amanda Price at the Treasury. The switchboard redirected the call to the House, as there was a debate under way which she had to attend. When they finally reached her, she had little real news, other than that she was quite convinced that some of the sovereign swap deals would be routed through London, so she was quietly ringing round to gather whatever intelligence she could. She also noted that Mac and his colleagues were now seeing a steady stream of pings into London, which were predominantly from North Korea, but routed via China. Amanda told him that GCHQ had been asked by the Americans to engage the UK's listening assets within the ECHELON system to add to their worldwide communications search. Apparently this was starting to yield results, but it would be a couple of days before anything definitive could be expected.

"You may not be familiar with ECHELON John, for the very simple reason that we deny its very existence. Colloquially, we refer to it as "Five Eyes"; its UK base is at RAF Menworth Hill in North Yorkshire. You may have seen photographs of the simply massive circular structures which are festooned with technical equipment. It's covertly run by the UK, USA, Canada,

New Zealand and Australia and is enormously effective, but completely top secret, as I'm sure you will readily appreciate. It monitors everything – and I do mean everything – that goes by phone, email, fax, satellite, you name it, across the entire globe. We tell the world that the internet providers are blocking our endeavours to catch the bad guys, but this is a total, and politically convenient, deceit."

She finished the conversation letting him know that Mac would be taking the next available flight to New York and asked if Charles could call her after the current debate in the chamber, which was not going the government's way, regrettably. They said goodnight and agreed they would be in touch again in a day or so.

Next John dialled Anne-Sophie's home number, expecting to leave a message, but joy of joys she picked up the phone. The pleasure of hearing her voice quickly turned to cold fury.

"Ah, Sir John, I'm so very glad you called. We are having a spot of trouble with the oil takeover that I need to bring you up to speed on. There is speculation in the press that we are dumping the deal onto the Chinese because we can't conclude the funding and you personally have abandoned the transaction. I've put our PR company onto it to try and quash the rumour, but Alasdair has somewhat put his foot in it, I'm sorry to report. He got embroiled in a bit of a row with a journalist after a long lunch and tonight's Evening Standard has a big splash on the business pages: "d'Abo's bank in trouble!" I gather the FT will also run a similar story tomorrow. It's not for me to say, but I think you should get home as soon as possible."

His mind began racing and running through the options available to him. If he left he would miss the Fed meetings, if he stayed he could lose the bank. No-brainer really. "OK Anne-Sophie, it's a total bloody nuisance, but I will see if I can arrange to be flown home overnight. I wonder how the press found out about all this. I can't possibly believe the Treasury leaked it, but I'll speak to Charlie before I leave. I'll email my itinerary once it's clarified and could you and George meet me at Mildenhall, or Heathrow if I'm flying commercial. Then set up a board meeting and a conference call with ICBC. Apart from all this excitement, how are you?"

"Oh, I'm fine, thank you for asking. The office is very quiet without you, but there are no other dramas to report. You literally just caught me before I was about to take a bath and turn in for the night. You'd be shocked if this was on Skype!" she purred flirtatiously, driving him to the point of absolute distraction. "Just let me know your flight plans and I will make sure we are there to meet you. I assume the rest of your trip is going well?"

"Lots of issues here, which I'll fill you in on when I get back. Get a hold of Seb and let him know my itinerary, plus any updates you may think he should be aware of. Until later, sleep well." He put the phone down and immediately went to the lobby to find Lewis and Charlie. The Chancellor was engrossed in meetings and on seeing John signalled 'ten minutes'. Lewis was propping up the bar chatting animatedly to the Brazilian delegation trying his best to get invited to next year's carnival, when John waved at him to come on over.

"Hello, Lewis, I've got a bit of a problem back at the bank with this bloody oil take-over we are engaged in. I need to get back ASAP, spend a couple of days trying to resolve the issues and wondered if I could use the plane? I've also spoken with the Treasury and they told me that two of the US banks in London and one of ours, HSBC I think, have received interrogatory pings from Asia." John, for the first time on the trip, felt weary and deflated. He ordered a whisky, but they didn't have his favourite brand, which made him decidedly tetchy. "Have you had any word from Sebastian?"

Nothing fazed Lewis any more, he had been battle hardened in an endless series of crises while at the Fed, especially over the past six years. He just adopted what he called his 'situation normal' pose and amiably rolled with the punches, as he often said to anyone who would listen. The only thing he could really describe as trouble, was the call from his new wife asking where the hell he was and would he be home at the weekend, as they had a very large dinner party planned. But hell, she sure was pretty, so somehow he would have to find the time.

"I'm sure the plane will be available, John. When would you like to leave, apart from immediately? Not quite sure where the crew are and whether it needs refuelling. If I can get you a flight plan for say three hours hence, will that suffice?" John nodded, feeling exhausted and wondering what in God's name the Financial Times would write overnight, while Lewis was already on the phone to the senior captain to confirm if they could accommodate the request, given the late hour.

John went over to Charlie and peeled him away from his discussions. "Charlie, I don't know whether you have been briefed, but all hell is breaking loose back in the UK regarding the take-over and reports in the *Evening Standard* that the Chinese may well withdraw. If my bank were publicly quoted on the stock exchange we would have a calamity on our hands tomorrow morning. As it is, we will have a highly damaging press story to deal with and smooth over, PDQ, before the bank goes tits up. I must ask you: did any of your people leak this?"

"Absolutely not, you have my solemn word John. Who did I wonder and to what end? Let's get some fresh air."

On the terrace outside Charlie mulled over what could be done to assist his friend. "I could issue a statement, I suppose, saying we fully support the merger. It would piss off the Business Secretary, but that's no bad thing. And if your bank needs liquidity we could discreetly provide that. Look, let me think about this. I could ask the Treasury's Permanent Secretary to draft something overnight. I presume you are going back to London to put out the fire?"

"I have little choice Charlie. Could you let Alison know, please? Profuse apologies and all that. Flowers and chocolates in the post. I hope to get this out of the way in a day or two, max. But, please, can you make enquiries within your department as to whom, if anyone is responsible for the leak?"

CHAPTER NINE

Lamma Island, D-14

CJ's junk was brilliantly silhouetted against the very busy harbour and the spectacle of Kowloon beyond, as his staff scurried back and forth serving drinks and canapés to the fifty or so guests who had boarded around six in the evening. Most, as requested, were dressed in very casual clothing, but Lyn was pleased to have made an effort, if only to delight Sebastian. The weather was its usual sultry self, very humid, but a very pleasant twenty-seven degrees centigrade. The background chatter was all about the forthcoming weekend's dinner parties, the volatility of the money markets and where the Hang Seng index was heading next and, needless to say, the latest gossip of who was sleeping with whom. Very typical cocktail party chit-chat in Hong Kong, thought Sebastian.

Lyn looked upwards in awe at Victoria Peak immediately behind them and asked Sebastian if he thought they could find time to visit it during their stay. He responded enthusiastically with a nod of the head and an equally ardent wave to the waiter indicating more champagne was required. Both of them had been clothes-shopping in the late afternoon, in preparation for the boat trip. Lyn had alighted upon a stunning cerise-coloured, pure silk, strapless dress in one of the endless shopping malls which are to be found more or less everywhere you turn in Hong Kong. Although she initially protested that this 'dazzling outfit was way too expensive for an army captain and a trip on a junk', Seb eventually persuaded her to try it on and forget the idea of shorts and flip-flops. In due course she acquiesced and emerged from the changing room to quiet applause from Seb, who held out his hand to gently kiss hers. "We'll take it", he said to the shopping assistant, while proffering his credit card. "You look absolutely sensational, Lyn darling, edible even! You'll knock them for six back in the barracks!"

He, by contrast, had earlier taken the default course of action in this part of the world, by going to see the Peninsula's concierge, asking for the hotel's tailor to come to the room and measure him for a new pair of lightweight trousers and a couple of shirts. Given the very limited time available for the poor tailor to work his miracles, he was astounded to be given the completed, perfectly fitting garments within a matter of hours. To say that Lyn was equally impressed with the tailor's work would have been an understatement, as some thirty minutes previously Seb had escorted her to the waiting car and a trip to the Royal Yacht Club, Hong Kong side, to board the junk. Reed and Bain were already waiting in the car, unsuitably dressed for the occasion in stock-issue security services suits, but Lyn noticed they were slightly on edge. She wondered why they seemed twitchy? They must have some updates to impart later this evening.

The chief steward was there to greet them personally when they all boarded the junk and to pass on the message that CJ was currently on the phone, but would like them to join him on the foredeck in twenty or so minutes. They decided to take a stroll around his truly magnificent boat. Glasses were periodically refilled and toasts were made, while Seb pointed out the cross-harbour ferry to Lyn, as it endlessly shuttled backwards and forwards, full to the gunnels with workers and tourists.

"The trip generally takes about an hour Lyn. I gather we are going to dine on the terrace of the open air restaurant, the Rainbow, which is famous for its endless list of fish dishes, cooked however you like. You will even get to select your own fish from the enormous tanks. Quite an experience, if you've never done it before! As we get nearer to Lamma Island, we should pass Aberdeen on the left, which is renowned for its hundreds of sampans. How's your Cantonese Lyn? A little bit of trivia for you: 'Sam' means 'three' in Cantonese, and 'Pan' means 'plank'; so a 'Sampan' is 'three planks', the original description of the boats used in this part of the world. And, as Michael Caine might have said, 'not a lot of people know that'."

"Michael who?" replied Lyn.

The steward came over and told them they were about to cast off. He also requested them to come forward as CJ had someone he would like them to meet.

"Such a beautiful vessel CJ", said Seb. "We are all honoured to be your guest on such a lovely evening. I've never really understood how such a glorious boat could be called a junk? It is, somehow, not quite apposite, don't you agree?"

"She's my pride and joy, Seb. You remember Sapphire? Just in case you are wondering, she is here in a capacity not too dissimilar to Lyn's. There is someone new I would like you all to meet, especially our friends Reed and Bain, whose government's help, I, or rather, we, may need shortly."

In the shadow of the foresail stood two men, one clearly a bodyguard of some sort, the other decidedly nervous, even apprehensive, about what would happen next.

"May I introduce Chang Jin-soo. For those of you unfamiliar with Chinese names, the surname comes first in this part of the world. Mr. Chang is a very senior banker from North Korea and urgently needs our help. In return, he is prepared to provide us with some very interesting information." CJ was as matter-of-fact as it was humanly possible to be, devoid of any emotion whatsoever. Mr. Chang, however, was sweating profusely, with his eyes continually on the move, examining every detail of the people in front of him, and any twitch or unexpected gesture from the guests that caught his attention.

"In a nutshell, Mr. Chang has asked for my help to defect, with immediate effect. If the authorities were to establish his whereabouts, they would hunt him down and kill him, without the slightest hesitation or compassion. Me too, for aiding and abetting him; probably all of you, as well. Given that he's been on the run for four days now, the North Koreans have probably already asked for Russia's help to track him down and bring him back, dead or alive. I am hoping that after you have heard what he has to say, you will use all your collective authority and contacts to see that he finds a safe place to live."

Bain and Reed were instantly on alert and transformed from happy-go-lucky party goers, into the professional agents they had trained all their lives to become. Jackets were unbuttoned and holsters instinctively checked. Lyn automatically patted her thigh.

"I presume we just have your friends on board, CJ? Even so, has someone thoroughly security checked them?" said Bain immediately, while Reed turned his back to the group in order to scan the face and movements of the people on board.

"I think you will find that is not a problem Bain. When I got Mr. Chang's call earlier, while we were at the China Club for lunch with Seb and Lyn, I made sure the crew were extra vigilant and everyone was vetted before we left. The cover of a spontaneous junk-trip was my idea, so that we would not be overheard. I also wanted to ensure we met in a very safe place." CJ beckoned Mr. Chang to move forward, while he introduced everyone to him. Given the gravity of the circumstances they were meeting under, the formality and ritual of it all struck Seb as more than a little absurd.

CJ continued, "Mr. Chang is – or more accurately, was – the managing director of Korea's Daesong Bank; in which esteemed role he was privy to endless political secrets and dark 'goings-on' in that part of the world. He also has another far more secretive role in what is now his ex-country.

Namely, he was also in charge of that 'can of vipers', known as Bureau 39."

Bureau 39 was very well known to Reed. The CIA Asian Desk endeavoured manfully to secretly monitor their activities on a daily basis, but more often than not it was a fruitless exercise. Here, therefore, was a prize almost beyond avarice for the Agency and something the United States would unhesitatingly trade good money, instant asylum and a lifetime of comfortable obscurity for. The US Treasury had long suspected Bureau 39 of being involved in counterfeit currency trading, especially the dollar and the yen and a steady stream of drug-related activities in the region. The result of which was the accumulation of a very substantial slush fund – some took a wild guess at US$800 million – with which to subvert anyone, or anything that threatened the interests of North Korea, which, in this part of the world, meant almost everybody. The CIA seemed in a state of perpetual frustration in respect of its activities, as they could never get to its core. They only saw the end results: assassinations, commercial espionage, spying of every variety and a widely dispersed network of *agents provocateurs*, informants, policemen and politicians, all of whom were handsomely paid to cause as much civil disruption as possible, whenever the need arose, which seemed often.

CJ resumed, "Chang has sought me out in the first instance because of information he has regarding opponents of the pro-democracy movement here in Hong Kong. Just so that you are aware, I have paid handsomely for the names he has given me and they will be dealt with in due course. It is the other half of the conversation that will be of most interest, or to be more accurate, most concern, to you all."

The party atmosphere coming from below was in stark contrast to the expressions on the faces of the group, which were now fully focused on what Chang had to say. In impeccable English he began to speak.

"When Kim Jong-un came to power in 2010, I thought for one fleeting moment that perhaps my country would find a way to be reconciled with the West. But alas no. If anything, life under the new *régime* has become considerably worse. I have foolishly been agitating the Supreme Leader to take a different path and restore human rights and dignity to our people. Instead he has imposed arbitrary imprisonment, starvation, public executions and genocide upon anyone who dares to challenge his will. My entire family, young and old, were rounded up last week and are now in prison, somewhere north of Pyongyang. I fear I will never see them again. My actions, by defecting, will certainly condemn them to death, if that has not already happened." He wiped a tear from both eyes and started to sob. Sapphire found him a drink of water and a chair. It was a while before he spoke again, during which time the lights of Lamma Island could be clearly seen in the distance. 'Twenty minutes to dock', thought Seb, 'then what happens?'

"I am deeply ashamed of what I have done", his voice almost cracking, "but I must find another life, another path. I am willing to provide you with, what I believe the intelligence community call, treasure: an undreamed-of insight into the inner workings of my country and its financial network. I have also absconded with twenty million dollars in hard cash from the Bureau. For that alone they will hunt me down for the rest of my life. I also have another confession to make. In 1996, I was seconded to Hong Kong to open the bank's first branch here. They would not allow my wife to join me and before too long I became infatuated with a colleague, a local girl and we had a daughter. When I was forced to return home, I immediately lost touch with them and, despite many efforts on my behalf, have not had any contact in nearly ten years now. Reluctantly, I have convinced myself that my life is over, or will be, very shortly. No one escapes. I want to ensure they receive this money and someone provides them with life-time protection. For me, I would like to seek asylum in America and if possible, if we can find them and they are willing to do so, to have them join me."

He cleared his throat, took another sip of water and came to the punch line, "The only trouble with this arrangement is that I know what is being planned in Beijing. Bluntly put, they are preparing to launch a blatant, all-out attack on the US dollar, which you will be unable to resist. My suitcases of cash may, therefore, end up as utterly worthless wallpaper."

Sebastian was the first to respond, in measured tones. "Let us divide your problem into two components Mr. Chang. First, and from my point of view, selfishly, I want to hear everything you can tell me about the intended assault on the dollar: especially, its timing and the method to be used. We need this information as a matter of the utmost urgency. Secondly, if you wish, I can arrange to have your funds transferred into sterling as a temporary measure, so as to give you some additional comfort and to indicate our utmost good faith. I am sure my government is willing to help and assist you to the maximum extent possible. Mr Bain here will probably need to confer with his colleagues in London, but from the look on his face I am assuming you will get a positive response to your requests."

The normally taciturn Reed immediately added, "Yes, I am sure I can marshal the resources of the CIA to that end, Sir, and get the State Department to confirm your asylum request overnight. May I make a suggestion, CJ? You good people continue to have dinner at the restaurant as if nothing had happened." Fat chance thought Lyn. "And let me take the junk back to Central, speak to Langley and find Mr. Chang a safe house until the powers-that-be decide what to do next. I'll send the boat straight back, so you won't be inconvenienced. Bain, I'm sure, will stay with the party."

"Everyone happy with that? Is that OK with you Mr Chang?" They all nodded in agreement, largely because no one had a plausible alternative suggestion and at least with this plan, Chang would be safe.

Once they had docked at the Sok Kwu Wan ferry pier, the guests casually left the junk and strolled, many without a care in the world, the few hundred yards to the restaurant. Within minutes of everyone disembarking, it set off back for Hong Kong, this time under engine power.

Two gigantic tables had been prepared and, at CJ's request, they were discreetly segregated from the other diners by a thin bamboo divider. Both Lyn and Bain were now decidedly on edge and felt utterly exposed to danger from every quarter, especially from the narrow street immediately adjacent to the restaurant. They both chose to sit facing the street, both regretting they had had champagne on the sail over.

Waiters scurried around offering to show them the endless tanks from which they could choose exotically coloured fish or massive lobster, squid, prawns and crab. Fingers were pointed, fish and crustaceans scooped out to their doom, while white wine and San Miguel beer were poured for the other guests, who were enjoying every minute of the experience, oblivious to events around them. The food arrived at the tables in no time at all, with everyone encouraged to try as many dishes as they wished from the restaurant's vast menu. Every time a dish was emptied, a new one would mysteriously appear and no-one ran short of something to drink.

CJ was a meticulous host and sauntered merrily around the two tables casually telling stories of his banking exploits, especially his recent golfing trip to Punta Baluarte in the Philippines. He returned to Sebastian and Lyn after about thirty minutes, to see they had not eaten a great deal and their glasses were still full. "Not enjoying the fried squid Seb? Then you must try the steamed crab, absolutely delicious; and for you Lyn, how about some spicy sea snails?" Her nose wrinkled alarmingly. "Ha ha, thought not!"

Seb looked up from his plate which the waiters had ensured was groaning with food, "I've sent an urgent message to my boss, Sir John d'Abo, via his secretary, to brief him on tonight's development. I gather he's *en route* to London to dampen the flames of some other crisis. When do you think we will get the opportunity to discuss matters with Chang, or will the CIA whisk him away so quickly we may miss the opportunity? There are endless technical questions I would like to put to him."

"I assume tomorrow Seb, once they have established him in a safe house, somewhere in Kowloon, I expect. I don't imagine they would wish to accommodate him in the American embassy, far too public. Besides which, they would never get him out. It would be a bit like that guy Julian Assange, holed up for years in the Ecuadorian embassy in London. My understanding of the asylum process is that a great deal of paperwork is involved and I'm pretty sure they will be forced to smuggle him out, maybe on your plane?"

"That hadn't occurred to me. I'll speak to Reed tomorrow, I'm sure the CIA will conclude that his immediate exit to safety should take priority over our mission here."

As dinner was coming to a very satisfactory close, CJ sent one of his minions to check if the junk had returned, who quickly reported back that there was no sign of it. He called the Yacht Club to ascertain if and when it had arrived, only to be told it had not even docked; nor had the captain called in for docking instructions, as was normal practice. In a rare moment of trepidation he gathered Seb, Lyn and Bain together to alert them to the news, while simultaneously phoning his contacts in an endeavour to track down where the hell the boat had ended up. He knew full well it could literally be anywhere and Chang and Reed already disposed of, tortured, held for ransom and goodness knows what else. Had one of his crew deserted him and been paid handsomely to turn a blind eye while the Russians or North Koreans attempted to recapture their defector?

He was now furious with himself for allowing Reed and Chang to return to Hong Kong, more or less by themselves and thereby provide the perpetrators with the easiest possible access to the largely unmanned boat. He pondered what to do next and how to get back to base? They took the easiest option and boarded the local ferry. The remaining guests were somewhat taken aback, but CJ gathered them together to explain that unfortunately the junk had experienced a mechanical failure and, deeply regrettably, they had to return home, in somewhat less glamorous style. He reassured his friends that he would make it up to them on their next trip together. Most shrugged their shoulders, noted 'these things happen', ordered champagne to 'take-away', whilst others were furious at having to travel home with the local riff-raff. Seb calculated that they would be back around midnight and phoned the hotel for a car to pick them up. CJ, meanwhile, was engaged in a desperate attempt to find his beloved junk and, more importantly, identify the miscreants who had betrayed him. They would pay dearly for their treachery.

The ferry lumbered its way towards the Central Pier complex at what felt like a snail's pace. Lyn phoned through the news to the local CIA office, to tell them that Reed was missing, presumed kidnapped or worse, while Bain contacted MI6. Everyone went onto red alert, agents were dragged out of their beds, their favourite bars, or anywhere they might be, to begin the manhunt to end all manhunts. No-one captures a CIA operative without being on the receiving end of the entire forces of law and order that the United States can muster. Meanwhile, Sebastian left a second message with Anne-Sophie to tell Sir John of the latest turn of events and asked that he phone back immediately, whatever the time difference.

As they arrived back at Hong Kong Island, CJ's car and men were waiting to whisk him away to his house on The Peak, where key members of his team had already assembled, ready to take instructions and commence a search. Bain was met by the local police and two of his MI6 colleagues and they immediately went into a huddle to plan a sweep of some of the more notorious bays and harbours, in an endeavour to find the boat and its very precious cargo. Lyn and Seb meanwhile hurriedly moved to the safety of the Peninsula's S-class Mercedes, waiting by the dock and asked the driver to get back to the hotel as quickly as he could. The chauffeur opened the rear passenger door and beckoned them quickly inside. It was only when they sat down did they realise there was another person in the front, holding a very large gun directly at them. The doors were immediately locked and a determined request made of Lyn to surrender her weapon, or be shot instantaneously. She handed her bag over without protest, thanking God that she had not also been searched, while Sebastian went ashen with fear and instinctively held her hand.

The man released the safety catch from his gun, crudely wiping saliva from his lips, his drug-induced pupils dilated to the point where virtually no white surrounds were showing and growled an instruction to the driver, "Mong Kok, immediately."

CHAPTER TEN

Berkley Square, London, D-13

The journey back to the UK was undertaken by Sir John d'Abo in a mixture of utter fury and – if someone, however inadvertently, had endangered his bank – murderous intent.

He arrived at RAF Mildenhall at eight o'clock sharp to be met by his chauffeur, George and by Anne-Sophie, who was looking every inch the impeccably dressed and utterly indispensible PA she had become. The drive back to the office was spent in virtual silence with John reading yesterday's Evening Standard and that day's Financial Times, which carried a front page story questioning whether the bank had lost its touch, or worse, much worse, was in serious, even terminal, trouble.

When he eventually put down the papers, Anne-Sophie quickly went through her diary entries for the day: an emergency board meeting had been called for midday; that, if required, Alasdair would see him immediately he was back in the office; Sebastian had called and asked if he could be in touch urgently; and overnight she had received a draft press briefing from the Permanent Secretary to the Treasury which was timed to be released at nine o'clock today, succinctly if abstrusely stating that: 'The rumours surrounding the Government's position in respect of the pending oil takeover have been misinterpreted. We are not hostile, but entirely supportive of a positive outcome'. At least Charlie was true to his word, he reflected silently.

When they eventually reached central London, John decided they would swing by his apartment so that he could quickly change and freshen up. It was the first time Anne-Sophie had been inside it and, in an effort to try and lighten the mood, expressed her delight at the mixture of contemporary and traditional furniture which she praised highly. It didn't help his mood one jot.

Back in the inner sanctum of his office at the bank, John began a round of heated phone calls to the editors of the Times, the FT, and the Telegraph, all of whom he knew well, expressing his outrage and disbelief that d'Abos Bank was being so maligned. The Treasury's press release had thankfully worked its magic and made his argument that – 'all was well' – much easier to accept by the editors. Although, to quash the story completely would require the Chinese bank, ICBC, to also confirm they had not abandoned the deal altogether; merely that they were seeking better terms. He would defer calling them until he had met with Alasdair, been fully briefed and concluded the board meeting.

Alasdair Tims had joined the bank over twenty years previously and was generally regarded by everyone as a safe pair of hands, even if at times he was far too prudent and cautious for the dynamic institution he was a part of. He was the *de facto* counterweight to the buccaneering style of the other directors. Moreover, he was always tasked with making a counter argument for not proceeding with some deal or other, but would always find himself in a minority of one when it came to a show of hands around the board table. Not many people would have willingly accepted this role, but he knew he was grudgingly respected by his colleagues for his integrity, even if the bank would have closed down millennia ago if they had adopted his style of deal-doing: which could be paraphrased as "let's pass on this one Chairman".

Besides which, he was too close to a very comfortable

retirement with his charming, if equally dull, wife and their three cats, to rock the corporate boat. It was inconceivable, therefore, that he could have placed the bank in jeopardy and, despite the previous day's 'two-bottle lunch' with the Evening Standard, he remained utterly convinced he had not said a word out of place. He replayed the bits of the lunch he could remember over and over in his mind: no, he categorically had not said anything inappropriate. Someone else must have 'tipped the wink' to those bastards in the press, but it sure as hell was not him.

The eight-man board of d'Abos bank comprised Sir John as the omnipotent Chairman and Chief Executive, three executive directors who ran various key departments within the organisation, and four non-executive directors who, in one form or another, were financially beholden to him personally. The latter group all recognised the part he had played in their lives and the utterly invaluable assistance he had provided in their past successes or, indeed, his role in protecting them from their corporate or personal misdeeds.

Ostensibly independent, the career and prestige of the non-executive directors within the Square Mile was entirely dependent upon the latest stunning transaction executed by 'their' bank, on which they could dine out for weeks afterwards. Their participation in any aspect of the 'deals', however, was threadbare at most, and, in all likelihood, the transactions were concluded before they even heard about them. Most were already very familiar with the UK honours system, being grateful recipients of one 'gong' or another, often achieved on the back of some moment of financial brilliance at d'Abos for which they ostensibly received the credit, at his gracious insistence, resulting in City adoration and subsequent decorations from the Queen.

As a rule, board votes were unanimous and unhesitatingly reflective of John's willpower and undisputed control over his bank; the only increasingly irrelevant fly in the ointment was Alasdair Tims, who cast the occasional vote against and spent the rest of the day being ridiculed by his colleagues for his conservatism. While the glittering offices of the bank were the epitome of modern-day sophistication and high technology, the board room was an oasis of dignified calm. Family portraits stretching back centuries hung on virtually every wall, while the present day board of the 'great and the good' sat their ever-spreading posteriors on exquisite Chippendale furniture, which would not be out of place in any of England's greatest country houses.

There was no need for an agenda, even though Anne-Sophie had circulated one which contained a single item for discussion: the future of the bank. As they shuffled into the room, suitably solemn, even sombre, everyone was fully aware from the newspapers of the need for a crisis meeting. They also, very grudgingly, had dismissed the idea that they would be the recipients of the usual utterly delicious post-board-meeting lunch prepared by Rosalind – for many the highlight of their culinary year.

Anne-Sophie gestured everyone to sit down, telling them that Sir John was presently finalising a call with the Wall Street Journal and would join them momentarily. She sat next to the Chairman's chair with notepad at the ready, while everyone else engaged in meaningless small talk about the weather; the Footsie 100; the forthcoming Glorious Twelfth shooting parties on their estates in Scotland; even the unrest in Hong Kong where they gathered Sebastian had been sent, transferred or exiled.

When John eventually entered the room, which immediately fell silent, he had a face like thunder.

"Bloody newspapers", he snapped, "that's the last time I give any of those blood-sucking leeches a scoop." He placed his folder on the board room table and poured a glass of water.

"Gentlemen: someone – and I quote directly from my last very heated conversation with the Journal, 'close to the bank' – has leaked the takeover story. The question is, who and why?"

"I am loath to suggest it is one of you chaps, as you would effectively be slitting your own throat here, but who else could it be? And if it's not you, then who the hell is it: the Chinese? Why would they do that; and indeed why would any of you do it? I'd like each of you to formally put on the board's record that the source of the story is not you."

To a man they denied it in turn; each solemnly repeating and affirming their undying allegiance to d'Abos. Alastair Tims recounted his regrettably boozy lunch with the Standard in great detail and – he fervently hoped and prayed – had eventually managed to convince all at the table that the leak had not emanated from him.

"I want to make it plain," continued Sir John in a voice full of menace, "that if I do eventually find out that the truth has not been disclosed today, I will vent my fury on anyone involved in trying to create problems for my bank. Meanwhile, we should all move into damage limitation mode and endeavour to contain this story gaining any more traction in the press. Direct anyone and everyone that you speak to, towards the Treasury's press release. Charles Sheer is expected back in a couple of days and I will make sure he also reconfirms the Government's position and his personal support. Just so that you are aware, I will shortly be speaking with the European head of ICBC in an endeavour to get the deal back on track, no matter what concessions it takes. Oh and, for the avoidance of doubt, if there is the slightest hint of a run on the bank let me know immediately and I'll have unlimited liquidity put at our disposal, courtesy of HMG."

The meeting had lasted no more than ten minutes. No one asked any further questions, all assumed their careers had hit the buffers: their personal gravy train was about to pull into the metaphorical station and stop stone dead. It was just possible of course that the deal could indeed be rescued; John was brilliant in a tight spot as they all knew too well, but at what cost to the bank, their reputations, their pensions. It was also perfectly possible that instead of being their protector, he would decide he had no choice but to lay the blame squarely at their feet. No one doubted his ruthlessness in business matters and the speed with which he would plunge the dagger into the back of anyone who crossed him. The non-executives left the building to have a very stiff drink at their respective clubs, while the directors at the coal-face went back to their offices and started planning to downsize their houses and lifestyles.

Anne-Sophie sat calmly at her desk in somewhat of a quandary as to what to do next that would help her boss, when the phone rang, startling her. It was an urgent call from Mr Mackenzie Gore, insisting he speak with the Chairman immediately, 'no matter what he is currently doing'. She put him through.

"Sir John, I've just been informed by my colleagues in the CIA that Sebastian Fortes has gone missing while in Hong Kong. At the moment we have no idea where he is, or whether this is sinister or he's out on the town overdoing the partying and not contactable. Either way, they have initiated the standard search procedures in such cases and I will expect a further update into GCHQ in two or so hours. I just wanted you to be aware that we may have an incident here and double check that you had not asked him to go somewhere else and not told us?"

"Good grief, Mac, I thought you chaps were supposed to be looking after him?"

"Hong Kong is now swarming with MI6 and CIA people trying to establish their whereabouts Sir John. If Seb still has his phone with him then we will be able to track him. That's the best I can offer you at the moment, I'm afraid."

"Their?" said John, even more exasperated.

"Yes, Captain Andrews is also missing. We presume they are

together, but don't know for sure. There is also the problem of the missing junk and a very important person, who links directly into your investigations on behalf of the Treasury. Amanda Price is coming over this afternoon to brief you personally. Meanwhile I am being temporarily relocated to New York tonight, taking the 6 o'clock BA flight, so as to join the US technical cyber warfare team. I am presuming that we will be basing ourselves at the Fed's offices. I'll re-contact you when I arrive."

"Missing bloody junk", he spluttered, "what in God's name are you talking about Mac?"

"Amanda Price will fill you in, Sir John. No names on the phone, but this person may well be pivotal to your investigations. He has also disappeared, hence Miss Price's personal visit to your offices. I'll be in constant touch from New York, but have to go now as I've a lot to arrange before my flight."

John sat at his desk in utter bewilderment. He pressed the intercom and asked to be put through to ICBC, then asked Anne-Sophie to check when Amanda was scheduled to come over and to organise sandwiches and coffee at his desk. He had only been back four hours and was already feeling jet-lagged and emotionally drained. The solitary highlight of his return was seeing his utterly beguiling secretary, matched, in distinctly second place, by a message from his wife saying she would be away at some equestrian event or other in Paris for the next couple of weeks. He hoped and prayed that he could keep his wits about him over the following few hours, which might turn out to be vital in saving his bank. The country, God bless it, would have to wait.

The European Chairman of ICBC, located in Luxembourg, was the epitome of inscrutability and double-speak on the phone: yes, their sincere apologies were offered for any disturbance they had inadvertently caused; they certainly had not deliberately intended to give the impression to the media that they were planning to withdraw from the transaction. However, their head office was insistent that the terms of the deal must be changed materially, in their favour, naturally, and – if they were to continue – a crystal clear commitment must be given from the UK Government that they would not block the takeover. They were preparing a revised 'heads of terms' which their lawyers would have concluded and delivered to him before the end of the day. If these were acceptable, then the deal was back on and they would issue a statement to that effect immediately. If they were not, then regrettably they would be obligated to withdraw. Classic, brazen, blackmail tactics, he fumed silently. I wonder if I can get Charlie to threaten to withdraw their new UK banking licence if this gets a spot rougher as the day goes along. That would immediately spike their guns, but it would also kibosh the prospect of the City becoming the hub of renminbi trading. Then again, in only a couple of weeks, this whole debate could be entirely academic as the world's financial system imploded. Hell, he needed a drink.

Amanda Price arrived, punctually, at three o'clock, to brief him personally on events in Hong Kong. She was widely acknowledged to possess one of the sharpest minds in the Treasury and although a little too prim and proper for his tastes, was none-the-less as equally formidable and ruthless as himself. In her, he saw a kindred spirit. John knew instinctively that one day she would rise to the top of her party, so she was most certainly someone to cultivate, encourage and charm on her way up the greasy pole of politics. Perhaps he should ask her to join the bank's board? She spoke, to his utter delight, with such precision and clarity, in her clipped upper-crust accent that she had acquired while at Roedean, where her Northern roots seemed to fall away like leaves in autumn.

"Sir John, I have nothing but bad news to impart to you, I'm afraid." She took a chair immediately opposite him across the partner's desk which dominated his office. "I gather Mac has partially filled you in already regarding Sebastian's unknown whereabouts. What he will not have mentioned is the attempted defection of a certain Mr. Chang, who is a very senior person indeed within the North Korean financial hierarchy and someone HMG has had their eye on for quite some time. We gather he has information which we regard as potentially vital in the unravelling of the possible currency attack, which GCHQ are increasingly convinced emanates from China and less importantly, North Korea. His defection may also be pivotal in other aspects of our political relationships with that part of the world, so it is vital the secret services get the opportunity to debrief him as soon as possible. The problem is, would you believe, he too cannot be found. Before he went missing, US and UK agents were about to interrogate him with Sebastian's technical help. But now everyone seems to have disappeared. We have deployed every security asset at our disposal in Hong Kong to track them down. However, as I speak, we are at a complete loss as to what is happening, who is involved, and why."

She leaned forward to put her papers on the desk before continuing, "One other thing I should mention in the context of today's newspapers: the Chancellor has made it quite clear to the Chinese delegation at the Jackson Hole summit that we fully support d'Abos Merchant Bank and will not stand in the way of the proposed oil merger. Furthermore, he has made it quite plain that the delegation must pass our Government's message loud and clear to ICBC in Beijing, that there will be consequences if this takeover is brought into the political arena. We have also been in direct touch with their Finance Ministry to re-emphasise this. The Chancellor asked me to make sure you were fully aware of our support and that he will make further statements, if necessary, on his return, which, he thinks, will be tomorrow."

"Thank you very much indeed, Amanda. Your public support of the bank is very reassuring news. Let's also hope that Sebastian's disappearance is only temporary." It was clear to them both that the meeting had concluded, so he stood up to escort her out of the office. "I am anxiously waiting to have the revised terms from ICBC sent over in a couple of hours or so. Perhaps we could make arrangements to have lunch tomorrow to assess developments? I could pick you up at the Treasury or the House, at say 12.30?"

"That would be a pleasure and, quite candidly, a most welcome, indeed joyous, relief from the preparations I'm embroiled in for the Autumn Financial Statement. I'll get my secretary to let you know where I will be and see you tomorrow."

Back at his desk he pressed the intercom, "Anne-Sophie can you pop in please? I'm going to have lunch with Miss Price tomorrow to follow up on this meeting, so could you book a table for two at The Ivy, shall we say one o'clock? And let me know immediately when the post room receives the ICBC papers."

As the adrenaline started to wane in his blood system, he started to feel very tired indeed and reluctantly decided that the best thing to do was to go back to the flat and grab some sleep. "On second thoughts, I'm going to go home and rest for a couple of hours. Could you bring the papers over at say six o'clock, and providing there is not a horror story to read and I've recovered sufficiently, I'd love also to take you out somewhere nice to eat and thank you personally for getting up so early this morning. I'll send George back with the car and leave the choice of where to go entirely up to you. My treat!"

Back at the apartment he was asleep within seconds. Two blissful hours later he was gently woken by George to let him know that he and Anne-Sophie had arrived with the papers and, penitently, would he need him tonight as he would dearly love to go and watch Fulham play their opening match of the season.

George was utterly thrilled and overjoyed when Anne-Sophie had given him two match tickets earlier in the day and frankly would probably have offered to resign if he had been denied an opportunity to see his beloved football team.

"You go, George; I'm sure we can slum it in a taxi tonight", he said, coming slowly to consciousness from his jet-lag. "Can you get Ros to organise a drink for Anne-Sophie and yourself, and let her know I will be out in fifteen minutes. Can you pour me a very large scotch, there's a good chap."

As he entered the drawing room, his eye was immediately caught by the delectable Anne-Sophie. "You've changed. You look stunning."

"Thank you, I took the opportunity to slip back home for half an hour and put on something more appropriate for the evening ahead."

"Now, what have these chaps got to say by way of a revision of the terms?" She handed him the already opened and date-stamped envelope. He took a seat on the sofa next to her, while George and Ros chatted amiably and competitively about football and how she was a lifelong Spurs fan who delighted in kicking "Fulham's butt" at every opportunity they had: her encyclopaedic knowledge even going so far as to remind him of their famous first win over Fulham in 1904. He took it all in good humour; after all he was off to the game in twenty minutes with his charming missus, a rare event indeed, with maybe even a plate of jellied eels to share like the old days!

George's smiling face as he left the room contrasted starkly with the demeanour of his boss, who was already deeply engrossed in reading the revisions to the transaction that Anne-Sophie had brought with her from ICBC and going redder and redder in the face with every clause.

"No, we can't accept this. We'll be the laughing stock of the City. Now what the hell do we do?"

As they were now alone, he walked over to the drinks

cabinet to refresh their glasses and continued speaking to her as if she was one of his most trusted colleagues, taking a moment to discuss the options open to him, as he saw it. Maybe she would have a view, he thought, or an unconventional response he could use.

"The problem is that the purchase price they are requesting our side to agree to, frankly, is an absolute steal. Everyone with a calculator will know that we've been screwed." He continued his deliberations out loud, talking to no-one but himself, "The only way I can presently think of to disguise this is by inserting some complicated formula for a very significant deferred payment should things turn out better than expected. I could say that we have a fundamental disagreement on the future direction of oil prices and this formula bridges the gap if I'm right and they are wrong. I'll argue they are going down, while they will argue they are going up. That sounds vaguely convincing and suitably plausible, don't you think Anne-Sophie? Would ICBC buy that?"

"I have no idea to be honest, Sir John, but if you can somehow establish a formula they feel comfortable with, then I would guess they would have no reason other than to agree." She leaned forward to pick up her drink and displayed a breathtaking view of her divine cleavage, causing him to be more than a little distracted in his train of thought.

"Let's not stand on ceremony tonight Anne-Sophie, I'm John. Pleased to meet you!" Shaking hands, they both roared with laughter, which lightened the mood, almost to the point of frivolity. "I'm ravenous, where shall we eat?"

"Well", she paused over-dramatically, "John", and still giggling, continued, "I have taken the liberty of preparing dinner for us at my flat. I just presumed you would not actually want to go out tonight, just in case the press and paparazzi were hounding you?"

"Is it far?" he replied, his mind racing with the completely unexpected possibilities this turn of events might lead to. Perhaps there was a God?

"I have been using my mother's apartment at The Lancasters, opposite Kensington Gardens, since I arrived in London. She rarely uses it, preferring to live most of the year in Monaco. It's exceptionally convenient and only a ten-minute cab ride from here. So, if that's all right with you, *saumon en croûte* awaits!"

Hardly believing his good fortune, heart racing with excitement, he enthusiastically grabbed a bottle of Bollinger and a bottle of Les Clos, Chablis Grand Cru, from the drinks fridge. This, he thought, should liven up the evening considerably and, quite possibly even complement the fish, not that he cared what they ate. They headed to the ground floor reception where the doorman had already organised them a taxi and off they shot in high spirits completely discarding the worries of the day's events. On the way over Anne-Sophie explained to him that her parents were exceptionally wealthy Parisians, but in his terms, were 'only' *nouveau riche, parvenu,* industrialists. So, while under normal circumstances, the lifestyle offered by a three-bedroom flat at the *uber*-sophisticated Lancasters was well beyond even her not-inconsiderable salary, it was comparatively painless when free.

They breezed into her apartment full of *bonhomie* and laughter: the first time John had felt truly alive in weeks, if not years. She almost purred while asking him to pour them both a glass of his already chilled champagne and retreated, hips swaying, into the open-plan kitchen to finalise supper. He handed her a bubble-filled flute and suggested out loud that her dress sense was delectable, undoubtedly *haute couture;* while silently reflecting how the cream, tight-fitting two-piece suit, enhanced her luscious figure. As she took off her jacket to reveal an almost transparent white silk shirt, her low cut wireless bra clearly visible beneath, he nearly fainted with lust.

"Do you find that living here is quite different from Paris,

Anne-Sophie? Certain aspects of France I adore, the wine especially, but the language and I never really got on." He moved onto the small Juliet balcony and stared over to Hyde Park and the Gardens directly in front of them. "The view from here makes quite a contrast to the facade I have of South Audley Street." He could already smell the delicious aroma of the food cooking. 'At least we have a magnificent summer evening to enjoy together', he thought. Now if I can only put my own 'sea of troubles' to one side, there could be quite some upside to this imminent *debaclé*.

"Yes, London is a fabulous city, John, but the romance of Paris is incomparable. I'll be absolutely delighted to show it you one day," she added provocatively, "if you're a good boy!"

"Now that is an offer I would be delighted to take up any time you are free. Perhaps we could take the Eurostar in the morning; I'll book a suite at the *George Cinq* immediately!"

The champagne was almost finished as she sauntered over to the poorly lit corner table to refill his glass. Her silhouette from behind was exquisite; her delicate waist contrasting with her stupendous breasts. She handed back his glass and moved to bring the salmon from the kitchen. Provocatively, but subtly, she brushed up against him as she placed the food down on the table; which had already been set for two, as if the whole evening had been meticulously planned. He, meanwhile, casually and skilfully uncorked the new bottle, smelt the cork, deemed it very passable and slowly poured the wine for them both, noting to Anne-Sophie that he had several cases of this vintage at home in the country, should she ever wish to visit when his wife was away.

He took an appreciative sip, "Nectar of the Gods, Anne-Sophie! I cannot begin to tell you how you have changed my life in the last few weeks. It's been an absolute pleasure to have you around the office, especially while all this turmoil at the bank has nearly overwhelmed us all. It's like I have been reawakened from a deep slumber. So, here's to your good health, our good fortune and a long and enjoyable time working and – who knows – playing together."

She raised her glass towards him, whilst simultaneously releasing her long auburn hair, letting it fall to her shoulders in what was clearly a well-practised move, calculated to drive any man to complete distraction. Her dark green eyes stared intently, even passionately, into his and at that very moment he knew that she would eventually succumb to him, possibly even tonight. John sat down opposite her at the comparatively small dining table, such that their knees had little option but to touch. She didn't move them so he pressed a tiny fraction harder to gauge her subconscious reaction. He was convinced she responded with the tiniest of gestures. The night was going very well indeed, he reflected!

"And to you John", she smiled, her eyes full of promise, and as if she was reading his mind, continued, "let's drink to a less stressful life, starting this very evening! As we say in France: *vivre pour le moment!*"

They both lustily downed their glass in one – something he would never, ever, do under normal circumstances. But in his entire life, consisting mostly of the utterly mundane and conventional, this was the most extraordinary of circumstances he had ever encountered: a simply beautiful young girl sat opposite who actually responded to him in a truly remarkable and flirtatious way.

She leaned over the table and tenderly but unexpectedly put both her hands on his chest, moving them slowly and deliberately upwards to seductively remove his tie, "We don't need that tonight, John." When she had finished he undid the top button of his shirt and cupped her hands, which she had not removed, kissing them gently on the palm. Anne-Sophie's beautifully manicured fingers transferred gently to his face, then were swiftly moved round to the back of his head, where she powerfully clawed her nails through his hair. It was as explosive a moment as he could remember in his entire life with the opposite sex. Absolute animal lust surged through his body as he pulled her towards him across the table and kissed her with as much passion as he could recall from his, deeply regrettably, far-from-misspent, youth.

With a deft movement befitting a ballerina, she quickly sashayed around the table and imperceptibly hitched up her tight skirt ever so slightly, so as to sit facing him with her legs on either side of his, while opening two further buttons on his shirt and kissing him passionately on the chest. She took his right hand and placed it firmly, roughly even, on her breast while whispering encouragement to remove her shirt and bra. Without a moment's hesitation they were both stripped to the waist, with John almost gasping for breath, devouring her breasts while almost being impaled by her pert nipples pressing hard against his chest; he, at least, was utterly lost in a world of silken oblivion.

She effortlessly moved his hand to her leg and encouraged him to slide it upwards, while breathing heavily into his ear and letting him know that heaven awaited. He could hardly contain himself and in a rare moment of sexual domination, largely unknown throughout his adult life, lifted her up off the chair and demanded to know where the bedroom was.

Anne-Sophie wrapped her long legs tightly around his waist, leaned backwards with an arched back that almost defied gravity and pointed the way with her feet. They fell onto the bed in a massive tangle of intertwined arms and legs. Regaining control, she slowly undid his trousers, sat astride his legs pinning his knees firmly to the bed and took him in her mouth while effortlessly starting to undo the zip at the rear of her skirt. As he looked down the bed at her delectable shoulders, all he could see was a blaze of her long auburn hair moving with such rapidity he almost lost consciousness with the pleasure of the moment. It did not take long before the broadest of smiles crossed his face. This would have been the pinnacle of any encounter with his young wife, many years ago and he would, in all likelihood, have then fallen quickly asleep, but not tonight. He was invigorated beyond his wildest expectations, had no idea where the energy had come from, no idea at all why he continued to have an erection fit to kill and apart from his well-practised missionary position, deeply regretted he had little variation in his repertoire with which to continue the evening.

It didn't matter: Anne-Sophie, while being thirty years younger, completely bewitching, yet almost predatorial in her demands and movement, seemed to have enough ideas and suggestions for them both. He removed her skirt and unbelievably small ivory satin thong, to cast his eyes upon her utterly, extraordinary, nakedness; not a hair in sight. He could hardly contain his pounding heart and breathlessness, having never had sex with a woman with no pubic hair in his life. Before he could make another gesture she had turned over, face down, delectable bottom invitingly raised slightly in the air, with her head buried deep into the pillow. Hesitatingly, even fearfully, he attempted something he had never experienced in his life before, but with Anne-Sophie's indescribably tempting and exquisitely toned posterior in front of him, he took his life into his own hands and with a vigour unbecoming of his age, exceeded his wildest expectations. Not only did it seem effortless and natural, she was actually enjoying it enormously judging by the initial murmurs, which quickly reached a crescendo for them both.

Never before had he experienced such pleasure; such utter contentment; such a sensation of being the happiest person on the planet. They lay down in each other's arms, breathless, while he gradually recovered his dignity. Maybe he still did have it in him. She slowly caressed his neck and softly nibbled his ear, praising him for his magnificent effort, thanking him for making love to her with such tenderness, mixed effortlessly with the occasional bursts of vigour and encouraging him to carry on. What seemed like only a moment later, he moved to be on top of her, with her delectable legs seemingly almost wrapped around his head: pushing, encouraging, demanding that he move faster and faster. His mind and body had become completely detached from the world as he now seemed possessed with a sexual dynamism he had never known.

The noise from Anne-Sophie was unbelievable, willing him upwards and onwards with every new thrust and movement. It was not long before he had his third orgasm in less than an hour, having been flung hither and thither across the bed, lost in the passion of the moment and her willingness to suggest everything he had ever dreamed about, but never found anyone that would let him fulfil his every fantasy. He only wished that he could capture forever the smile of absolute contentment and happiness on his face, which he saw beaming back at himself from the large mirror on the wall.

When eventually he collapsed back onto the bed he was almost lost for words; surely this was the most beautiful moment in his life, which he was now convinced must, absolutely must, have the gorgeous Anne-Sophie in it forever. Her brazen sexuality, hidden daily beneath her demure persona at the bank, was in complete contrast to her indescribably seductive body. While her youthful *joie de vivre* was beyond anything he had ever experienced – no triumph in the City, no matter how much money it made for him, could match this moment. It had to last forever; he made a silent oath that she must henceforth be a permanent part of his life, not just his secretary. Perhaps if he offered to promote her, buy her this apartment, move her in to South Audley Street, the options buzzed through his head. What a day this had been. Never in his wildest dreams could it have ended this way, wrapped in the arms of the most sensational woman he had ever encountered. He was overcome with feelings and sensations he had never before experienced and on a whim of euphoria, he recklessly put a proposition to her.

"Anne-Sophie, darling, I realise you may feel that what I am about to propose is completely crazy, delusional even, but I would like you to become a much bigger, indeed permanent, part of my life. I desperately want you to stay in London with me. If you like, I can buy this apartment from your mother and you can have your own place."

For an instant he was back to being a major-domo in the banking world again, and although he knew instinctively that what he had to say might slightly spoil the mood, he felt unhesitatingly that it could be the key to a lifetime of ecstasy with her. "As you well know, I've been running around the globe like a madman these past few days – which, now I think further about it, may have a hidden upside for me – us. There is a big crisis about to hit the financial markets which I can take considerable advantage of by applying some sophisticated trickery in the foreign exchange market; which, by good fortune, I just happen to have unrivalled inside knowledge of. I can very easily make the few million it would take to persuade your mother to sell. Does that appeal to you?"

"Oh, John, that would be absolutely marvellous and a dream come true; every new girl in town needs the protection and love of someone as powerful and strong as you. My mother never really liked this place anyway, so I am sure she would be most willing to let me buy it from her. But how could you possibly afford to buy this, it's probably worth four or five million pounds?"

In a fit of probably unnecessary bravado, he replied, "A mere bagatelle, darling. I'll use the bank's money, or, more accurately, the Government's money, to short the US dollar in a couple of weeks' time. The transaction will be completed in a snap of a finger and we will make absolutely millions upon millions; we could buy the whole block! You'll have your apartment by lunchtime on August 22nd; I can assure you of that!"

"You actually would be prepared to do that for me, John? Really, you love me that much?" He was once more lost in a blizzard of overwhelming lust as she moved, gracefully, from his side of the bed to sit languidly astride him; seductively moving her hips in a slow swaying rhythm, her breasts undulating mesmerizingly in front of him, just tantalisingly out of his reach.

He somehow managed to get the words, "It would be my absolute pleasure" out, before exploding inside her, utterly spent.

It was by this time, well past midnight, and in a moment of chivalry – probably unbefitting the debauchery that had taken place that evening – he suggested that he should really go back to his flat, get some sleep and he would see her some time in the afternoon, after his lunch with Amanda Price. She kissed him tenderly, wrapped her silk kimono around herself while he dressed and with her arm around his waist, sauntered slowly to the door and one last lingering goodnight kiss. She opened the door to let him out and he walked purposefully to the lift, still thinking it was a miracle he still had an erection at his age. She blew him a kiss and he disappeared into the lift and a taxi home to catch up on his much-needed beauty sleep.

Anne-Sophie moved back to her rumpled bed and carefully tidied the sheets, then placed her folded clothes neatly onto the nearby chair, smiling contentedly. She casually sat once more on the edge of the bed recalling the events of the evening, gracefully smoothed out her very rumpled hair, picked up the phone and pressed 'redial'. When the unidentified recipient answered, 'hello', she simply enquired:

"Did you get all that?"

CHAPTER ELEVEN

Mong Kok, Kowloon-side, D-12

The Mercedes carrying Sebastian and Lyn sped with indecent haste through the harbour tunnel, driving deeper into Kowloon, where it violently screeched to an abrupt halt. Such a beautiful car was utterly ostentatious and completely out of place in the seemingly derelict, featureless, tenement buildings of Mong Kok.

Outside the dreary facade stood three or four men who immediately and without ceremony or words, roughly dragged Sebastian and Lyn out of the car. In a squeal of tyres the car then rapidly returned to the Peninsula Hotel, before its absence could be noticed: the driver knowing that his status in the triad had improved immeasurably as a result of his work tonight. Neither of them knew where they had been taken, or who their assailants were. Lyn's training in Special Forces could not help them for the time being, but in due course she would seek these people out and cold-heartedly deal with them.

They were escorted, arms locked tightly behind their backs, up the dimly lit stairs into a room so filled with smoke their eyes immediately began to stream. The stench almost caused them to retch. Once inside they were both quickly re-bound, gagged and brutally, callously, thrown onto the floor where Sebastian seemed to crumple, having been temporarily knocked out by the fall. When they eventually regained their senses the men had disappeared behind the locked door, but thankfully they did seem to be alone. Lyn had prepared all her life for such situations and although bruised, she felt in control of the situation, however bleak. I've had much, much, worse in basic training she allowed herself to momentarily reflect. She quickly established that there was little chance of escape from the windowless, almost empty, room other than via the way they came in. But she also reasoned that because they were still alive, the bad guys must have some other purpose for them.

Sitting up, she quietly gestured to Seb to position himself back-to-back with her and see if either of them could move their hands to untie their bindings. After what seemed like an age of tugging, pulling and twisting they managed to loosen one of the ropes sufficiently to release Lyn who quickly undid both their hands and feet, before gesturing to Seb to be quiet with a finger to her lips. Whispering in his ear, she said; "Are you OK, no bones broken I trust? Amateur hour thankfully, Seb. These guys may be thugs, but they have no idea how to tie a rope. They wouldn't survive five minutes herding cattle out on the ranch. And they didn't even frisk me! Let's get out of here. You know the rules; if it gets ugly, I take the bullet."

He gradually came to and tried to make some sense of what had happened over the past twenty or so minutes since they docked at the ferry terminal: "Where were the others?" he wondered out loud and, "Where the hell are we?"

"No time for that just now, Seb, we've got to get out and fast, before they come back. We only came up one flight of steps, correct? And we entered the room from the right as we faced the door. So once we get out of this room, head left down the stairs and by whatever means possible get back to the hotel, which I am guessing is due south of here. Then we get the cavalry and kick these guys' asses." He nodded in agreement, even more in awe of her than he ever thought possible.

Lyn hitched up her by now filthy, badly torn dress and removed her small side arm from her thigh holster which they had failed to detect. "I hope nine bullets will be enough to get us out of here. Stay behind me at all times Seb and if I tell you, then run like hell in the opposite direction from the bad guys."

He had no time to reply when a loud shot rang out as Lyn casually put a bullet into the door lock, bursting it apart and kicked it open in one very-practised move. Gesturing him to follow her, she moved stealthily forward with her back against the wall towards the stairs, the Glock 27 raised to shoulder height. As she got to the top and peered down, two of the men were running quickly upwards, guns in hand. She was down to six bullets by the time the two thugs even realised they had been hit and, almost certainly, fatally wounded. Seb stepped gingerly over their bodies, while she unceremoniously kicked them very hard to ensure they were indeed stricken. As Lyn ventured carefully into the street, an immediate hail of bullets came their way; one hitting her in the upper arm, drawing blood. She stepped rapidly back into the stairwell to establish that Seb had not been hit. It was far from easy to estimate how many of them there were outside, or indeed where the gunfire had emanated from. Terrified people enjoying a pleasant evening stroll were fleeing in all directions to avoid the gun fire, adding to the confusion, limiting her ability to establish where the gunmen were hidden.

"I'll draw their fire and you bolt like hell the other way." Adrenaline pumping and completely oblivious to her wound, she exited the door into another stream of gunfire encouraging him to make indecent haste as she dashed heroically forward. With a cry of "Come on Sundance!" ringing in his ears, Sebastian raced in the opposite direction and blindly rounded a corner, only to run straight into an outstretched fist and was out cold.

Lyn meanwhile charged down the street with bullets ricocheting off the nearby walls of the narrow street, but luckily they all thankfully missed her in the general hubbub and confusion. By the time she turned around, Sebastian was gone and the thugs had melted away into the endless backstreets and corridors. She rapidly retraced her steps, trying to assess where Seb had hidden, shouting his name at the top of her voice. But to no avail. He was nowhere to be found.

Reasoning that he had escaped and fled back to the hotel, she walked briskly into the nearby main street, mentally noting its name as Tung Choi, and flagged down a passing guy on a moped, flinging him ruthlessly and emotionlessly to the floor. She leaped onto the bike, her ripped dress incongruously flowing behind her as she sped forward. Unsure of which direction to set off, she let her instincts guide her and headed at full throttle towards the brightest lights she could find. Slamming her brakes on very hard at the first traffic lights she came to, Lyn shouted at a rather startled young couple, "Where's the Peninsula Hotel?" They pointed a terrified finger down the street and off she charged.

As she drove around the sweeping grand entrance to the hotel, flinging the bike to the floor and almost knocking people flying, she stormed into the lobby, blood still dripping from her arm and went straight to the concierge's desk. Dramatically holding her by now empty gun straight at the head of the floor manager, she shouted, "Call the police and get them here immediately."

Then as an afterthought, "Show me where the chauffeurs take their rest breaks."

Forcing the normally very dignified manager to run, they entered the chauffeur's room where she quickly singled out the miscreant driver, went over to him and with one blow knocked him out cold. "Restrain him till the police come."

As she took the lift to their suite, very elegantly dressed guests backed rapidly away at the sight of her blood-drenched, utterly ripped clothes, her by now filthy face, blazing eyes and the menacing gun still in her hand. When she got to the correct floor, after what seemed an eternity, keyless, she banged on the door without reply. Lyn dragged one of the chambermaids over and forced her to open the door, by which time the hotel's security staff were charging along the corridor, not quite sure whether to help or – seeing the cold fury and controlled determination in her eyes – try manfully to detain her. Thankfully one of them instantly recognised her as Captain Andrews and, drawing breath, they collectively concluded it was better to provide her with whatever assistance she required. They entered the room together, but Sebastian was nowhere to be found.

She went into the bedroom and immediately phoned Bain at the MI6 offices in Mid-town, fortuitously catching him at his desk despite the hour and briefly explaining what had happened. Lyn asked him to get over to the hotel immediately, with back-up if possible. She then put a secure call through to Colonel Sanford's *aide-de-camp* in Mildenhall and reported the night's events, asking for top priority surveillance of phone and internet traffic via ECHELON when they identified the miscreants. The ADC noted that the Colonel was currently at sea, but he would hopefully get the message within the hour. He also told her that Reed had not reported in as usual that evening and the CIA were organising the modern day equivalent of a posse to scour every inch of Hong Kong. It was clearly going to be a long night.

The hotel's doctor knocked on the open door intent on bandaging the gunshot wound, which he quickly established was superficial, despite the copious amounts of blood. Reluctantly Lyn sat still while he completed sterilising the wound, finishing the running repairs and leaving as quickly as he had arrived.

Within moments the local police entered her room and were quickly brought up to speed by Lyn. They told her they had arrested two of the drivers, not just the one with the bruised cheeks and very black eye and they would be taking them to the Central Police Station for interrogation. The Inspector added that he expected they would undoubtedly reveal nothing whatsoever for fear of being subsequently assassinated. However, in circumstances like these, they might well hand them both over to the security services, who had slightly more assertive methods, to get to the bottom of what had happened this evening. She also asked them to please arrange to send the bill for the damaged Vesper bike to her room and to let the person she stole it from know that she was very sorry for the rough treatment she had meted out to him.

When Bain arrived with two colleagues she managed to relax slightly, while instinctively reloading her gun with the bullet clips she had kept in the safe, "Good, now you're here we can go back and undertake a thorough search of the area for Seb. Do you know where Reed is?"

"Not as yet. We have the entire police force out looking, but there are literally a million places the junk could have gone to, including – if they had planned this properly – Macau. If they have ended up there, it's going to be even more difficult to track them down. To be honest Lyn, I fear for Chang Jin-soo's life. If he is not dead already, then he will almost certainly be in chains and being dragged back to North Korea as we speak. But I can't see them deliberately eliminating Seb or Reed. My guess would be that they will use them as a bargaining chip to thwart your endeavours to stop the currency attack. These guys rarely mess with the CIA as they know full well that it always brings vengeful reprisals."

Bain also thought it prudent to un-holster his weapon and check that it too was fully primed; feeling quite certain that it would be in use before the night was over. While Lyn went into her room to change into combats and more suitable shoes, now hell-bent on seeking revenge and getting Sebastian out of whatever scrape he now found himself in. She reluctantly threw her new dress into the bin, incongruously and gently kissing it goodbye as she did so.

"OK team, let's head off to Tung Choi Street, due north I think. Do you know it? I'm certain that's where the gunfight took place. I think I will recognise the building once we get near."

"Yes, I know that, it's close to the Goldfish Market. Should take us no more than ten minutes." Bain led the group to the door while instructing one of the hotel security staff to stay in the room just in case Seb called – or more optimistically – returned. Within no time at all they were on site, but however hard they searched there was precious little sign of Sebastian and the locals had naturally not seen or heard a thing. Bain called the local police inspector now running the case, to ask him to begin a house-to-house search and start questioning any of the residents who they deemed suspicious or to have any connection with the local bad guys. The latter point might take days he reflected as, in some shape or form, they were all suspects.

Immediately the call to the police was concluded, Bain's phone rang abruptly.

"CJ here, Bain. Bad news I'm afraid old chap. They have found my junk beached in Tangjia Bay about twenty minutes ago. You may not be familiar with the precise geography, but that's just a few miles north of Macau City. It has been set alight and, from what I gather, neither Reed nor Chang are anywhere to be found. It's probably a write-off. I have sent some of my people down to investigate and will be back to you in a couple of hours as soon as I have further information. I have some excellent accomplices there who are dedicated to our cause, so we should get to the bottom of this quickly. My presumption, for what it's worth: expect to find Reed in a ditch somewhere very badly beaten up and to never see Chang again."

"Thanks CJ, keep in close touch as the night goes along please. You are probably aware that it's like the missing persons bureau here; Sebastian is also AWOL. Can you get your network into action on this as well? See what they can sniff out?" He turned to Lyn to explain what he had just heard, "Looks like we have a full-blown crisis on our hands here. I had better report to London and Langley, and then set up a co-ordination centre at our offices. Do you want to come back with me, or scout around here a little longer?"

"I'll stay. Can you leave the guys just in case they return and I need more fire power?"

"No problem. Get them to drop you back at the hotel, or at my office, when you have finished up here. I've no doubt the forensic team will be with you shortly, but don't hold your breath on anything significant being discovered. See you anon." Bain moved to his car, adding, "Don't worry unduly Lyn, we will find Sebastian."

Lyn continued to scour the streets and nearby buildings for another hour, by which time the crime scene detectives had arrived and departed, with only bullet cases to examine. In a quandary as to what course of action to take next, she headed back to the hotel and some much needed sleep. Hotel security stood guard outside the room for the rest of the night. She asked to be called at 6.00am and was instantly asleep.

Bain spent the rest of the night on the phone with London and his colleagues in the CIA, both locally and in Langley, who were apoplectic with rage. At about 4.30am the video conferencing facility sprang into life. Colonel Sanford was on the line from the USS Washington.

"Bain, we have had some encouraging news for once. One of our scout teams in Macau has found Reed, who's in bad shape, and Chang who is thankfully alive, just. First indications are they have been badly beaten, but judging by the scene when our guys caught up with them, there must have been one hell of a fire-fight. Two dead bodies, including the junk's Captain and one of their group badly wounded. We have him under interrogation. Reed has a bullet in the right leg. Chang has been shot in the chest, but the medics think he will live. We are immediately getting him a thousand miles out of the way and air-lifting him to our recently reopened naval facilities at Subic Bay in the Philippines, where we can treat his wounds and begin his debriefing. I also gather that Fortes is missing. We have engaged 'Five Eyes' to see if we can pick up any unusual phone or email traffic referencing him. We may get lucky, who knows. No doubt GCHQ will contact you in due course with any updated Intel."

"That's great to hear Colonel. I'll call off the search for Reed and Chang and refocus our resources on locating Sebastian."

Sanford continued, "I'm making arrangements to fly up to Hong Kong in two days once I have sorted out a few matters here. Can you relay that to Captain Andrews please? The Pentagon has just ordered me to get some boots on the ground to support your team, just in case. They are extending the scope of Operation "Intrepid Guard" to include the current situation in Hong Kong. I intend to bring two Navy Seals from here on the Washington who, amongst other deadly arts, are communications specialists. I've already contacted your counterparts at the MOD in London and they will relocate a three-man SAS team currently embedded in the Chinese mainland. We may well need their local knowledge to track down Fortes. If all goes to plan we should all be with you by mid-afternoon on August 12th: which is D-10, so time is getting increasingly critical."

"Thanks again, Colonel. We will await your visit. Just let me know if there is anything you need. I will be talking to Lyn when she wakes up in a couple of hours to bring her up to speed." Bain was starting to feel the strains of the day catching up on him and allowed himself a loud yawn while doing some stretches to loosen up a little. He was delighted that his great friend Reed was OK and that henceforth he would probably be able to beat him at last at their weekly squash game: assuming he had the decency to now have a limp to rebalance the tally of losses he had accumulated over the years.

At around 7.00am he called CJ to let him have the news on the demise of his junk and the 'termination' of its Captain. Needless to say, he already knew – word travels fast in this part of the world. He was planning to go down to Macau at lunch and extended an invitation to join him. "Bring Lyn as well if she is not too preoccupied. I've just bought a new Azimut 77 speedboat: amazing what you can get at short notice in Hong Kong! I'm arranging a crew as we speak, so we can be there in no more than a couple of hours. We can stay overnight at The Venetian and return tomorrow. I want to say goodbye to the junk and get my hands around the neck of the bastard who has betrayed us."

"That works for me, CJ. I will get a note through to Lyn, grab a couple of hours of shuteye and presumably see you at the Yacht Club. Tell me – are all Morgan Stanley bankers so rich?"

"I'm a member of the 'Lucky Genes Club', Bain! My honourable father has made pots of money in China, which is ironical really given my present antagonism towards them. See you shortly."

Bain walked slowly across his cramped office to where the only really comfortable chair in the entire place was strategically located for such nocturnal occasions, he slumped down, managed to send a brief explanatory text to Lyn and after setting his alarm, instantly fell asleep.

CHAPTER TWELVE

New York & London, D-11

The executive offices of the Federal Reserve are located on Liberty Street, in the very heart of the financial district of downtown New York, directly opposite Chase Manhattan and a stone's throw from Wall Street. The building, constructed as long ago as 1924, is typical of many central banks around the world: austere, purposeful and fortress-like. However, the distinguishing feature of the Fed, which is well beyond the boast of the endless other central banks throughout the world, is that it holds over 8,000 tonnes of gold in its vaults. The staff will very proudly point out to anyone within shouting distance, that it has more bullion than Fort Knox; engendering a sense of awe and wonder from the very moment you enter the lobby.

Mackenzie Gore had just arrived on the red eye from London and had yet to enter its hallowed portals for the first time. He had been in the Bank of England often as part of his job tracking down villains within the financial community and over the years had become convinced that the world of international banking was, as he delightfully put it, full of exceptionally dodgy characters. He was more accustomed to tracking down and punishing individual miscreants, so was relishing the challenge of pitting his wits against the entire population of China. Following an endless stream of technical correspondence with Alex Cadbury at SQT over the past week, it was very clear to him that he was in the presence of an exceptional talent. Possibly even an extraordinary mind in the mould of say Alan Turing. They had eagerly bounced a series of ideas across the Atlantic and now would be meeting face-to-face for the first time.

As Vice Chairman of the Fed, Lewis Moyns had all the privileges that his elevated position within the organisation demanded, especially the most desirable perk of all, a corner office. He would often be found contemplating whatever new challenge had landed on his very full plate, while gazing at the Manhattan skyline and the tip of the Freedom Tower a few blocks away. All new visitors to his office were treated to the same, utterly terrible banker's joke: "and this, ladies and gentlemen, is the Fed's famous Discount Window."

Thankfully he had made it home from Jackson Hole the previous day and managed to temporarily pacify his new wife with an enormous bunch of flowers. She had almost forgiven him for missing the dinner party at the weekend, but he was sure this whole sorry mess would require another trip to the Caribbean before she was placated. As his mind drifted towards the delights of Mustique and his adorable bride on their recent honeymoon, his thoughts were abruptly broken by the entrance of both Mac and Alex; who, being the punctual people they were, had arrived at exactly the same time.

Lewis gestured them to sit at the conference table. "So, what do you guys have for me?"

Mac was the first to respond, "Well, quickly running through a few important matters to set the scene: the number of pings into London has increased dramatically in the last few days, but no foreign exchange transactions have been executed as yet. I gather that's the same story in New York. GCHQ is focusing its efforts on those pings emanating from China and have managed to isolate the location where they are coming from to Guangzhou. This location has been confirmed by an independent sighting, from one of Mr. Cyrus Jian's associates, of a large quantity of computer equipment being surreptitiously taken into a warehouse in the dead of night. We're sending in a few of the boys to take a closer look. Meanwhile, Alex and I have been putting our heads together on the problem of penetrating their super computer, which we strongly suspect will be used to flood the FX markets with sell orders for the dollar on August 22nd. I'll let Alex give you an overview."

"We have managed to hack our way into their computer system. It was remarkably easy, as a matter of fact. Clearly, because it is being used for weather-forecasting they have neglected to install the usual high security measures we would expect to find. I'm confident that within a day or so, we'll have penetrated their coding and should be in a position to prove to the world what they are planning. Once we are in a position to report back on that, we can then go into a more proactive mode and write our own software to either stop it happening, or manipulate it to our own ends. However, we have yet to figure out what approach we should take and will probably need guidance on how to, metaphorically speaking, 'cut them off at the pass'. Either way, we're confident that we're getting close to clarifying the problem very shortly. It goes without saying that we need to keep our powder dry until the very last moment on the 21st or 22nd, and to avoid tipping them off that we're on to them. But I'm sure that between us we can dream up something suitably fiendish, or decidedly harmful, to ensure they never try this again."

Lewis phoned through to his secretary and ordered some coffee and donuts for everyone, while continuing, "I've organised office space for you here, with access to lots of 'techy-stuff' for you guys to play with. Langley is also sending up a couple of its people to assist you, should you need it. Just so that you're aware, I am going up to Connecticut later to chat with Goodwood Capital on the potential problems caused by the dollar swap rollovers confronting Brazil and the rest, which I think we may have an elegant solution to. My boss has briefed the White House on developments, because we may need to prepare an urgent statement for the President should the Chinese decide at short notice to change the implementation date."

Lewis showed them to the interconnecting pair of offices he had allocated to them, made a few perfunctory introductions to the staff he had organised to provide them with any help they needed in navigating their way around the building. Turning swiftly, he then went downstairs to his car for the two or three hour journey to Westport. On the way up, he spoke to Alison Fletcher who was just finishing her week of meetings at Jackson Hole, having said goodbye to the UK Chancellor about an hour ago, who was returning to London. They discussed the forthcoming appointment with Goodwood and agreed their approach. She asked him if he could make a first attempt at a draft statement for the President, which he said he would be delighted to do after he returned from the trip.

The Goodwood meeting was concluded remarkably quickly, given the huge sums involved. Lewis reflected that when it comes to dealing, unflinchingly, with zillions of dollars, it makes sense to work with the biggest and best in the country, indeed the world. The problem was really very simple. Brazil, Singapore and Japan had to roll over a vast quantity of foreign exchange liabilities maturing on the same day and replace them with new ones. The problem was that their counter-party was China and – should the Chinese central bank decide to play rough – they could demand extortionate terms, or simply cause a default to occur. Under either of those circumstances, the countries involved would immediately be under enormous pressure on the international markets and could, in the worst of cases, find themselves with a run on their currencies, a massive drain of their reserves and goodness knows what else.

Lewis, speaking with the full authority of the Fed board, had proposed that Goodwood step into the breach and replace China. The Fed would back-stop the transaction, guarantee no losses would occur and if they did, they would cover them and, in due course, they would make arrangements with other parties to take the dollars off the hands of Goodwood at a later date. As they would never be placed in a position of risk, they agreed, unhesitatingly, to the plan. Together, they reviewed the list of banks through which these arrangements would be channelled, which were located in either New York or London. High level, exceptionally discreet, conversations had taken place with each bank in turn and they were all now making preparations for the switch over to Goodwood. Documentation was being prepared to deal with the new counter-parties and, everyone agreed, a smooth transfer could be more or less guaranteed. A series of technical meetings were then scheduled at the Fed's offices and in London at the Treasury to finalise the precise details.

On the drive back to New York he managed to relax a little for the first time in the past couple of weeks, even asking the driver to find his favourite country and western station on the radio while closing his eyes for 15 minutes' sleep. As he dozed, he reflected that at least this part of the puzzle was now – please God – satisfactorily put to bed without too much drama. If only the rest were as simple.

He also took the opportunity to call John d'Abo briefly in London, to update him about today's meeting and the safe arrival of Mackenzie Gore.

Earlier in the day, John had met with Amanda Price for lunch at The Ivy, located almost adjacent to Covent Garden. He went there frequently with clients and was always assured of a table well away from prying eyes and ears. He urgently needed to discuss the latest counter-proposal from ICBC on the oil take-over. His primary concern was to ensure that the Government didn't waver in its support of d'Abos Bank and he was pleased to receive a string of reassurances from her that this was indeed the case. Over coffee, she also readily concurred with his strategy for some sort of adjustment formula to the eventual acquisition cost, dependent upon oil price levels. It was quite clear, she said, that oil prices were increasingly volatile at the moment and temporarily heading south given the slump in worldwide demand. There was disarray at OPEC, general political instability in Asia, and the incredible success of fracking in the US; which she hoped could be repeated in the UK. By great good fortune, she was aware that a Government-sponsored report on 'The Future of Oil Prices' was due to be published in a couple of weeks' time, and promised to see if they could accelerate the publication date. It would, she reassured him, vindicate the bank's position.

John had not slept at all well, following his vigorous exertions the previous evening – which made him smile every time he thought of it; which was more or less continuously. As lunch was drawing to an end, he moved the conversation onto two interrelated topics he wanted Amanda's views on.

"When I last spoke to Charlie, he was kind enough to say that should we be experiencing any liquidity issues at the bank, to let him know and he would organise a temporary loan for us. I've had the chaps at the bank look at our maturity dates and I think we would be wise to ask for £100 million to cover us for a couple of days between August 20th and August 24th, just in case it all becomes very volatile. Do you think that could be made available, Amanda?"

"Of course, I don't see that as a problem," she readily replied.

"Do you mind if I keep this, more or less, between Charlie, your good self and me. I don't want to raise suspicions at the bank, or elsewhere, that we have a problem. It's just me being super-cautious. Is that OK?"

"Again, not a problem, John. There will be a few formalities and signatures needed. If you pop over to the Treasury in the next couple of days, I'll have the documents prepared for a temporary loan facility."

"That's wonderful, and really appreciated, for endless reasons." John was already turning on the effortless charm for which he was rightly famous. "One final thing for you to think about, Amanda: as you may have gathered, I really am a big fan of your work at the Treasury and believe you will go very far indeed in Government. You are probably aware that we have never had a woman on our board and I wonder if you would consider taking on such a role in due course. You probably think such an appointment would cause a conflict of interest right now while you are in the Treasury; but perhaps later in your career, say after the next election, or if we do, or don't, get through this present crisis and you need a change of scene? With any luck I can get Charlie to approve it?"

"I'm pretty sure he wouldn't do that John, but you're very welcome to try and use your undoubted charisma to persuade him. I'll certainly consider it if we are out of office at the next election, or God forbid, I get moved to 'Ag and Fish'. It would be nice to see the world from your perspective, so consider my response a firm 'maybe'."

"Excellent Amanda! One more glass before you go back to the House? George can drop you off."

"Better not John, as the Chancellor is due back any moment and we have a great deal to discuss. I'm sure he'll be very pleased that you should be able to resolve the oil business, hopefully! In any event, I'll probably see you very soon to sign off the loan facility." She stood up to leave and was given a goodbye kiss on the cheek, before adding, "Very bad news about Sebastian, let's hope they find him soon. It's all getting a little fraught don't you think. I've asked GCHQ to keep me informed and should I hear anything, you'll be the first to know."

John sat down again and immediately sent a text to Anne-Sophie, who was having a day off, following the exertions of the previous night, "See you later around 9.00pm. Oh and, by the way, I have solved the apartment purchase. Big hug xx."

CHAPTER THIRTEEN

Macau, D-10

CJ and Lyn sat next to each other on the flying bridge of his new Azimut speed boat as they raced along at thirty-five knots down to Macau intent on getting to the bottom of what had happened the previous night. By contrast, Bain, who had a childhood fascination with engines, which had never left him, was below deck enthralled in the power and majesty of the three massive diesel engines propelling the boat forward at incredible speed. For Lyn the trip was a wonderful and much-needed distraction from fretting about the welfare and whereabouts of Sebastian. The sheer exhilaration and adrenaline rush, as they bounced along the water, took her back to some of the behind-the-lines missions she had been involved in over the years. She was quite convinced she would be called upon to bring this hard-acquired skill-set back into action again very soon. CJ's mood, however, veered from total joy at being able to play with his new toy, to vengeance at the loss of his old one. At the dock, they were met by a phalanx of cars and bodyguards, which CJ had arranged to take them, initially, to the scene of the crime and then to the hospital to see how Reed was progressing.

The junk was by now a burned-out wreck, with nothing salvageable. Indeed it looked like it had been looted, or someone had already gone over the boat, inch by inch, searching for anything that could incriminate him and his pro-democracy movement or – far less likely – given the state of the junk, was worth stealing. CJ knew full well that he was not at all welcome in Macau; indeed he and his entourage had to maintain a constant vigilance while there, just in case they became the next victims of China's intention to quash all political rebellion. Thankfully, he did have well-placed supporters here who could be counted on to assist him in getting to the bottom of what had happened. What was very clear, however, was that there were no clues to be had at the beach; only Reed and the injured crew member could fill in the blanks of what happened that night.

At the hospital, Reed's private room was protected by two extremely menacing guards, courtesy of his CIA compatriots, who had taken up their station a few hours previously. They were let in, without ceremony, to see his leg heavily bandaged and his face badly bruised. He was at least able to watch the TV through the one good, non-blackened, eye – a rare treat in his profession – and catch up on a re-showing of this year's Hong Kong Rugby Sevens, which he had missed due to being on yet another assignment and the evening's racing from Happy Valley.

He beamed broadly at Lyn as the others entered the room, when they all seemed to realise, in unison, that they had neither brought magazines, flowers nor grapes. Maybe next time, she thought: in his business, indeed in my business, there was always bound to be a 'next time' in hospital.

"The consultant said we can take you back to Hong Kong tomorrow Reed if you feel up to a bouncy boat-ride back: CJ has already replaced the junk with something far sexier, faster and sleeker. You'll be very impressed, I'm sure. Oh and Bain here has thoughtfully booked a squash court for you both in a week's time; he suggests we bet heavily in his favour!" Lyn was full of bonhomie at seeing him in such good form, despite the gunshot wound in the leg.

"So, what happened?"

Reed raised himself slightly in the bed, and enquired,

"Firstly guys, is Chang OK? Before I was wounded, he took a bullet which looked very bad. I gather he's been taken from the hospital here, but my guys outside don't seem to be in the loop as to where to?"

"Yes, nothing to concern yourself about unduly", said Lyn, "he's been airlifted to the main US Naval Base in the Philippines. We understand that he was operated on overnight and the bullet satisfactorily removed from a lung I believe; and, although he is in poor shape, the prognosis is that he will pull through. I'm told he'll be able to chat with us in a day or so."

"Well, that's at least some good news." Reed winced slightly as he moved his leg, before continuing, "CJ, it's my opinion that your captain was implicated in this up to his neck. We thought we were on our way back to Hong Kong but it quickly became apparent that we were heading almost due south. I went down below to find out why, when I got belted on the head from behind by one of the crew, and was out cold. The next thing I knew, I was coming to on a beach and seeing the junk on fire directly in front of me, no more than ten yards away. Some bastard then began pistol-whipping me, almost for fun and screaming 'America Scum' at the top of his lungs. I was urgently looking around to try and figure out where the hell we were; but all I could see was that we were in some bay, Christ knows where."

"I noticed that Chang was close by and from what I gathered, in pidgin Cantonese, they were waiting for a motor boat to arrive to take him somewhere. I just assumed they were having fun, kicking me around before they shot me. Thankfully, the guy who kept hitting me was momentarily diverted when the boat hove into view, while the rest of the crew were making quite a commotion, endeavouring to direct it to land where we all were. He was distracted sufficiently long enough for me to take the opportunity to knock him to the ground and grab the gun. It didn't take the rest of the crew long to realise what was going on. Then the bullets started flying in all directions. I managed to shoot the captain stone dead and winged one of the gang. As the others fled in the boat, a bullet hit Chang square in the chest and I took one in the leg." He leaned over to take a sip of orange juice from the bedside table, while Lyn moved from the foot of the bed to a nearby chair.

"Over in a flash, really! Off they all vanished, out to sea. Then the local police arrived and I was taken to this hospital and had the wound to my leg bound. When they realised who I worked for, the mood changed for the worse, but at least they had the decency to call my office in Hong Kong and the guys outside arrived within the hour. All in a day's work, as they say at Langley. I'll definitely take you up on the offer of a ride back tomorrow thanks: the food's dreadful and don't get me going on the nurses."

CJ moved round to shake his hand warmly, say a sincere 'thank you' for his heroics the previous night, and bid him a fond goodbye. "I'll even let you steer my new plaything, Reed. We're off to have, shall we say, more than a quiet word with the crew member you winged and will either see you later tonight, or, failing that, we'll pick you up from here at ten o'clock in the morning?"

Formalities concluded, they headed back to their rooms at the Venetian hotel to freshen up and see if Sebastian had miraculously reappeared anywhere. An hour or so later, after receiving no news whatsoever, Lyn put in a secure call to Colonel Sanford. Bain, meanwhile, accompanied CJ, as they headed out to see what could be elicited from the surviving crew member, who was now in the safe custody of MI6.

Sanford was still on board the USS Washington preparing to leave for Hong Kong the following day. Kit was being assembled and briefings held with his small team of communications specialists. He and Admiral Farley had been in constant touch with the Pentagon over the past couple of days, as the scope of their mission expanded considerably. The Joint Chiefs of Staff reiterated their considered view that they were experiencing a co-ordinated series of actions aimed at destabilising the south-east Asian region. Consequently the 7th Fleet was ordered to increase its level of readiness from 'amber' to 'red': Farley was tasked with containing the Chinese expansion into the Spratly Islands and Sanford, incongruously, to somehow resolving the looming currency crisis. Ominously, the Joint Chiefs added a direct command to Sanford: 'by any means possible'.

The aircraft carrier's eavesdropping group had been ceaselessly monitoring the radio waves and internet traffic in a determined attempt to find the whereabouts of Sebastian, or Fortes as Sanford habitually called him. Thus far, their efforts had revealed nothing whatsoever, but it was quite clear from the volume of traffic between certain groups and individuals that they keep a special eye on, especially the cell code named Foxtrot, that it had increased significantly. Foxtrot was well-known to the team, but they moved with such frequency that they could never be tracked down to one location and dealt with.

"They always make a mistake, Captain Andrews", he said in the telephone call with Lyn, "but now that we have got every agency in the western world focused on this and related events, I am sure we will track Fortes down soon. By the way, we are almost certain that we have identified where the banking pings are coming from and its Guangzhou and Pyongyang, in a ratio of about twenty to one. The UK Special Forces unit that we were sending down to you from inside China has been diverted to check this out further. I've asked them to report into you when they have 'eyes on'. I leave at 0600 hours tomorrow; I want to check out Chang at the military hospital and see if he has anything important to say, then I'll rendezvous with you towards the end of the day assuming nothing intervenes."

"Thank you, Sir. I'll be back in Hong Kong around noon

and continue the search for Fortes there. I may have further news as the evening progresses. We saw Reed earlier today, who, I'm pleased to report, is recovering well. It's our intention to transport him back with us when we leave tomorrow. By the way, it now seems clear from events here that the North Koreans have initiated a determined effort to get Chang back, and according to a conversation I had with CJ earlier, the members of the pro-democracy movement are being increasingly harassed and threatened. Intimidation is most definitely in the air and getting more intense. My gut tells me that they may try to eliminate CJ prior to the planned major demonstrations on August 20th. We're all on a high state of vigilance here." With that she signed off and in a rare moment of femininity over the past two days, decided a long soak in the bath might prove beneficial.

CJ had no idea which crew member had survived and probably would not recognise him at all when he clapped eyes on him shortly. He had considered the captain – who had been a member of his staff for nearly four years – to be a loyal, reliable and dependable friend; however, his faith in whom to trust had been thoroughly shattered by recent events. His personal security had been strengthened considerably, especially in Chinese-dominated Macau, whose population was becoming increasingly unsympathetic to his democratic ideals; and although Bain was the epitome of an understated English gentleman, with impeccable etiquette and old colonial-style charm, he was very pleased to have him by his side. You always underestimate the quiet ones, he thought: Bain's physical presence would dominate most men, especially the local thuggery who, no doubt, would shortly come to regret messing with his friend Reed.

On arrival together at the safe-house, where the crew member was being detained 'at Her Majesty's Pleasure', CJ asked for a moment alone with the miscreant who had caused so much trouble. "In this part of the world, as I am sure you may be aware, Bain, we have a very apposite phrase for this encounter. We call it, 'closing the door and beating the dog'. So if I could just have ten minutes with him, we may get to the bottom of this."

Although CJ was a much lighter build than his companion from London, it would not be obvious to the casual observer that he was in fact a fourth-dan black belt in Taekwondo and more than capable of looking after himself. It was, thus, ironic that the Korean martial art he had practised, more or less all his life, would shortly be ruthlessly applied to the reprobate now in front of him, on his knees, begging for mercy. After ten minutes of anguished howling, banging and crashing, he emerged smiling: his ex-crewman lying on the ground out cold.

"Thank you for turning a blind eye to that, Bain. Sometimes you get to the bottom of matters quicker this way. I now gather that the offending members of the crew were paid handsomely by the Russians to get Chang back to North Korea, preferably alive, but in a body-bag if necessary. Can you make some sort of arrangement to find the whereabouts of his girlfriend and child please? I'm sure they will be next on the list. Better to get them out of the way while all this is still in play. Also could you let the Hong Kong police know that there will be two or three bodies of my crew washed ashore at some point and to get their names, as they refused to join the kidnapping? I intend to see that their families are suitably rewarded for their honourable deaths on my behalf."

"Yes, I'll attend to all of that CJ. As a matter of protocol, I have already started a search for Chang's Hong Kong connections, especially his second family who I think are a major kidnap risk unless we get to them first. I'll also alert the navy in the Philippines to double the guard on Chang. Presumably there is nothing more to be gained here? Let's see if Lyn fancies dinner."

Back safely at the Venetian they called Lyn from the lobby to get her to join them. Bain disliked the casino intensely, having a pathological hatred of gambling inherited from his father. But, in the hotel's favour, it did have some fabulous restaurants which he had visited often: especially the Fogo Samba on St. Mark's Square, which serve fabulous Brazilian steaks and endless, coma-inducing, Caipirinhas, which he was very partial to after a hard day's spying. Under different circumstances they would undoubtedly have finished the evening dancing on the tables, but, until Sebastian was found, the mood was more sombre and reflective. They were still nowhere nearer getting to the bottom of the mysterious workings of the money markets, which they had assembled to solve less than two weeks ago and if the timetable was to be believed, they now had precious little time left to resolve the matter. They retired to bed around midnight absorbed in their own thoughts.

CHAPTER FOURTEEN

Westminster, D-9

The Chancellor of the Exchequer's rooms at the House were, quite frankly, in need of considerable repair and refurbishment: as indeed was most of the Palace of Westminster, which over the years had been very badly neglected and was gradually falling into a state of unseemly decay. However, given the current mood of austerity within the country, it was not politically expedient to spend the public's money on such fripperies. The Chancellor was reluctant to approve such vast expenditure and the consequent disruption to activities in Parliament, which he readily acknowledged in private, overrode common sense. The roof of the Chamber wasn't quite leaking as yet, but who knows what it would be like in a couple of years time when countless billions would have to be thrown at the problem. He often remarked when pressed on the subject at Treasury Questions, that should The Elizabeth Tower – home to Big Ben – collapse, this might well be the only way to accelerate the process.

Sir John d'Abo had entered these hallowed portals many times in his glittering career, often brought in by his good friend Charles Sheer to help solve 'yet another bloody problem in the City'. Sheer often tried to persuade him to enter politics, flattering him that he would make a wonderful Foreign Secretary, but was rebuffed on every occasion with the same reply: 'It's the Chancellor's chair or nothing, Charlie and there is no vacancy!'

They were there to discuss the events in Jackson Hole, from

where the Chancellor had just returned after his meetings with the Chairman of the Federal Reserve and what they should do next. The strategy for containing the Sovereign swap problems for Brazil, Singapore and Japan now seemed to be agreed by all the participants; with just a modicum of technical work and cooperation needed with a couple of the UK's clearing banks which would be handling the transactions. Both Charlie and John agreed that China would be both shocked and very 'pissed' when they realised what had happened in the event that they press for harsher terms and were simply repaid from another source they had lined-up. Ironically they would then end up with even more real dollars in their central bank coffers rather than billions-worth of Treasuries held as electrons in the equivalent of a computer vault. If China's plans succeeded they could be papering the walls of every building in the Forbidden City with even more worthless dollar-bills very soon.

With that issue seemingly off the table they turned their attention to August 22nd, which was less than two weeks away. GCHQ had sent a technical briefing memo through, saying that they were now very clear indeed that the ping-traffic did emanate from the vast super-computer system in China, but there were no other clues as to the perpetrators' true intent or timing. Lots of well-educated guesses, but, as yet, nothing unequivocal. They also noted that Mackenzie Gore and Dr Alex Cadbury were deeply embroiled in the task of hacking the computer system they all now agreed would launch the attack. They were cautiously laying the groundwork for the infiltration of suitable 'data wiping viruses', should the need arise in due course. The briefing went on to explain that this highly destructive class of malicious software, codenamed STUXNET, would render "the enemy's" computer system inoperable. So, before the electronic trigger was metaphorically pulled, incontrovertible evidence must be obtained that points the finger squarely, unquestionably and undeniably at the

Chinese. Till then, no action was to be taken: this was to be a decision entirely left at the discretion of the President.

Meanwhile, Lewis Moyns at the Fed had sent an urgent communiqué to the Chancellor, at the behest of some of his fellow board members, three of whom fell into the 'Conspiratory Theory Group' on more or less every issue. It suggested that London should keep a very close eye on the inner workings of the Euroclear organisation, where China held most of its US Treasuries and where they could be bought or sold effortlessly in the billions off their computer screens.

Based in Brussels, Euroclear, as the name suggests, acts as an administrative intermediary between buyers and sellers which functions as the clearing house for this form of transaction. As John and Charlie were all too aware, ever since Euroclear launched its much-hyped Global Collateral Highway in the summer of 2012, strange things had been happening, once again off the radar, with massive purchase and sale orders of Treasuries being initiated and acquired by anonymous parties. The Fed and US Treasury had been increasingly alert to these movements and keenly watchful as these activities grew, theorising that they could be part of a concerted plan they clumsily code-named: 'De-Dollarization'.

There was a growing suspicion amongst a certain cohort at the Fed that many of the world's economies, led, naturally, in their minds by, Russia and China, were intent on dumping the dollar as the world's reserve currency. This would fit in neatly, they argued, with forthcoming events on the 22nd (real or imaginary, who knew?) and so needed close scrutiny on the ground by d'Abo and his team. They posed the awkward question: could China also be simultaneously intent on destabilising the US Treasuries market as well as the dollar foreign exchange market? This was as potent a threat as they could conceive and one that, in their considered opinion, must be stopped at all costs.

John continued, "This note from Lewis is very interesting

Charlie. Over the past year, I've had a couple of memos from the guys on our trading desk, who've also noticed something odd going on over in Brussels. I'll do some digging and get back to you. Now, two other subjects close to my heart: as you are probably aware we still have no idea where the hell Sebastian is, so we are more than a little in the dark regarding up-to-date information from Hong Kong. I gather Colonel Sanford is due to relocate there at any moment, which may shed some much-needed light on developments. Also, just so that you are aware, I have put a suggestion to Amanda that she may wish to join my board in due course."

"Ha ha, not a chance John: she's destined to be PM one day. Nothing, or no one, will quench that ambition, not even with all your charm. Best of luck, however! Fancy a snifter before lunch?"

The antique wood panelling of the Terrace Dining Rooms are an ideal place for Parliamentarians to entertain their guests and Charlie had invited a couple of his senior Cabinet colleagues to join them. With unrivalled views of the Thames, the terrace was a haven of peace and a glorious place in mid-summer for a preprandial short stroll in reasonable privacy. John was introduced to the Secretary of State for Defence and the Foreign Secretary, both of whom he was already on 'nodding acquaintance' terms with, having bumped into them both at countless functions over the previous years.

Over lunch, Charles Sheer explained that they were all here at the behest of the Prime Minister, who wanted them fully briefed and up to speed on what d'Abo was doing. He noted, while drinking a glass of claret, that their departments might well be called into action at any moment; and the much-vaunted COBRA Committee initiated to co-ordinate the government's response to the situation, should it get that far. Both of the distinguished guests were well-acquainted with the political and military problems confronting their departments in this part of the world, but they were utterly unaware of the financial dimension.

It did not take long for all concerned to be in agreement that trouble was indeed brewing and contingency plans for such an eventuality should be brought forward immediately. The MOD could quickly relocate a couple of Type 45 destroyers to work alongside the 7th Fleet, if required and they had already ordered a cadre of SAS to be on standby should their services be needed. It certainly would not be difficult to stage a joint military exercise in the region at short notice. They all nodded in unison.

The Foreign Secretary was, by contrast, frankly, utterly delighted, in his typical Machiavellian way, to learn about the financial interventions to assist Brazil, Singapore and Japan that were being initiated, using the major London banks. This, he mused, might herald untold diplomatic benefits as a *quid pro quo* for the UK's involvement, however modest. He was a past master of exaggeration and hyperbole, so was already thinking through what his ambassadors could wheedle out of their counterparts in these countries in response to our indispensable contribution to saving their respective economic skins. The Foreign and Commonwealth Office's approach to the Chinese, however, would have to be completely re-evaluated, assuming there would be conclusive evidence forthcoming at some point. If Hong Kong were to become the diplomatic equivalent of a 'no-go zone', economically and politically, it would have profound implications for the government's interests in that part of the world. He needed to consider HMG's response to this very carefully indeed.

They finished lunch over coffee around 2.30pm, just as the Division Bell sounded giving them fifteen minutes to vote on some matter or other. The entire table found themselves staring contemplatively in silence at the never-ending riverboat activity on the Thames, directly in front of them, each absorbed in their own thoughts and what they had to do next. It was deemed appropriate that they would all meet again in a couple of days' time. Then they could assess their respective departments' readiness and exchange briefings on their considered responses to the threats and opportunities that today's news had brought: each inwardly reflecting that there were more of the former than the latter.

John was quickly back in the tranquillity of the Bentley, being driven out of Parliament Square by his chauffeur George, while the others stayed on at the House to continue the more mundane duties of government. On the short journey back he phone Anne-Sophie and asked her if she had plans for the evening?

"Why, John, darling, it's nearly that time of the afternoon that we French delightfully describe as *cinq á sept*, the hours between five and seven when lovers meet after a busy day at the office."

She giggled on hearing John almost choke with delight in the back of the car.

"It's a national homage to pleasure and all things sensual; it's also how my parents began their lifelong assignation. Shall we see each other at the apartment for champagne and frivolity? I'll wear something very special for the occasion!"

"Perfect, Anne-Sophie. I'll be there, sharp, at one minute past five!"

"Can you go via South Audley Street George? I just need to pick up a couple of papers and freshen up." On entering his flat, John poured himself a large brandy, checked the post and the phone messages. Odd, he thought, two messages from an unknown international caller, both blank. He took a quick shower and changed before heading out of the door with George who was still arguing football trivia with Ros the chef. She was still taking inordinate pleasure in goading him about Fulham's loss the previous evening.

Ninety minutes later, John was escorted to the lift in Anne-

Sophie's building by the concierge, the excitement of the evening ahead and its inevitable physiological affect, making him a tad embarrassed when trying to walk casually. His rejuvenated libido was making him almost light-headed, the anticipation of the forthcoming events betraying his usually dignified manner. Without question, he had changed immeasurably as a result of the previous encounter, going virtually overnight from care worn to care free, from distinguished banker to devil-may-care lothario. If the mounting troubles with the Dark Pools and now the bloody Collateral Highway, whatever the hell that was, didn't finish him off, another night with Anne-Sophie between the sheets almost certainly would.

He stood, mouth agape, as the door opened to reveal her posed provocatively, wearing only a diaphanous negligeé, with a black silk ribbon tied in a big bow around her neck, the ends resting tantalisingly on her aroused nipples and a matching, almost non-existent, G-string. His desire was almost uncontainable.

"Christmas has come early, John!" she beamed, "make sure you don't!"

Here was a man who, up until this point in his life, had felt sex was almost a perfunctory duty: pleasurable, certainly, mechanical and mundane unquestionably - but something he would never really describe as exhilarating, thrilling, pulse-racing, or, at its simplest, a sensation which overpowered his body and mind with raw lust.

These newly discovered sensations were just overwhelming to him and were, in his view, undeniably, joyously and, utterly, life-changing.

'Congress' – as he old-fashionedly referred to it during inappropriate conversations with the chaps at the club, late into the evening, after far too much to drink – with his charming but increasingly cold wife Isobel, had become routine and was gradually, remorselessly, becoming a thing of the past. Yet here was someone, standing virtually naked in front of him, her stupendous figure enhanced immeasurably by the delectable frivolity of a ribbon. To him, she was indescribably vivacious, adorable, and above all, very, very, young. All of which took his breath away! Once again, he was overwhelmed with the desire to possess her; the default position of a very wealthy man.

"The chilled champagne is on the dining table, or would Sir prefer my version of an *amuse-bouche* to start the evening? The literal translation of which", she whispered provocatively, "as I am sure you will become very familiar with as the evening goes along John, darling, is 'mouth amuser'. I can also accommodate bite size should you prefer."

She held his hand as they moved into her bedroom, arms around each other's waists, the champagne and two glasses being scooped up in one practised move as they passed them. By contrast to the previous evening, the commencement of their love-making was slow, tender and passionate, pausing only momentarily for a refreshing glass of what he endearingly called fizz, "to keep my pecker up": a phrase she had not heard before; and one which, when explained, caused much hilarity.

Intermittently, she would provoke him into a frenzy of desire, by the simple expedient of nibbling his ear, while breathing so heavily he could almost feel her heart pound against his chest. John tingled at the touch of her skin on his, the smell of her perfume, the fall of her hair upon his shoulders, but above all, above everything in the world, the animalistic, wholly uninhibited, approach she took when in the bedroom. He believed with all his heart that he had at last found love, albeit in the least expected place: his own office. Circumstances had thrown them together; it was meant to be.

After an hour, she slowly arose from the bed and sauntered, naked, into the kitchen to bring a previously prepared plate of smoked salmon and another bottle of Krug. They drank, laughed, gently mocked each other's accents, told stories of their past and started to discuss their future together.

"I had lunch at the House of Commons today Anne-Sophie, some dreadfully complicated mess with the Chinese I won't bore you with. I did, however, get confirmation from my dear friend, the Chancellor, that I can temporarily borrow some of Her Majesty's Government's well-earned cash, make a little overnight investment, buy this wonderful apartment from your mother and return the money intact to HMG the next day before anyone knows anything about it!"

"That's fantastic news, John. Are you sure you won't get into trouble on my behalf?"

He shook his head decisively, to indicate 'no'. "Oh, by the way, what news of Sebastian? Everyone I speak to in the office would really appreciate an update from you on where he has been these past couple of weeks. I've casually said he's working on a very secret M&A deal in Asia and will be out of touch for a while. I've left dangling in the air that he's also working behind the scenes on the oil deal helping Alasdair. I hope that's OK?"

John sat up in bed, took a bite of the smoked salmon and refreshed the glasses, "That's a very helpful response. Regarding Seb, we will just have to finesse the issue for a while until, please God, he turns up somewhere. He's simply vanished Anne-Sophie. Christ knows where on earth he is right now; I just hope he's safe!"

Still endeavouring to regain his composure following the past hour's vigorous exertions, he consciously tried to calm his heart rate, fan his flushed face and breathe more steadily, before he managed to continue. "Oh and yes, the largesse of the Chancellor has ensured you will have this flat within a couple of weeks. Tell your mother that you will certainly take it off her hands, just let me know the price and her account details. I'll make arrangements to wire the cash on the 23rd."

"*Je t'aime,* darling John, my mother will be flabbergasted

and delighted in equal measure. We must go to Paris, or Monte Carlo, or wherever she is presently and meet her very soon."

"There is the little matter of my wife to resolve first Anne-Sophie. But that's tomorrow's problem." He picked up his mobile phone and called the car "No need to wait George. Be back here at eight sharp, please."

Although he didn't get very much sleep during the ensuing few hours, he exited the apartment in the morning feeling rejuvenated and ready to take on the world. Safely ensconced in the back seat of the Bentley, he was passed an envelope from George, marked 'confidential', which had been delivered to the house earlier that morning. He opened it to see that the Chinese bank ICBC had, with very minor – and totally acceptable – amendments, agreed to his revised terms for the oil takeover. "Well, well, well: that's a gratefully received blessing-in-disguise", he thought out loud. "I wonder why they capitulated so quickly?" He would take the very unusual step of inviting Alasdair to lunch as a 'thank you' for making the drafting changes and for getting this problem off his desk; although goodness knows how he managed to do it. He would then make arrangements for the very good news to be splashed all over the front pages.

John silently rejoiced that d'Abos Bank was back in business after an almighty scare for a few days, but immediately realised that this news might cause a bit of a problem securing his short-term loan from the Treasury. His 'run on the bank' excuse would start to look a little thin. So, after further thought, he decided to defer the press briefing until he had the funds in the bank, argue with Amanda Price that he should keep the money until after the 22nd, 'just as a precaution, you understand Amanda; a perfectly normal and prudent action that any bank would take in this position'. With that settled, he relaxed and headed to the office.

CHAPTER FIFTEEN

South China Sea, D-8

On the bridge of the USS George Washington, the ship's two senior officers, Colonel James Sanford and C-in-C Admiral Farley, were deeply engrossed in a private discussion as they looked at the weather charts, which indicated that a serious low front was approaching their sector. From their vantage point high up on the carrier, it was patently clear from the white tails and the increased swell of the sea, that the wind was getting up. Probably force 5, they guessed. This was compounded by the clouds on the distant horizon, which looked decidedly dark, brooding and unquestionably menacing.

Sanford wanted to ensure he could undertake the trip from the Washington to the US military base in the Philippines before it became impossible to fly: he felt it was increasingly imperative to get back to Hong Kong and *en route* look in on the injured Chang Jin-soo, the North Korean defector he wanted to question more thoroughly. After consultation with the carrier's chief meteorologist, they concluded that they had a window of a few hours of reasonable flying time available to them later in the day. The Admiral placed a call to the Air Wing Commander instructing him to prepare two Saberhawk helicopters for the trip "I think it's best to deploy two in this weather James, just in case you have to ditch and you need help. You can swim can't you?"

"Just a little, Admiral", he smiled. "I'll assemble the team; departure in, say, one hour?"

"By the way, Jim, we received a signal saying the Royal Navy is indeed sending two of their newest Type 45 destroyers to join the Carrier Strike Group. They should be here, or hereabouts, early tomorrow, depending upon what happens with this storm. I can't wait to have a look around them when they rendezvous; pity you'll miss them." He pulled out a couple of photographs from a file to show him what was on its way. "Impressive, eh!" He continued the briefing.

"I don't think it will be a typhoon this early in the year, but you can never be sure. Also, while you're here, I wanted to show you a couple of reconnaissance satellite photos we got in about thirty minutes ago. They show Fiery Cross Reef, located more or less in the centre of the Spratlys and a recently-completed man-made structure which, would you believe, is nearly two miles long and a thousand feet across. What's your professional opinion?"

Sanford took a long, considered, look. "Aircraft landing strip! Absolutely no doubt about it, Sir; if I'm not mistaken, there appears to be a couple of dredgers to the East, which look for all-the-world like they are constructing a new harbour." Sanford recoiled from the photos in utter amazement. "Once the Pentagon analyses these photographs further they'll unquestionably conclude that this is a brazen escalation of military tensions in this area."

"My thoughts exactly", said Farley. "The reef is about 500 nautical miles south west of our current position, so I have decided to set course for there as a precaution. I've signalled Central Command to that effect thirty minutes ago. Fortuitously, the Brits are coming north from Malaysia, so they may get to the area before we do."

"So, my dear friend, I wish you a pleasant flight, although given the weather, I doubt you'll think that it was by the time you land. I'd like my helicopters safely back in one piece please, as soon as you can. We all look forward to having you back on board before too long James to celebrate your promotion to one-star General properly. Oh and finally, I have impressed upon the guys from the National Security Agency at Fort Meade, Maryland, to redouble the efforts of the ESCHELON team to find out what has happened to your guy Sebastian Fortes. I will pass on whatever they find as soon as it comes in." They said a fond goodbye, saluted each other, then shook hands warmly.

It certainly was a bumpy flight, but for an experienced air force pilot like Sanford it was all in a day's work. The newly commissioned Saberhawk helicopters were remarkably agile and swift machines, more than capable in these conditions; but by the time they were an hour into the flight they entered much calmer conditions and positively roared into Philippines' airspace to land in precise formation at naval headquarters at Subic Bay, the 'Ride of the Valkyries' subconsciously playing in everyone's head.

On arrival, he immediately tasked the two Navy Seals, who were to accompany him on the mission, with getting them a ride on anything that was going to Hong Kong the following day. He then gave an order to the helicopter pilots to refuel and head back to the carrier at the first opportunity. Meanwhile, Sanford made arrangements to visit Chang in the nearby military hospital.

The hospital ward had armed guards posted day and night to ensure no further harm befell its extremely valuable patient. Sanford felt reassured that the atmosphere on the private ward was quite menacing but reassuringly protective. Chang was still in post-operative recovery, so had tubes and monitors everywhere as he lay on the bed, almost motionless. There was an armed navy nurse in constant attendance and the very large room seemed a haven of peace in an increasingly troubled world, especially for Chang; who was now, probably, a very wanted man indeed. As he entered, the attending nurse was just administering what he assumed was some form of pain relief, as Chang's eyes opened and he managed a brief smile.

Earlier, Sanford had changed into military uniform and now, with a customary salute, formally introduced himself to Chang. "My name is Colonel Sanford, Sir; I am on secondment from Strategic Air Command Europe and have been asked to visit you to discuss the closing procedures for your defection. Plus – assuming you are happy to do so – I would also like to establish any other information which may be relevant to our efforts to get to the bottom of what is going on in your country, sorry, your ex-country, with regard to the US dollar. You'll be pleased to know that the US Secretary of State has signed off on your intention to defect and the moment you are well enough to travel, we will get you State-side and into a secure place to recover. I'm sure you will appreciate that everyone in the State Department, the Military and the Treasury is keen to learn as much as possible from you."

Chang was slow to respond and decidedly breathless, the wound to the chest – as the grimace on his face clearly revealed – was still demonstrably very painful. In a very low tone of voice, he thanked Sanford for his sincerely appreciated help with the move to America and asked for a piece of paper. On it, he slowly and painstakingly wrote the names of the seven senior members of China's Politburo who were covertly behind the intended attack on the dollar, due in only a few days' time. By doing so, he sealed their fate. He also wrote the precise address of North Korea's cyber-crimes unit, a large and growing rag-tag collection of computer geeks who liked nothing better than to cause as much mayhem in the West as possible. Finally, with what might turn out to be the most valuable information of all, he managed to drag from deep within his memory the secret bank co-ordinates of Bureau 39, which extended throughout the world and the false account names they used to disguise its corrupt and subversive purpose.

Sanford knew, immediately, that this last piece of information was gold dust. It would enable the Security Services, at long last, to monitor where the funds in the North Korean 'terrorist slush-fund' were going, who the recipients were and equally importantly, had previously been. Additionally, and at the proverbial drop of a hat, it would allow them to monitor any large or unusual movements in the accounts; if deemed a sufficiently serious threat even close the accounts; and, who knows, even close the banks themselves. As for the computer guys, well that was someone else's concern; and the Politburo names, well such matters were well beyond his pay grade. He thanked Chang profusely and said that, while he was in Hong Kong he would use all his authority to ensure that every resource he could muster would be directed at finding his long-lost girlfriend and child. Chang was weeping silently as Sanford left the room.

Back at the naval base's communications department, Sanford quickly relayed the information he had received to both the Pentagon and to Admiral Farley on the USS Washington. Both came back almost instantaneously with their unalloyed joy and deeply-felt appreciation at receiving this priceless level of detail. Sanford quickly brushed off the praise coming rapidly in his direction, saying he was only doing his job. As they discussed the implications of what they had received from Chang, instructions were already being dispatched to countless intelligence officers to drop whatever they were doing and 'mine the data'. They were directed to prepare confidential reports, make suggestions, initiate counter-measures and, where appropriate, to recommend strategies to foil the enemies' purpose. He also suggested that they consider relaying the banking details to Cadbury and Gore, currently to be found at the Fed's New York office and see what bright ideas they had to use this information as part of their Deep Pools enquiry. When the conversations were finished, he placed a call through to Captain Lyn Andrews in Hong Kong to confirm his arrival tomorrow, and asked for a meeting to be set up with CJ, Bain and, if Reed was also up to it after his injury, him as well, to assess what to do next in regard to their still-missing compatriot.

His Navy Seals team soon reported back that they could hitch a lift on one of the civilian planes which routinely visited Hong Kong carrying US military, leaving around 10.00am. With that settled, he decided to grab some much-needed sleep.

As they flew up to Hong Kong, he allowed his mind to wander and explore the very realistic possibility that Sebastian might well be dead. Then, in the way that only a dispassionate military man can do, he decided that they needed an immediate replacement. The question was, who? He would put a call into London when he landed and seek d'Abo's council; and if that approach didn't yield any results, he would somehow cajole CJ into this vital role. It was very clear, from the daily TV coverage, that the pro-democracy movement was rapidly heading for yet another major confrontation with the authorities. The protestors were meeting progressively more violence on the streets, intimidation in their homes or offices and harassment, of every kind, from the police during ostensibly peaceful demonstrations. Perhaps there was some more proactive way Sanford could assist their cause in return for CJ's greater involvement: after all, he was a senior banker himself and, equally importantly, had men on the inside in China's central bank.

Upon landing Sanford and his two team members immediately went to CIA head-quarters in the Central Business District of Hong Kong Island in order to make a long series of calls using their secure telephone lines. It would also be an opportunity for them all to be brought up to speed by his counterparts at the Pentagon and to gauge progress, if any, on penetrating the Chinese computer systems – which they all presumed would be used in the much-anticipated assault on the dollar. He left a message for d'Abo, who was neither at home, nor in his office. Eventually, he caught up with Lyn on her cell phone while she was once more scouring the back streets of Mong Kok for any clue as to Seb's whereabouts. Needless to say, she had discovered nothing new at all.

No one would ever dream of describing Colonel James Sanford as warm-hearted or mawkish. Quite the opposite in fact. Brutality, bloodshed and savage violence, all undertaken strictly in the line of duty, were never far from the surface in his world. Years of military training and an inordinate amount of time spent behind enemy lines, made him impervious to sentimentality or emotion. But Lyn was one of the soldiers under his command and needed his help: he could clearly see that she was struggling to deal with Sebastian's prolonged absence, or worse fate.

They decided to meet after lunch, when CJ would be free, and have a full-scale review of the problems they faced. He determined that, one way or another, they would not stop until they found Sebastian, dead or alive.

Reed was in remarkably good humour, considering his badly bruised face and his recently acquired pronounced limp, which now necessitated a walking stick. Although his fitness was not up to 'operational' standard as yet, he felt that he should contribute to the group's activities, even if he would probably have to sit this one out from behind his desk. Sanford introduced him to the two communications experts he had brought along from the USS Washington and asked if he was happy to tag along with them as they began their investigation into Sebastian's disappearance. Reed had not previously had any operational reason to use the ultra-secret ESCHELON surveillance system, so he was excited at the prospect of discovering its capabilities in the company of acknowledged experts. Regrettably, they had, so far, drawn a blank, but he was told this was quite common at the start of an enquiry. Once the computer system started to refine its search optimisation techniques, the Seals were supremely confident that Sebastian would be located.

CJ arrived with Sapphire around three in the afternoon, bringing with him news that one of his pro-democracy supporters in Guangzhou had been found murdered that morning: his bullet-ridden body having been unceremoniously dumped in a skip. This was the unfortunate man, he reminded everyone, who originally tipped them off about the new computers being installed in some disused factory in the middle of nowhere. He didn't know him personally, but this callous and brutal action clearly demonstrated that they (whoever 'they' would ultimately prove to be) had no compunction in killing someone to keep their nefarious endeavours a secret.

A replacement for this brave man had already been identified and would be put on station shortly. However, he would be under strict instructions to keep a very low profile and in no way endanger his life, nor draw attention to the possibility that 'they' were being systematically watched. He had also sent word to his two sympathisers who worked deep within the central bank to take extra security precautions and, for the time being, only report back sparingly. This would cut off a vital supply of information to CJ and the team, but he expressed his hope that signals intelligence would gradually fill in the gaps.

He also told them of an unconfirmed report – coming from one of the endless shopkeepers in Mong Kok – that some dark-haired Gweilo was bundled into a car after the shooting incident which Lyn had been involved in.

As was the way of things in this part of the world, comparatively large sums of money would have to change hands in order to clarify the matter further with the witness. He nonchalantly added – although they all knew this instinctively – that it would be pointless involving the local police force: better to apply their own methods to get to the bottom of this sighting. However, it was the first encouraging news they had received and, as one would expect, this lead would be pursued with heart-felt vigour, no matter what the cost.

CJ ended his briefing to the group by saying that the rally on Sunday the 20th of August would go ahead, even though many of the protestors were now fearful for their lives. The number of riot police was increasing daily and their presence was distinctly menacing and threatening to the mainly student body of supporters. Despite the massive concerns they all had, their unflagging belief in democracy for Hong Kong outweighed their personal safety.

Sanford was quick to respond that he would immediately endeavour to galvanise the politicians in Washington into giving their unequivocal support for the demonstration. Bain nodded his agreement to the course of action being proposed, while Reed promised, somewhat tongue-in-cheek given his gammy leg, to stand shoulder to shoulder with CJ, armed to the teeth if necessary.

"Best you sit close to your desk, Reed", Sanford instinctively ordered the CIA man. "I want answers to where Fortes is by tomorrow; let's give ourselves a target of twenty-four hours to find out where the hell they have taken him. I'll get my communications team up to full readiness by this evening and we should have the three-man SAS squad here from the mainland very shortly to help beef up our efforts."

Sanford took CJ to one side and quietly asked, "If necessary, can we call upon Sapphire's local knowledge of China, just in case they have whisked him over the border?"

"Of course; you only have to ask", he replied. "She's at your disposal day and night. There is more to her than meets the eye, Colonel, as I'm sure you'll find out to your advantage very soon."

"I know, CJ, believe me; I know."

Chapter Sixteen

The Federal Reserve, New York, D-7

Dr Alex Cadbury sat facing his bank of computers on the fourth floor of the Federal Reserve building in downtown Manhattan, chatting amiably over yet more coffee and donuts with Mackenzie Gore. Although it was around noon on a bright mid-August day, within their shared office – which was deliberately kept pitch-black – their intense level of concentration was palpable. The only exceptions to the contrived darkness being one small desk light to avoid them spilling their precious supply of caffeine and a row of four computer screens which they were staring at attentively. They had installed two, what turned out to be, very uncomfortable camp-beds in the adjacent room and switched their work routine to coincide with the time in Beijing. Both felt like they had not slept for days and were, in the eyes of the man from GCHQ, starting to resemble bearded hippies desperately in need of a shower. The frenzied scene in front of him simply reminded Cadbury of the late nights spent finishing his doctoral thesis at Harvard; papers and mess everywhere.

They were running through the overnight results of their own covert analysis of the security systems being employed by the Chinese super-computer, Milky-Way 2. It would be an understatement to say that they were not impressed with their own modest progress. Following two days of intense effort, they had finally gained access into the millions upon millions of lines of coding driving the computer. They had already become heartily sick of deciphering complex equations dealing with China's weather forecasts, which made endless projections and pollution forecasts for what seemed like the next millennium. They had yet to find anything incriminating: but, as they both reluctantly acknowledged, they had barely scratched the surface.

"Are there any brilliant search algorithms up your sleeve which we can use to speed up this process, Alex? It's bound to be hidden somewhere, unless they're using a remote server to dip in and out." Mac absentmindedly held out a match to enable Alex to light his pipe, which had reappeared after a four-year absence; such was the need in his mind to find the answer to their puzzle via nicotine. Mac, on the other hand, was simply hallucinating for a pint of warm beer, lovingly served in one of his favourite pubs in the borders of Scotland where he grew up. His home town of Jedburgh, and Mary the delectable barmaid, seemed a million miles away.

"It has got to be something like that, Mac, for the life of me I can't find any coding here which bears any link to the dollar, or Treasuries, or currency swaps, or sneaky, devious, dastardly deeds: just bloody weather forecasting equations. I can only guess they may have used codenames, but I have tried the Latin term for every damn cloud formation and variations on the theme of precipitation I can think of and still absolutely zip, zilch, nada! Perhaps we can get some of your famous Bletchley cryptologists involved? There must be one or two still left?"

"I increasingly think we are looking at this the wrong way, Alex. We know from the CIA Intel reports that there is some secret installation in the clandestine warehouse in Guangzhou; chances are that this is where they have located a powerful remote server and, consequently, there is no coding at all on the mainframe. Just maybe the odd gateway. In which case, we have to switch tactics and direct our efforts towards infiltrating that system. We can deploy the so-called Boomerang Routing programmes to track where, exactly, their messages leave China and establish by which route they get back: pound to a penny it's via Taiwan. Then we can decide how to stop the information reaching New York and London. But just to be on the safe side, let's conjure up some nasty little wee beastie to spike their guns at precisely 9.30am Eastern Standard Time on 22nd August."

"That's easily done, Mac; subversive software, using the Chinese language programming environment, is in preparation by the boys at Langley as we speak. But I don't want to initiate its use until the very last moment, just in case we get rumbled and give the game away, agreed?"

"Reluctantly, I think that makes sense. Can I suggest that you go back to painstakingly re-analysing the data we hold on the original pings and try again to triangulate where they came from? If they emanate from the coordinates of the warehouse, I'm pretty sure we can find our way into their server."

Mac continued, "I don't know whether you saw the long memo which came in overnight? We have had reams of data sent to us relating to the secret bank accounts for this clandestine agency called Bureau 39, based in North Korea, I gather. Perhaps we can start getting to the bottom of that later today?"

Alex tugged deeply on his pipe and exhaled, gradually working towards the perfect smoke ring. "No idea what level of information or detail you've been given, but we're here to serve our respective masters, so just fill me in and kindly get more, very strong, coffee. I always thought forensic accounting into dodgy bank accounts was one of your specialties, Mac. There is always something unexpected when you lift the lid, my dear friend, especially if there are corrupt politicians and businessmen involved. I'll just set in train the hunt for this Chinese server and then help you focus on the audit trail of these bank account transfers. The golden rule of computing by humans: they always make a mistake. So let's find it."

Three hours later on the top floor of the building, Lewis Moyns was being shown into the Chairman's office in order to review progress. His allocated responsibility was to ensure that all contingency planning for the anticipated events – scheduled in their collective minds for only eight days hence – were well in hand.

"Morning, Alison." Lewis confidently strode up to her desk, sat down with his usual nonchalant air that comes with wearing cowboy boots at the office and tapped the password into his tablet computer. He was instantly onto the secure page, marked 'FBI Top Secret', which held the latest updates from the various agencies of Government. In the past few years he had briefed the Chairman of the Federal Reserve so many times on some crisis or other that he had become a little blasé about impending catastrophes; but not today.

"Firstly, Chairman, let's get the two items of good news out of the way. From all the reports I've received from the Military, the State Department, the CIA, the FBI, GCHQ, the list is endless; it would appear that our increased level of surveillance of the Chinese has not been detected by them, as yet. May be only a matter of time, of course, but, so far, so good."

He pulled a large red handkerchief out of his pocket and blew his nose violently.

"Summer cold, sorry Alison! Got a bloody temperature too. The very last thing I need right now."

"Secondly, we have begun analysing the bank account data provided by this guy Chang from North Korea. I've asked Dr Cadbury also to take a look at this and he's been very quick to provide much more insight into 'who', and 'what': more of which in a moment. However, our in-house guys here have said it's absolute gold dust; while, according to this morning's email from the Treasury, they describe it as the ultimate 'mother-lode' of cyber intelligence. The banking instructions, apparently, emanate from an élite spy agency called Bureau 121, another damn Bureau I'm afraid, Alison! These guys have got more of them than Macy's! Anyway, I'm told that despite their undeniable sophistication and long list of computing black arts, this information should enable us to get inside the heart and mind of the organisation: indeed, to the very core of their operation. The CIA tell me that they are beside themselves with joy!"

Lewis took a glass of water and swallowed some 'quack medication' given to him by the Fed's in-house medical team to ward off the impending bout of flu, thinking privately that a shot or two of bourbon would probably be more effective! After another snivel from his increasingly tender nose, he began another round of coughing and spluttering.

"Take it easy for a moment, Lewis. While you compose yourself, let me put you in the picture from my chair. I got a couple of calls earlier this morning from the White House and the National Security Agency: the President has let it be known that he wants and, I quote, 'our invaluable input', while they consider a range of retaliatory options. Should the need arise, the NSA is working through several potential responses to what they now fully concede, is a looming geo-political crisis. Apparently, the President has put the 7th Fleet on red alert and may take the unprecedented step of sending the Vice President to Hong Kong shortly to, as he put it, 'Up the political pressure' on the Chinese over the democratic protests."

Having regained his composure Lewis managed to continue, "So, to summarise the problems: one, we have no idea where Fortes is and, given that he is privy to some vital information, we need to find him very quickly indeed. I gather Sanford is spearheading that endeavour; two, we need Fed Board approval to provide SQT with over a trillion dollars in immediately-available funds to purchase the Chinese paper in the event that we do not find a solution to their computer-hacking efforts. By the way, we should also prepare to provide every assistance necessary to our money centre banks, just in case they get caught in the fall-out and need emergency cash very quickly. I assume neither of these matters will be a problem?"

Alison nodded her approval.

"I'm pretty confident we have the sovereign swap rollovers covered by Goodwood Capital, who inspire confidence whenever I have chatted to them in the past couple of days. All we need to do now is focus on Rumsfeld's delightfully insightful 'Unknown Unknowns', and hope they don't bite us in the ass, if you'll excuse my turn of phrase!"

"Do we need to more actively involve the White House as yet Lewis? I've got several members of staff working on your draft for the financial section of a possible presidential speech on the 22nd, should we need it. I have no doubt at all that we will require a hundred re-writes before it's ready for broadcast. I'm sure you'll appreciate that the President's Chief of Staff is also 'working up' the text dealing with the politics and any military dimension that is set in train. So let's just focus our people on their immediate tasks and the Fed's specific responsibilities. And for light relief, maybe we should get Donald in for lunch?"

One of the many phones on the Chairman's desk rang, abruptly breaking their train of thought. It was Alex Cadbury: "We've found something you may care to take a look at. We'll be up in say, ten minutes if you and Lewis are free? I just need to print a few pages of coding for you to see."

Alex and Mac entered the room together, each with a very broad grin, and armed to the teeth with laptops and papers. Alison looked up: "If you could just leave the pipe outside Alex."

They all huddled around the laptop brought in by Mac, who immediately received the outcome of a sneeze by Lewis at very close quarters. "Nasty cold you've got there, old chap. I'll make you a hot toddy later: my dear mother's recipe includes both whisky and brandy. It will blow your head off. Anyway, to business! We've had two breakthroughs that warrant your attention. The first is what we call a 'specific identifier' which shows conclusively that the Chinese are up to something. If you look at these lines of code you can clearly see a header entitled, 'Dollar Termination', which I think we can all agree is odd for a computer dedicated to the weather. It links to an external computer and acts as the gateway to another server, which we think we can now gain access to within say 24 hours. Then I assume we will have chapter and verse for you on whatever it is they are planning. We then need to have a frank discussion on what to do about it. One option is to surreptitiously put some malware into their computer, which we can encode with a time-bomb capability. If they do trigger something, then we can basically download most, if not all, of their relevant files for subsequent proof of their actions and simply erase everything on their system. It's really a question of how retaliatory or vindictive the US Government wants to be: which, I'm assuming, is not to leave a smiley face as a screen saver?"

"That's fascinating, Mac. Can you get this into report form as soon as possible please? I need to circulate it to a whole host of people and get some feedback on the question of what to do with this information. And the second thing you have found?"

Alex continued: "I wanted also to show you this 'quick and dirty' analysis of the banking data you asked Mac and me to look at. The first thing to note is that it's definitely North Korean in origin. There are cross references to Bureau 39 and Bureau 121 everywhere. Interestingly Lewis, this will take us back to our rookie days, when we tried to fix this particular banking problem together. Do you remember discussing with me, what seems like years ago now – 2005 from memory – when we collaborated for the first time in an attempt to close down Banco Delta Asia for money-laundering? I'm not sure what you were doing at the time, Madam Chairman, but BDA, as it's known, is located would you believe, in Macau and was accused of being the front for a host of nefarious and reprehensible money-laundering scandals. I thought we had closed it down Lewis, or at the very least constrained its US dollar activities; but it would appear they are back in business."

"Jesus, Alex, I don't believe it!" spluttered Lewis. "I'll be damned. I'll get the old files out immediately. Can you get any recipients' names? What companies are involved? Transferred amounts, timings and so forth, so we properly nail the bastards this time?"

"In short order, I'm sure we can Lewis. However, we haven't got that far yet, but our friend Chang has done us a considerable service. I hope we're looking after him appropriately? He deserves a Congressional Medal for this. I'm going to contact the relevant departments of the security services and establish a multi-agency task force to get you this information as soon as it's revealed. We can undertake the entire dollar account tracing and transfers we need right here at the Fed, but we need to overlay that with the political and military dimension, which is way beyond me. I'm assuming you wish me to share this immediately with the UK Government, as I'm quite sure they can make a significant contribution to retrieving the data?"

"Of course," interjected Alison. "The sooner, the better, please. Get someone to put the appropriate security clearance levels on it. I want this completely nailed down and fully documented before, shall we say, the 20th, for obvious reasons. Can I tell the White House that this is achievable?"

"I sincerely hope and believe so Chairman. Our only request is that we have unfettered access to whatever computer resources and Chinese coding specialists we need, whenever we request them."

"Ask, and ye shall receive, gentlemen! Whatever we have is at your disposal. And I'm sure it's not beyond the wit of man also to rustle up a barber and a shower! You guys really do need to get out more." In all the years that Lewis had known Alison, that was the nearest he had seen her get to having a sense of humour. Maybe she felt the tide had turned.

Alex and Mac left the meeting to continue their deliberations knowing full well that they might have seriously over-committed themselves: but, as they said in the lift on the way back to their office afterwards, they both liked a challenge and they certainly had one on their table now. They had less than a week to untangle the conundrum of how to outgun the fastest computer in the world. Then, somehow, they had to surreptitiously install within it a failsafe solution that would ensure the dollar didn't come out of this with a bloody nose, or worse. There were going to be some long nights ahead.

CHAPTER SEVENTEEN

Hong Kong, D-6

Colonel Sanford had assembled everyone in the CIA's briefing room, which was very covertly tucked away in a relatively obscure office block in the Central Business District of Hong Kong. They were there in order to welcome the newly-arrived SAS team and to introduce Captain Andrews, Bain and Reed and their counterparts from US Special Ops. To say the latest addition to the team looked battle-hardened would be an understatement. The SAS cadre had been undercover in mainland China for almost two months, tracking a particularly dangerous international terrorist cell, who the Generals in Hereford felt needed particular attention, for which read: 'removed from theatre'. Although no one needed to ask, it was patently clear that the outcome of this particular mission had been satisfactorily accomplished, hence their availability for their next tour of duty. The three-man team was by now a well oiled unit, with considerable experience of covertly crossing borders all over the world: perfect for what lay ahead.

"We have a formidable collection of specialists and firepower around the table and with your joint approval, I would like to add one more, uniquely qualified, resource. Could you send our guest in, please?"

It was difficult to know who was more shocked: Lyn, Bain or Reed, as CJ's previously demure, almost invisible, companion, Sapphire, joined them.

In contrast to her previous appearance at lunch, where she was the very epitome of Asian elegance, dressed utterly alluringly in her cheongsam, she was on this occasion wearing a tightly fitting, grey T-shirt, with some indecipherable military emblem on the sleeves, combat fatigues and army boots, with her jet black hair in a ponytail. 'Fearsome' would have been an understatement.

"Let me introduce ex-Major Hui. Prior to her change of allegiance to the West, about five years ago, she was previously stationed with China's Special Forces unit with the code-named 'Falcon'." He beckoned her to join him at the front of the room before continuing.

"Sapphire, as she now prefers to be called, is an acknowledged world expert in emergency evacuation tactics, something I feel we may need as this mission progresses. As well as working for CJ and the democracy movement, she reports directly into Delta Force's senior command at Fort Bragg. She is without question an invaluable local asset here in Hong Kong. So much so, that a decision was made some years ago to restrict this information to only a few extremely senior personnel which – I'm sure you won't be too offended by this Reed – didn't include the local CIA desk. I've sent the appropriate files demonstrating her re-calibrated loyalty and full US security clearance to all the agencies represented here today. I can unequivocally and personally vouch for her unwavering loyalty and, when required, utter ruthlessness. Indeed, we have successfully worked together in the past; but where and when is, for the purposes of this discussion, classified information."

Lyn was the first to speak, "Wow, Sapphire, you really are a dark horse. Unbelievable! I'm in total shock! Anyway, welcome aboard and thank you very much indeed for joining the search for Sebastian."

Reed just kept muttering 'son of a gun', 'son of a god-damned gun', subconsciously acknowledging that – in his business – a tightly-held secret was a sign that all was well with the world.

"Good, now let's get down to business." Sanford pulled out a series of mission files and distributed them to the team.

"Lyn, there is a modicum of good news which I want to impart to you first. Overnight reports from ESCHELON suggest they have picked up mobile phone traffic which indicates that a prominent hostage has been taken to a town or city close to the Hong Kong – China border. No specific location has been established as yet, so we could be talking ten miles or a hundred; but I'm sure we'll have that locked in before too long. Our satellites are currently scouring the known safe houses by the border for signs of unusual activity and I am fully confident that we'll refine the search and get a very precise fix of where he is shortly. If we do find indications that Sebastian is still alive; it is my intention, or to put it more strongly, I have been directly ordered, to get him out, irrespective of the consequences to those in this room."

He carefully fixed his cold, piercingly grey eyes on each of the individuals in front of him; slowly and deliberately reconfirming to himself that he had chosen the right team to address this problem head-on. The atmosphere within the room intensified significantly, with all involved anticipating what role they could shortly be playing. Everyone sat in absolute silence.

"To use an SAS expression very familiar to our new colleagues here, we have to 'Find, Fix and Extract' in an operation which does not allow for pleasantries. As yet, we have no idea what level of security he is being subjected to, but, we must assume that it will be very well-fortified and dangerous. They want Sebastian off the chess board while they play out whatever game they are embarked upon; it's our job to get him back on the field, if you'll excuse the mixed metaphors. With the exception of Reed, who is reluctantly forced to sit this one out, I'm assuming everyone else is on board with this. Life expectancy, if this goes wrong, is limited."

"We're all with you, Sir," said Lyn, to unanimous agreement from everyone present.

Sapphire stood up to address the group, strategically positioned in front of the large map of Shenzhen Province on the wall behind her. Lyn realised that, in all the times they had met her, she had never actually spoken in their company, while Reed was feeling somewhat ashamed, for he had assumed she was just arm candy for CJ. As for Bain's vicarious thoughts, as he gazed at her in awe, well, they were not those of a gentleman!

In a calm, authoritative and almost lyrical tone, she continued the briefing where Sanford had left off.

"If we are successful in locating Sebastian we will have to move immediately, day or night. So we are all on a fifteen minutes alert from this point forward. I can get us across the conventional border into China without undue trouble and I shall be able to arrange for suitable transport to be waiting on the mainland to take us close to the target. I have no concerns at all that we have assembled sufficient military skills and hardware to overwhelm whoever is holding him captive and, providing we can arrive unobserved, I am completely confident we can extract him in one piece. If there is to be a problem it will be on the return journey, especially if we are inadvertently detected. I have thought carefully about the possibility of a helicopter pick-up, but that is just about as provocative and dangerous as you can get in this part of the world; so we will, how do you say in English, 'Yomp' our way back, if we have to."

As everyone was looking at the individual files in front of them, Sanford drew the meeting to a close with his, by now, familiar call to arms. "I want you all thoroughly to check your weapons, physically and mentally focus, study your maps and routes back should we become separated and run through everything in your files in the minutest of detail. I'll call another meeting when further Intel arrives."

He saluted them and concluded, "Let's get our man back on the team! Dismissed."

★ ★ ★

Within two hours they were once more getting re-seated around the briefing room table. The comparatively intimate space they occupied was, by now, bristling with the electricity and tension such occasions engender.

"OK, we're on!"

The chatter grew quieter as Sanford started to unfurl a series of detailed maps and asked everyone to gather round.

"Once we've finished here, be prepared to leave at 2100 hours which is just over two hours from now. Our colleagues at Langley and GCHQ have both confirmed a positive location for the whereabouts of Fortes and I've been authorised by the Secretary of Defence, no less, to extract him with all possible urgency. And, in deference to our comrades from the UK, I've also had a communiqué from the commanding officer of 22 SAS confirming your approval to engage. Now we've got the bureaucracy out of the way, I'd like Sapphire to run you through the plan we've devised, take any questions and suggestions, and then allocate teams. Sapphire, if you please."

"Thank you Sir. I want to commence by saying that we would appear to have had an immense stroke of good fortune, in that Sebastian is being held in the densely-forested area known as Yangtai Mountain. This is just to the north of the city of Shenzhen, which in the scheme of things is not too far away from here. I've discussed our options with Colonel Sanford and we are of the view that we can get pretty close by via speed boat and then by rib to this point here on the map. It's called Qianhai Bay and, if you look carefully here, there is a convenient little inlet running to the south, which has very little urbanisation; so with any luck, we should arrive unobserved. I estimate that it will take us fifty or so minutes by speedboat to get to our drop-off point from here. We can beach there and be picked up by my contacts relatively easily and be driven to the forest. Say another twenty minutes. We then hike a couple of klicks and we are at the target, which is a comparatively small house absolutely in the middle of nowhere. It's an odd choice of location to hide anyone because it seems so isolated, so let's approach the target with our customary caution."

She looked up from the maps before continuing. "I don't need to remind everyone that we would be going in completely blind as to their firepower, combat personnel, communications capabilities beyond their mobile phones and so forth. If all goes to plan we should be there around midnight, so good cloud cover. Fifteen or twenty minutes of action, then reverse the route and back here in time for breakfast."

"Thanks, Sapphire. We'll leave one of the men from the Washington to secure the rib for departure and one from the SAS unit to guard the transportation at the drop-off point. That leaves the remaining seven of us, who, together, will spearhead the assault. Lyn, Bain and I will form the first unit; Sapphire, together with our three remaining specialists, the second unit. Team Two will initiate the assault using flash-bang grenades courtesy of 22 SAS, then proceed to secure the perimeter and exit route. Simultaneously Team One will enter the building and extract Sebastian. We have authority to shoot to kill, as no doubt do they. We have about an hour to study the photo reconnaissance of the site and thirty minutes to collect our gear. Pick up your night goggles after this briefing. Any questions?"

Sanford sat down to only one enquiry from Lyn. In the past couple of days her emotions seemed to waiver like a roller-coaster ride, from being emotionally drained, to being energised into fearsome retaliatory action: "Suppose he's already dead, or gets killed in the fight, what then?"

"Then we bring our comrade home, anyway, anyhow. Let's get to work."

The sun had just set as they headed off to board the speedboat which would take them into Chinese territorial waters. After they had left the crowded traffic of Hong Kong harbour, a decision was made to turn off the navigation lights and proceed in darkness to their rendezvous point. Sapphire had, by now, contacted her colleagues in Shenzhen who quickly confirmed that they would be waiting for the group from nine o'clock with three Transit vans. Although China regularly patrolled these waters, Sapphire and the SAS group had undertaken similar trips on many occasions. Keeping close to the shoreline, they arrived at the bay without incident and were able to scramble down into the two ribs, rucksacks laden with armaments of every conceivable variety.

Once safely ashore, the ribs were hidden away in the undergrowth and one man left behind, while the others continued by road through the crowded streets of Nanshan; hidden inside the anonymous builders' vans that would take them to the forest, some fifteen miles away. They were on schedule, arriving shortly after 2300 hours. The trip had gone without incident thus far and, as predicted, there was heavy cloud cover, which they all deemed perfect for their mission.

There were endless paths and roads from which to enter the mountain area. Under normal circumstances the Yangtai Mountain was a much-loved local beauty spot and a place to take the children at weekends to pick flowers, go for a hike or take a leisurely bike ride. Tonight, however, the six people left under Sanford's command would undoubtedly be disturbing the tranquillity and serenity of the forest. With consummate professionalism, they moved swiftly and silently forward, into ever closer proximity to the house where they hoped to find Sebastian. They had at their disposal the most sophisticated infra-red scanning technology available to the SAS team, the use of which enabled them to quickly ascertain that there was only one guard outside the building, who appeared to be casually smoking and drinking from a can of beer on the veranda, a further six-pack at his feet. He appeared not to have a care in the world. Inside they could see the figures of two men located in the first room you would enter, and one more, presumed to be Sebastian, in a room at the rear. Sanford beckoned Sapphire over. They went into a quiet huddle and in whispered tones agreed that, in military terms, this looked straightforward. They decided upon a two-pronged assault: first step, to silently take out the externally positioned guard by stealth – one muffled shot would do it. Then, overwhelm the two men located inside with stun and flash grenades, while crashing through the door with rapid fire. Simultaneously they would enter through the rear of the house into the room where the third figure was to be found.

When everyone was primed and had moved into their allocated positions, front and rear, Sanford fired the first lethal shot. This was the signal to charge the building, hurl the grenades through the glass, smash down the doors and with pinpoint accuracy befitting their years of training, eliminate the two additional miscreants holding Sebastian captive.

Lyn, meanwhile, hurled herself through the rear window, gun in hand, crouched down on one knee and saw a crumpled, dishevelled Sebastian crudely tied to a chair. She quickly went over, kissed him gently, despite the newly grown beard and whispered, 'Thank God you're safe Seb. I'll be back, don't move'. Lyn immediately raised her gun and went into the main room fully anticipating more trouble. Her eyes immediately met Sapphire's, who was by now standing over the two dead guards, a whiff of smoke emerging from the barrel of her gun.

"All clear?" shouted Sanford, to be met with almost instantaneous replies of "Yes Sir" from within and without the building.

"Get Sebastian ready to leave Lyn, we depart in one minute."

Sanford quickly double-checked the rooms of the shack; endeavoured to ascertain the identities of the guards, without success. He scanned the tables and cupboards for radios or anything that could – in that brief moment between the start and finish of the operation – have betrayed their presence, but could find nothing. Satisfied that all was OK, he ordered the team to assist Lyn with Sebastian's departure.

One of the SAS members removed his bindings and ran a quick physical check. It was clear he had been badly beaten and was undoubtedly groggy and in shock, but he could seemingly still walk without undue problem. As quickly as they had arrived, they left. However, within half a mile Sebastian was staggering and acting incoherently: he would have to be dragged or carried the remainder of the way to the waiting vans.

The drive to the estuary was anxiously undertaken at what seemed like snails speed, but it accomplished their primary objective of being undetected on the busy roads. They were quickly out of the vans, which immediately left, as the team scoured the area for any sign of activity. All was quiet. Without dignity or ceremony, Sebastian was flung into one of the ribs, which immediately shot off to the speedboat waiting, unlit, in the bay. It took the strength of three men to drag his limp body over the side of the boat and get him safely on board. They took him below and gave him a brandy. Immediately he vomited it back up and then fell into, what to the untrained eye, appeared to be a coma.

Safely back in Hong Kong in the very early hours of the morning, Sanford quickly dispatched the much-anticipated debriefing reports of the night's events to the various agencies involved. The key item being that Sebastian was back in their custody, secure and safe, although what had transpired since his disappearance was, as yet, a mystery.

Not a word had passed between the members of the team

throughout the entire journey back. Over a number of very stiff drinks, courtesy of the CIA's considerable stash of liquor reserved for such occasions, and with the adrenaline still pumping through their veins, the buzz in the debriefing room was palpable. The multi-national group raucously concluded (somewhat immodestly) that, providing Sebastian was OK, this was a text book example of how to conduct a recovery mission. The single military issue left on the table was what retaliatory action the Chinese would now take when they discovered he was missing and they had three dead guards to dispose of. It could only mean further pressure being put on the pro-democracy movement at their rally in three or four days' time.

The task ahead of them now was to establish what had happened to Sebastian in the intervening six days. Sanford quickly decided the safest place to take care of him was in the CIA building itself and, on this occasion, to bring the medical care to him. While the others celebrated their undoubted success this evening, the main question occupying his mind was whether their actions would accelerate the timetable for the attack on the dollar. Hopefully he and Sebastian would have a more detailed conversation together later in the day when he came to from the deep sleep he was now in. The doctors had given him a strong sedative earlier, put him on a saline drip and left him to recuperate. Lyn had slipped away from the celebrations with the team, telling them that she would join them on another occasion. Tonight she would stay by Seb's bed just in case he woke up, presumably frightened and utterly disorientated. She had to remind everyone that he was a civilian and would be badly affected by his capture and interrogation.

Sapphire thoughtfully took a large drink into Sanford's temporary office, where he sat in silence diligently typing yet more reports.

"Do you ever stop, Jim?" she asked. "I thought tonight's mission was a bit like the old times in Tibet. Do you remember when we had to evacuate those 'persons of interest' together in rather a hurry? Ten years ago was it, how quickly time passes. Now that was an adventure, it never once occurred to me that top-gun pilots like you could ski so well across those passes. And to crown it all, I gather they are about to make you a General."

She lifted her glass, handed one over to him, and made a slow, almost sultry, salute.

"I presume the reports don't mention the two days R&R we managed to sneak in afterwards", she continued. "It seems an eternity since you showed me that deliciously wicked trick with your tongue. I simply cannot believe the cock-and-bull story that the monks taught you that, you rascal. I always thought triple-tonguing was for virtuoso trumpet players."

She raised her glass once more, "To wonderful memories", as they stared intently at one another, momentarily taken back to another place and time.

"So what do you say Jim: we've a couple of hours to kill before we have to report in again, and my apartment is only fifteen minutes away. Suppose I show you some of the best off-piste action in Hong Kong and you can work your magic flute trick again. It's been quite a while since you took me all the way to top C."

CHAPTER EIGHTEEN

London & New York, D-5

At 11.45 exactly, the Prime Minister left his private office in the Palace of Westminster, flanked by his entourage of special advisors and walked briskly through the labyrinth of corridors to the weekly bear-baiting ritual that was PMQs.

The House, as usual, was full to overflowing with the assembled throng of parliamentarians in their ritualistic, boisterous mood. The noise was utterly deafening as the PM entered the chamber, his party wildly cheering and waving the day's Order Papers in a sign of tribal support. The opposition, as you would expect, booed and brayed their scornful contempt of the Government. The PM took his place on the front benches and, as was the case on more or less every Wednesday since he was elected, he sat next to the Chancellor and placed his copious briefing notes, known colloquially as the 'Plastic Fantastic', on the dispatch box in front of him.

Conjecture on the early morning news bulletin by the BBC's political editor suggested that he had been tipped off overnight that the Prime Minister might leave office at the next election. Given the unedifying din, it was difficult to know therefore, whether his own troops were in full agreement with that course of action, or vehemently opposed. He turned around and gave the assembled masses on the Government benches a broad Cheshire Cat grin.

Turning to Charles Sheer on his immediate left, he almost

had to shout at the top of his voice to ensure his Chancellor could hear him above the commotion. In such a febrile atmosphere, if you were more than two feet away, you would not be able to catch a single word that was said between them.

"Charlie, I'm going to announce a mini reshuffle later this afternoon. Been thinking about it for some time. I'm going to promote Amanda to be the Chief Secretary to the Treasury, so can you let me have a couple of names for her replacement, if you could, please? She's doing an excellent job, it's a big promotion, so I'll invite you both over to Number 10, say at five tonight, for a celebratory drink. It'll make a great photo opportunity for the early evening news broadcasts. As a result I'm moving your present number two, Birkett, to the Home Office, so your power base across Whitehall will continue to grow. No objection I take it? You'll need your protégés to be well entrenched across various departments in anticipation for when you take this seat." The Chancellor nodded his approval, "Good move," was all he managed to get out.

The Speaker rose and the House fell silent, "Questions to the Prime Minister."

After he had carefully manoeuvred through the usual 'six-question punch-up' from the Leader of the Opposition, the questioning then switched to the back benchers. The Member for Portsmouth South, the proud home of the British Navy since 1194, as he would frequently remind the House, got to his feet to ask:

"Could the Prime Minister tell my constituents why two of our most advanced warships, HMS Defender and HMS Dragon, are being simultaneously redeployed to the South China Sea, when they thought they would be home for Christmas?"

Although the PM did not immediately respond, he was more than a little shocked that such sensitive information was now in the public domain. He rose slowly to his feet, shooting a quick glance at the Chancellor as he did so, "I'm sure the Honourable Member for Portsmouth South will fully appreciate that we do not comment on operational matters, no matter how routine. This is a long-scheduled exercise, which we periodically undertake in conjunction with the US and Philippines' navies in that part of the world. I will make arrangements to ensure that the Secretary of State for Defence speaks with you personally later in the day."

Apparently satisfied, they moved on to more mundane subjects and in another twenty minutes the weekly ordeal was over. Walking back to their respective offices, the PM asked the Chancellor if he could have a brief word in private. "Charlie, how could he possibly have known that we were repositioning those two destroyers? Can you get the MOD to double check our security procedures? There can't be more than three or four of us who were aware of this information."

"Will do, Prime Minister. By the way, have you heard that Sebastian Fortes has been recaptured, if that's the right phrase?"

"Yes, I had a note about it in my red boxes. CIA looking after him, I gather. Let's talk further about it at 5 tonight. Perhaps we should have d'Abo along as well; I can then gauge progress directly from the horse's mouth. Can you arrange that?" And as quickly as he arrived, he was dashing off to yet another meeting, shouting down the corridor over his shoulder, "Jolly good. See you all later."

★ ★ ★

Downing Street was abuzz with journalists and camera crews, alerted to the imminent reshuffle and the consequent walk of shame for those who had been unceremoniously fired from the Cabinet and the walk of unalloyed triumph for those who had made it one, or more, notches up the greasy pole that was politics.

Exactly choreographed to coincide with the five o'clock

chimes from Big Ben, Amanda Price and the Chancellor exited Number 11 for the very short walk to Number 10. They could very easily have gone via the interconnecting corridors, but this was one occasion where they wanted the oxygen of publicity. To the assembled hacks and politicos jostling with each other for the best photograph or interview, Price was undoubtedly a rising star, if at times too aloof in their view for her own good. Her progress to Chief Secretary could probably have been anticipated in say three years time, so this early elevation to high office was a 'scoop' worthy of the evening news and tomorrow's papers: if such a term could correctly be said to reflect a well-signalled leak from one of Number 10's special advisors.

They walked together to the speaker's lectern with its endless microphones placed directly in front of them, while, as was normal on such occasions, everyone present simultaneously commenced shouting indecipherable questions at the Chancellor and his protégée.

Standing behind them, by a distance of ten feet or so and therefore out of direct TV camera shot, was Sir John d'Abo. He hovered nonchalantly and quietly in the background, feigning disinterest, accompanied by a couple of the Treasury's more junior members of staff that had also been invited to the celebrations. To the delight of the waiting media, Charles Sheer immediately poured effusive praise upon the undoubted talents of his newly-promoted colleague, joking that he had already had a spare set of keys cut for his own office, just in case there was a further rise in her meteoric career before the weekend. The new Chief Secretary simply waved and smiled enigmatically. Playing the long game, she deliberately took no questions, despite the pleadings from the journalists behind the barrier. Within a matter of only a few minutes the Treasury team had moved seamlessly into the opening door of Number 10, pausing momentarily for the obligatory photograph and flourish of hands raised in triumph.

Such was the intensity of the media scrum's focus on Amanda Price, no one apparently had recognised or acknowledged d'Abo's presence, with the exception of one reporter who covered the banking sector for the Times. With the well-practised nose of a hack looking for a story, he conjectured out loud, "what on earth was Sir John d'Abo doing here tonight? Most odd!" He wondered if the bank was in trouble again? Unlikely, he thought, otherwise it would have been a very clandestine meeting well away from the glare of a hundred press men and women. So, it would follow that there was something else brewing. He decided it was best to make a quick call to his editor.

The reception rooms of Number 10 are ideal for such formal occasions, bringing a sense of grandeur, decorum and history to the proceedings, but, given the beautiful autumn evening, it was decided to hold the private reception in the rear courtyard garden. When the Chancellor's entourage was deemed – by the countless flunkies on duty that evening – to be all present and correct (and those assembled had been poured a glass of rather dubious red or white wine), the PM sallied forth into the midst of 'his people'.

With well-practised skills accumulated over a lifetime of politics he worked his way casually around the people in the garden. The more junior members of the government first, to make them feel special and to engender loyalty; the middle ranks next, to conspiratorially whisper some harmless state secret into their ear, which instantly made them feel part of the inner circle; and, lastly, the guests of honour.

A witty speech of admiration and praise was made by the Prime Minister, extolling the considerable qualities of his newly-installed member of the cabinet. Warm applause on the new appointment was followed by glasses being raised in a toast to good fortune and robust health; and, formalities concluded, the various guests began chatting amiably amongst themselves.

John, Charlie and Amanda were engaged in animated conversation about the looming financial crisis scheduled for only a few days hence, a pressing topic that was never far away from any of their thoughts, despite the jollity of the occasion, when the PM eventually joined them.

Were it not for the gravitas implicit in his office, the country's Prime Minister for the past nine years, one Christopher Compton, could easily be mistaken for the actor Harrison Ford, but without the obligatory Fedora. Many of his enemies and, indeed, some of his close friends, had over the years felt the metaphorical lashing from his whip if they somehow managed to upset him. Distantly related to Pitt the Younger, who in his far-from-modest eyes was nearly as formidable a leader as his good self, Compton was both photogenic and superficially congenial. He was also possessed of an endless stream of seemingly spontaneous witty ripostes that had served him well throughout his parliamentary career. It was an open secret within Government and Civil Service circles that you crossed him at your peril, but progress was relatively straightforward if you were reasonably competent, suitably sycophantic and unswervingly loyal. Amanda Price was unquestionably brilliant and a very praiseworthy addition to his team, but he knew her loyalty was to herself alone.

"So, John, what have you to tell me? Will there still be a world to govern on the 23rd, or should I start looking for another job before the election?" The PM's tone of voice was not unlike the head boy addressing some snivelling first-former in one of the country's more established public schools.

In his heart of hearts, John had convinced himself that – deeply regrettably - there was no resolution to the crisis they faced. No-one had proffered any form of solution to the looming dollar catastrophe; he had been massively side-tracked with the problems at his bank; his far too vigorous private life was taking its toll on his energy levels; and his colleague, Sebastian had only recently emerged from captivity goodness knows where. Lamentably and reluctantly, he had concluded that this was a hopeless endeavour. Such a direct question from the PM had, however, left him no choice if he wanted to hold onto the loan facility he had negotiated with Amanda Price. With little room for manoeuvre, he felt duty bound, compelled even, to say:

"Well, I sincerely hope so, Prime Minister. We have teams working on the problem here, in New York and in Hong Kong."

Somewhat exasperated by the reply, the PM brusquely added, jabbing his finger directly at him, "Yes, but do we have solutions, John? I, we, you, need solutions." He paused for effect before adding, "Let's see, today's the 17th, so you've only got five days to work your undoubted genius. Anything you need, anything at all, just let me know." With that he took Amanda's arm and, almost conspiratorially, moved her a few feet away for a private conversation.

"The PM's a bit tetchy tonight Charlie, wonder what's got into him."

"He thinks the Government is leaking like a sieve. A comment at PMQs seems to have him more than a little rattled. I don't think it's directed at you John: more probably, at me. Plus he's called a COBRA meeting for Friday afternoon, which has upset nine-tenths of the attendees, as they have probably had to cancel their weekend. I won't say 'mutiny' is in the air, but they are all very annoyed. He also wants me to brief the cabinet tomorrow and get formal responses to the situation from the MOD and the Foreign Office. Given that this will be quite a bombshell to virtually all of my colleagues, I think they will be profoundly shocked by the precarious position we find ourselves in. We don't want another bloody Soros debacle on our hands." He took an unusually large gulp from his glass of tepid, possibly corked, white wine and wiped his brow, before continuing. "You'll readily appreciate John, that I'm rather short of the PM's 'beloved solutions' and may well get crucified in cabinet. Let's hope that you and your technical chaps can come up with some brilliant way out of this dilemma quickly, otherwise I may well be handing those keys over to Amanda rather sooner than I had anticipated."

"For what it's worth, we have some of the brightest minds on the planet working on this, Charlie; I'm sure they will come through in time. I don't need to impress upon them the urgency of the situation, but I'll make a round of calls tonight and send you a note first thing in the morning."

"Great. Look, when this shindig is over, come back with me to Number 11, have a nightcap and we can sign the documents for your bank's short-term loan facility. Amanda left them in my study earlier. We can also check if there's any update on Sebastian."

Within half an hour, they had moved next door, duly completed the formalities of signing the loan agreement and, over a very convivial brandy, had chatted amiably together about old times, reminiscing about events in their forty-odd years of friendship. One of the Chancellor's staff made a call through to GCHQ, where they eventually established that there was nothing new regarding Seb, who was apparently still sedated. And finally, with a hearty slap on their respective backs, the friends departed to their evening engagements.

Meanwhile, George, and his beloved Bentley, were duly summoned from nearby King Charles Street to collect their lord and master at the front gates.

As John casually strolled towards the entrance into Downing Street he had made a quick call to Anne-Sophie, asking her to meet him later at his apartment, "say in a couple of hours' time, and then could you please type up the results of the conversations I'll be having with the States and Hong Kong?"

He finished the call with, "…and bring an overnight bag. It could be a long night!"

For once, his mind was not entirely absorbed by her physical assets, but on the Treasury loan document, now safely tucked into his jacket pocket. John had convinced himself that, with the purchase of her mother's apartment, this surely would be the 'icing on the cake' in their blossoming relationship. Tomorrow he would draw down the £100 million from the Government's coffers and surreptitiously place it into the foreign exchange market. Besotted and without an ounce of scruples, he would selfishly bet the lot against the very thing he was charged with resolving, thereby simultaneously betraying his country, his bank and – not that he particularly cared – his wife.

As the Bentley moved serenely along an unusually busy Whitehall, heading towards The Mall and home, neither of the car's occupants had noticed the unmarked car carefully tailing them at a distance.

CHAPTER NINETEEN

Hong Kong & New York, D-4

Sebastian finally came to his senses around six-thirty in the morning, the alarm clock blinking by his bedside showing it to be Thursday, 18th August. He had been missing for over a week. Slowly and gradually, he became aware of his surroundings. The room seemed very bright and to be overwhelmed with the delicious aroma of freshly-brewed coffee, which jolted him back to reality. He had no idea where he was. All he could feel was pain and bruising everywhere.

Blissfully, his first image was the enduring smile of Lyn: still in her Army fatigues; makeup-less; patiently sitting by his side, holding his hand. She looked decidedly weary and drained at the end of her all-night vigil, with the strains of the rescue mission clearly visible. After days of captivity, beatings and precious little food, Seb prayed that this was not a cruel deception. His mind gradually began to clear, as he recalled the blinding flash and incredible noise he had experienced as he was evacuated from the house where he had been imprisoned. No, he convinced himself, the apparition next to him was indeed Lyn. He could also see that he was attached to various machines, drips and monitors; but inside he felt warm, safe and above all – for the first time in his life – he felt truly loved.

"Welcome back darling! You gave us all one hell of a fright going AWOL like that! I think the boys want to put you on a charge! I know you've only just woken up and probably feel utterly dreadful, but – duty first – do you feel up to a short chat with Sanford? He's extremely keen to run through what happened. Are you happy for me to call him in? He's especially interested to establish whether you learned anything about your captors; but, probably more importantly, whether you were forced to divulge any information on our nascent plans; and, if so, what?"

"Of course, Lyn. Ask the good Colonel to step into my new office!" He looked more intently at the clock and date. "Looks like I've been away for a full week? God, it seems longer; I've completely lost track of time." Then, with a twinkle in his eye, he added, "Do you like the beard and black eyes?"

"No! It's hideous: I'll get a razor." She surreptitiously slid her hand under the sheets, "Just checking the crown jewels are still intact!"

"You're incorrigible. Any sign of life down there? And when you've finished, can I get something to eat? Would you believe I have an overwhelming craving for Marmite on toast!"

They smiled tenderly at each other; she bent over to kiss him on the forehead and left the room to call Sanford and the on-duty doctor, who was the first to arrive.

"Ah, Mr Fortes, well, I'm pleased to say there doesn't appear to be any long-term damage, although – as I am sure you are more than well aware – you have been beaten up quite badly. Nothing we don't see in A&E every Saturday night. You'll be right as rain in a day or so." He glanced intently at the bleeping medical paraphernalia which appeared to the untrained eye to be attached to every orifice on Sebastian's body and looked over the nurse's chart. "Good, your vital signs are all stable. Lots of TLC for him if you please Captain Andrews. You can have him back by tonight."

The doctor and Sanford sidled past each other at the entrance to the temporary medical centre. "Will he live, Doc?"

"Probably until sunset....say in fifty or so years"

"Excellent! Morning, Lyn. How's the patient?" Sanford seemed more relaxed and congenial than she had ever seen him.

"Some bruising, no broken bones and I'll leave you to judge whether he's delirious and confused Sir. We've only briefly chatted, so I've nothing really to report."

"Yo, Sebastian!", Sanford interjected enthusiastically, Lyn and Sebastian shot a glance at each other, immediately noticing this was the first time Sanford had ever used his Christian name. "I hope they are looking after you OK? We need to chat about what transpired while you were missing, as time's running out and we are decidedly short of leads. Firstly, what information, if anything, did they extract from you?"

"To be honest, Colonel, I'm not at all sure if I divulged anything useful or even vaguely lucid! I just played dumb. It wasn't heroic of me, either; it's just that the whole thing was conducted in very broken English and, because I didn't get much sleep, I wasn't exactly coherent. For the first couple of days they focused their questions on my relationship with CJ and the pro-democracy movement. I said repeatedly that he was helping my bank with a business transaction. Sometimes they seemed to accept this, other times they just flew into a rage and just kept punching me again. Occasionally, there were five of them, sometimes three; all clearly Chinese. The two visitors asked all the questions, while the other guards just stood around and callously did the hitting. They also spent quite some time asking me what I knew about computer hacking: to which I just shrugged my shoulders. Oh, and they seemed to be aware that I was part of a team led by my boss in London. They kept banging on about that, asking if he was my close friend.

I just kept saying over and over, 'of course he's my close friend, but I'm here for the oil deal'. After several hours of this, they literally 'upped sticks' and left! I couldn't quite determine whether they were frustrated and annoyed that I seemed just a very small cog in a very big wheel, or I had simply nothing of relevance to say."

"OK Sebastian, if you think of anything else, anything at all, just get in touch immediately. I gather you're going back to the Peninsula tonight, so we'll make sure you're guarded day and night. Look, you'll have to excuse me – I'd better go and report in. I'll probably pop round to the hotel tonight, just to make sure everything is fine. If you feel up to it, let's have supper together. I'll bring Sapphire – you've a lot to thank her for! Oh, and by the way, I don't know if you can recall Chang?" He nodded to say he did.

"Well, after an intensive search we have found his nine-year-old daughter and wife; or is it partner? Not entirely sure. Anyway, they were living in Stanley. Your compatriot Bain eventually tracked them down. I have been instructed by the State Department to get them out of Hong Kong, with immediate effect and told to use your plane to move them to the Philippines. Hope that's fine with you? They'll leave later tonight, en route to the States. The aircraft should be back tomorrow."

Sanford casually made his customary salute, turned on his heels and left.

"OK, soldier boy, let's get you out of here. I'll get the nurse to untangle this mass of wires and unplug you from these infernal machines. Tell me Seb, did you get any impression they really knew what we were all doing here? Are they focused on CJ, or the dollar? They went to a lot of effort to whisk you away to the mainland. Then they seemed to lose interest in you. We really have not made a lot of progress since you unceremoniously left us in the lurch. Everyone is a little despondent, to be honest. I know the guys at the Fed are desperate to speak with you. Shall I set up a conference call for tomorrow morning? I'm sure the Colonel would also like to listen in."

★ ★ ★

It would not be an exaggeration to say that Alex Cadbury and Mackenzie Gore were having a torrid time making any progress with cracking the computer code employed by the Chinese super-computer. They had poured every ounce of intellectual energy they possessed into solving the problem in front of them. However, they both readily acknowledged that – apart from massively expanding their now extraordinarily detailed knowledge of the Asian weather system – they could not find the elusive coding that was going to do the damage in the foreign exchange markets. Without that, they were effectively flying blind in a snow blizzard.

But, as is often the case in such matters, they had a most welcome and entirely unexpected stroke of luck. They were, by now, fully plugged into the dollar trading desks of most of the major banks, both in the States and Europe and had established an alert system to forewarn them of any unusual activity, or indeed the much-anticipated mass onslaught. The latter was causing both of them many sleepless nights, if for no other reason than that – continuing the military jargon, which they now felt just tripped naturally off the tongue on every occasion – they had not as yet assembled the computer firepower to work faster than their rival's incomparable machine. If they were just one minuscule, infinitesimal, fraction of a second late in countering the threat, then they might as well not even try. They were engaged in their own race to zero.

They reasoned that if they could somehow corral two or three of the largest computer systems they had access to, metaphorically wiring them together in sync, then they would at least stand a chance. However, their counterparts in the security agencies foresaw a major problem with this approach. They were very reluctant indeed to grant them unfettered access to, say, Langley, or GCHQ, or their preferred solution:

both. This would mean the spooks having to stop work on all the other vital activities they were ceaselessly engaged in, which they were naturally loath to do.

Pressures and the attendant appalling bad tempers from all concerned, were rising with each day this decision was not made. Both knew full well that the stress this engendered certainly did not help either of them to maintain a clear mind, or to think creatively, or laterally: a commodity in very short supply at the moment. They firmly believed that the appropriate computer linkages could be accomplished on a technical level, but there was no unanimity on when to grant them full access to the machines, other than a general agreement that it should be at the very last possible moment.

Mac picked up his ringing mobile. It was Ponsonby, one of his jollier, frightfully English, colleagues, in GCHQ; which, quite frankly, was the last thing he needed right now.

"You may be interested to know, old fruit, that Barclays has just recorded a new type of ping into their dollar trading desk at Canary Wharf. Your friends in China have just taken the pesky ping process one vital step further. Lovely alliteration that, don't you think. Would you believe, they have actually had the impertinence to place a firm order to sell dollars – I gather about two hundred and fifty million – but then they cancelled the instruction in less than a millisecond after it was made!

Very impressive, I must say. I'm sending you the data files right now. Normally you could easily miss this type of activity, for the simple reason that nothing actually happened and the order wasn't executed, but given the circumstances, the boys here are all over this like a rash. We are now putting all our efforts into tracking this message down to the originating server. Just wanted you to be 'in the loop' the moment that we were alerted to this new development. I'll be back to you and Alex as soon as we have run this particular fox to its lair. Tally ho and toodle pip!"

Mac's jaundiced response to his friend was a simple, exhausted, thank you. As he was endeavouring to decipher this most welcome breakthrough to Alex, they both saw the encrypted email come through on the bank of screens in front of them.

"That's great, Mac: I'll get the FBI, the CIA, the NSA, and any other bloody acronym you can think of, to work on this as well and, if he's available, we'll even rope in the Archangel Gabriel. If we can just get behind whatever Klingon cloaking device they are using, we'll zap the bastards."

In the intense concentration of their office, Alex's humour and ready wit had not surfaced for quite a few days. So the news was a welcome relief to the hours of grumpy head-scratching, unwelcome road blocks and countless dead ends they had endured. He looked at his watch, feeling thoroughly drained and jaded: hell's teeth, it was five-thirty in the afternoon. He felt pretty confident the sun must still be shining, although neither of them had been outside the building in days.

"Right, call up that reprobate Lewis and tell him to raid the petty cash! He's going to buy the first half dozen rounds! We'll meet him at Brady's Bar in five minutes."

Brady's is a famous Irish bar on Maiden Lane, just a couple of minute's walk from the Fed's office, and is frequented by countless bankers and Wall Street types: it is 'the' watering hole of choice before the commute home. Tonight was no exception: the place was heaving as usual, especially as they were showing some vitally important baseball game which had everyone roaring their approval loudly and frequently.

"Barman, if you would be so kind. A pint of Guinness for Mac, a double bourbon for Lewis and I'll have an exceptionally large tequila slammer....no! On second thoughts, better make that a single malt, please. This guy's paying!"

"So, what's got you two young whippersnappers out of the office for the first time in a week?" enquired Lewis, as he handed over the corporate credit card. "Must be something momentous, or are you just desperate for a drink on Uncle Sam?"

"We're pretty sure they have significantly overplayed their hand Lewis. They have put in and then immediately cancelled, a sell order for two hundred and fifty million bucks. The consequence being, that we can now, almost certainly, trace this back to the original server. Providing we can get past their firewalls, we should be able to conclusively prove who is behind this, and insert something very toxic where the sun doesn't shine."

"Well, I'm glad they taught you something useful at Harvard, Alex! Do you have a realistic timeframe for this, guys? It's getting real close to the 22nd and I've got the White House on the phone ten times a day pleading for news. If you don't mind, let's wait until tomorrow before we tell anyone about this. I don't want to raise false hopes with the higher orders; my ass has been kicked enough already this week."

Lewis got them another round of drinks and they moved away from the bar towards a comparatively quieter corner of the room, which had a free table.

Mac was the first to voice his concerns softly as they sat down: "We really do need formal endorsement of our 'rules of engagement' from someone high up the chain of command Lewis and very soon indeed please. Assuming we can eventually crack this, we need clear guidance on how far to take our response. Do we simply wipe their super-computer of all its data and permanently put it out of action? Or something less aggressive? If so, where do we draw the line? And assuming we can tunnel our way into it, when do we push the button? Before they strike, or after? And if it's after, then we need to move with unprecedented speed the moment they decide to act. The trouble is we cannot be one hundred percent certain we will be quick enough to prevent a global financial panic.

Statistically speaking, Lewis, the odds are not stacked in our favour."

"OK, I'll speak to Alison tonight and get you some guidance. She's bound to have to run this through a thousand people. Personally, I'd kick their sorry ass, but I'm not the voice of reason here. How long do you think it will take you to configure the computer system necessary to match their speed? I take it we will still need to take this course of action, even if you can eventually figure out where the 'sell orders' are coming from?"

"It would be a very wise precaution to take, Lewis. We need that as an insurance policy. Let me come back to you with a better estimate of the down-time we would need to accomplish a stable and usable connection between the various agencies' computers. Obviously, we will endeavour to keep this to an absolute minimum. But we must devise a very robust circuit breaker of some sort in order to stop their 'sell orders' flooding the market on Monday next."

Alex raised his glass to his mouth and in doing so caught a glimpse of the three of them in one of the pub's mirrors: "Compared to the beautifully suited and booted bankers around us, Mac, we are starting to look a tad feral. I'm amazed they let us in here frankly. Perhaps we'd better get back to the office and save these guys' skins from the impending Armageddon. Thanks for the drinks Lewis; it's been a most welcome break."

With that, they downed their glasses and got up to walk slowly back to the Fed's offices. When they were out of the noisy bar, Alex continued:

"By the way, Lewis, we are also making great progress on tracking down the vast number of participants in the Bureau 39, Bureau 121, money-laundering matter, emanating out of North Korea. Your boys on the floor below us have done a wonderful job sorting out what sums got transferred to what accounts, the specific dates, and (most importantly) to whom the money was sent. You're going to be amazed. I don't recognise half, or even a tenth, of the names on the list so far, but there are one or two humdingers. I am having the tracing team check, double-check and then re-check the list again, as it's absolute dynamite. Plus, it's all being routed via our old banking friends in Macau."

Lewis was meandering along Maiden Lane, absorbing this welter of new information when a text message came through, asking if Mac and Alex could make a conference call with Hong Kong in an hour. They entered the Fed's offices and went up to the Vice Chairman's office to await the call.

★ ★ ★

The previous evening had seen Sebastian being formally discharged from the doctor's care and transferred to the comforting and most welcome embrace of Lyn. They had effortlessly settled back into their rooms at the Peninsula Hotel, had a memorable hour of relaxation in the Spa and booked a table for four at Gaddi's to sample their world famous Challons pressed duck. Lyn pleasantly concluded that the patient was at last beginning to recover his *joie de vivre* and following his earlier stone therapy massage, was already moving his limbs with more fluency. The black eyes were fading, the beard had thankfully been removed and his hair cut. It wouldn't be long before he was back to his old self, judging by the hand resting languidly on her thigh.

Over supper Sanford meticulously ran through the past week's events to establish that no point, however minor, had been missed. He kept coming back to the curious reference – in his eyes at least – to John d'Abo being a "close friend". This seemed to have no bearing at all upon the reason for his being taken prisoner, which both he and Sapphire assumed was Sebastian's association with CJ and the upcoming protest march on Saturday. Was this the 'dog that didn't bark' he wondered. As no-one could find a suitable or coherent explanation, they moved on to dessert and a full-blown replay of the night of Seb's recapture. He had absolutely no idea of Sapphire's previous military background and to be told she had eliminated the two guards inside the house simply flabbergasted him.

Lyn had arranged for them to have a series of sequential conference calls with New York, Langley and d'Abo's bank, starting at seven the next morning. By the time the waiter was serving them coffee, they were both starting to flag somewhat and she was regretting her organisational enthusiasm for breakfast meetings. So they retired to bed early and blissfully enjoyed an hour of very slow lovemaking involving the minimum of movement. It seemed much more than a week that they had been apart, but their desire for each other had grown immeasurably. This was definitely 'the one' she thought.

The calls to the States followed the routine debriefing sessions that Lyn and Sanford had been through a thousand times in their career, post a mission. Although their counterparts were meticulous in their questioning, neither the Army nor the Federal Reserve teams managed to elicit anything new or insightful from Sebastian. The rescue had gone exactly as planned, mercifully there were no casualties on our side, Fortes was back in safe hands, but they had not advanced their understanding of the enemy's intentions one iota. Nor had they added to their ability to counter the looming threat. There was an increasing air of hopelessness and desperation attached to their conversations.

It was after midnight when they eventually reached John in London. He too had been very actively involved in transatlantic calls all evening, pausing only briefly to dictate his notes to Anne-Sophie, who sat silently and patiently by his side through the passing hours.

"Hi Sebastian, a hearty welcome back! We have all been worried sick here. I gather you've incurred some unsightly bumps and bruises, but nothing a stiff whisky won't fix, I'll venture? Very pleased you're safe. So, are we any further forward at your end? I have minor bits and pieces to update you and your colleagues on from here: someone is fishing at Barclays with sell orders that go in and are immediately retracted and the oil takeover seems back on track, although, obviously, we won't know whether that has been a monumental waste of time until next week. You may also be pleased to know that Amanda Price has been promoted to the cabinet. However, I gather from my conversations earlier tonight that we have got absolutely nowhere with our efforts to break into the Chinese super-computer. All in all, a bit of a calamity really! I'm writing up a report for the Chancellor, but unless we have something more concrete by way of a plan, well…."

He trailed off into silence, while Anne-Sophie, by now changed into her negligée, came over and put an arm around his shoulder. He patted her hand, more to comfort himself than her.

"Sir John, let's not be overly downhearted, even at this late stage. I've had a detailed chat with Alex and Mac who are confident they will resolve the matter. They have written the spoiler programme they intend to plant inside the Chinese machine and are just painstakingly ploughing their way through the coding to find a way in. It's frustrating, certainly, but they are methodically working the problem. Please tell everyone in the office I'm fine and will be back with them for a celebratory drink on the 23rd or 24th."

And with that, they all said 'goodbye', promising to keep in constant touch as events unfolded in the few days left to them. John, wearily, went over to Anne-Sophie's desk and finalised his report to the cabinet. As a matter of courtesy and protocol, he also sent a copy of it to the Chairman of the Federal Reserve. He was far from happy with its gloomy conclusions and lack of 'solutions'. Sebastian's upbeat comments and, in his view, false agenda of hope, simply went straight over his head.

In order to protect his own increasingly precarious position, should no way out of the problem be forthcoming in the time left to them, he decided to finish the update with a suggestion to find a political solution urgently to the impending débacle. He hoped that by surreptitiously passing the buck to Whitehall, hidden deep within a long paragraph on page eighteen of the report, he would somehow avoid the reputational damage that would surely follow if it all went disastrously wrong.

CHAPTER TWENTY

South China Sea & London, D-3

First light broke on Friday 19th August to a day of beautiful clear skies, unlimited visibility and agreeably calm seas. The languid and leisurely ascendency of the sun on the far horizon was in sharp contrast to the frenetic activities on-board the USS Washington. The entire ship's company and its substantial air-wing, were now at battle stations and steadily making preparations for what they all anticipated would be a major altercation with the Chinese navy. Operation "Intrepid Guard" was now in full force.

The Carrier Group was gradually and purposefully snaking its way northwards through the Spratly Islands; the typhoon of a couple of days ago, now a distant memory. Despite the hour, Admiral Farley was perched on his traditional, if incongruous, wooden Captain's Chair, located centrally on the bridge. He was fully immersed in the study of his charts, when he received a signal from the Executive Officer of HMS Dragon.

It told him that the two British destroyers were now on station fifty nautical miles due south of Fiery Cross Reef, the focus of the bitter dispute over territorial conquest by the Chinese. It went on to say that they had detected nothing new by way of enemy surface vessels on their radar and satellite systems, apart from what appeared to be a couple of smallish supply ships heading their way, and superficially, all seemed quiet. He asked the signals officer to reply with an estimate of when the Washington would be in a position to rendezvous with the British contingent and then, purposefully, left the bridge. He immediately went to the 'situation room', two decks below and assembled his senior commanders. The, by now, constant roar of jets taking off and landing, created a reassuring and comforting effect amongst the carrier's crew, as the officers sat down in their tropical whites to hear what their commander-in-chief had to say.

"I've been weighing up two main options currently being war-gamed at the Pentagon", Farley commenced. "Firstly, do we adopt the Kennedy solution, employed in the Cuban Missile Crisis during October '62 and blockade the Reef to all Chinese vessels; or secondly, do we play hard ball and immediately go in with the marines, retake the place and raise the Philippines flag? Both approaches are equally provocative and confrontational. The question before us therefore is: how will the enemy react under each scenario?"

Like most Admirals since time immemorial, he had hawks and doves on his staff who argued for wildly different approaches to the threat they each perceived. The barrack-room lawyers amongst them urged him to seek a United Nations Resolution of some sort, as an international seal of approval for their actions, while the opposing faction demanded firm pre-emptive action before this potential conflict escalated any further and engulfed the entire region. Unlike a good many commanders in the field, who invariably took their decisions single-handedly, Farley positively encouraged debate amongst his staff. Like an erudite professor at the end of a rather boisterous tutorial, he then summed up the mood of the room.

"Ladies and gentlemen, a moment of silence, please. I thank you all for attempting to elucidate your respective and, if I may say so, diametrically opposed positions. It's good to have a forthright discussion and I'd like to show my appreciation to everyone for their contribution. So, here is what I am proposing to do. Firstly, I want to remind everyone that China has signed a Declaration on the Conduct of Parties in the South China Sea. By building on Fiery Cross Reef and, for that matter, attempting to reclaim Johnson South Reef for similar military purposes, they are in breach of this international agreement. Their actions are simultaneously belligerent and intimidating to this region's stability.

Within a thousand mile radius of Fiery Cross you have Indonesia, Brunei, Malaysia, the Philippines and Vietnam; all therefore easily reachable by fighter jets if an operational runway is established there. Judging by their plans, the military base they appear to be building would be twice the size of our installation on Diego Garcia in the Indian Ocean. So, we have to stop this happening, as it is a very serious threat to the interests of the United States. I don't need to remind everyone here that diplomatic solutions have been attempted, but they have simply fallen on deaf ears. We are now tasked with implementing a military solution."

The Admiral paused to let them digest this position statement, prior to continuing.

"Before revealing the broad outline of my plan, I want also to draw your attention to something that I have been discussing in the strictest of confidence, with Colonel Sanford: namely, a possible attempt by the Chinese, scheduled apparently for August 22nd, to destabilise the foreign exchange markets. This is only three days from now, but it is pertinent to the situation we now face.

We know the aircraft carrier, Liaoning, is heading into theatre, with a mini Battle Group of half a dozen ships and it would appear that its arrival will intentionally coincide with, what the Chinese hope, is massive disruption to the US dollar on that day. It is not difficult to predict they will wish to escalate their conquest of these reefs quickly under the umbrella of chaos in the financial markets."

He brought a map of the region up onto the wall-sized screen behind him.

"So, to the operational plan: we are expecting a contingent of the Philippines commando brigade to land on board shortly, fifty men. They will, symbolically, spearhead the mission to retake Fiery Cross and to give us some political cover for our actions. Secondly, we know from our intelligence sources that the Liaoning's senior naval commanders feel that she is vulnerable to submarine attack. The helicopter and air shield at her disposal is not fully functional as yet, a consequence of leaving the dry dock at least two months early to spearhead this mission. More fool them! So, I am proposing to do something out of left field. Given the lengths to which we go to keep such matters top secret, I am going to let it be known that our nuclear submarine, 'The City of Corpus Christie', is now fully deployed on active duty in the region. That should make them sit up and think twice! I've asked the State Department to deny the rumour, started by us, naturally, that the submarine is in these waters. Nothing like a denial to demonstrate the opposite and make them feel we are concealing something. It would not surprise me if their Battle Group starts a spot of serious zigzagging as soon as this information goes public in a few hours time! I have also been in direct communication with the Japanese military high command and asked them to effectively surround the disputed Senkaku Islands, which they have willingly agreed to. Hopefully, this co-ordinated action will split the Chinese forces, or at the very least, cause them to have to look two ways at once."

Lots of questions followed from the assembled specialists, who were now huddled around chart tables and making plans for their respective teams to go into full-blown action. It had been quite some time since the 7th was engaged in such a mission, so the mood was boisterous and the conversations animated. They would be with the Brits by noon. The carrier's air-wing was already deploying helicopters to scout ahead and provide cover and the Philippines commandos would be with them shortly. The assault would be scheduled for five in the evening to give them good light to land and darkness soon after to consolidate their position. Satellite reconnaissance had put the number of men on the reef at no more than two hundred and there was little sign of any defensive capability or military personnel. They expected to meet little resistance, only engineers and construction workers drafted in to complete the runway.

★ ★ ★

John d'Abo's day had started with him in exceptionally high spirits. He had thoroughly enjoyed a very enthusiastic twenty minutes of exceedingly energetic sex with Anne-Sophie and was ready to take on the world once more. His despondency of the previous evening, now a distant memory.

Over breakfast he checked his computer to confirm that the funds from the Treasury had been cleared into his private account at the bank and were now securely lodged in his name. He picked up his mobile to immediately have a quiet, decidedly conspiratorial, word with the bank's finance director. His ability to bully his staff was legendary, but he had to ensure that everything – absolutely everything – relating to the transfer remained secret. He went to great lengths to impress upon him the unflinching requirement to never, ever, disclose the inward transfer, or what was subsequently done with it, as a matter of grave national security. For d'Abo, such an intimidating conversation was a proverbial 'piece of cake'. With that part of the day's jigsaw puzzle firmly in place, he set off to the office while Anne-Sophie went to her apartment to change into more formal business clothes.

After running through the morning mail and email traffic,

he put a call through to Charlie Sheer to make sure he had received the cabinet briefing memo and to ask whether he required anything further from him. "Only a way out of this unholy mess, John", was all he got, somewhat tersely, from the Chancellor.

He then called Barclays Bank and asked to be put through to one of their senior managing directors dealing with foreign exchange matters for Ultra High Net Worth customers of the bank. He had had regular dealings with the institution over the past thirty years in a private capacity, but what he was about to propose would – he knew well – come as quite a shock.

"Ah, good to talk with you again, Sir John. Buying another bank are we?"

The unctuous, utterly insincere, tone of voice came naturally to someone who spent his entire career sucking up to billionaires. John gritted his teeth at the audacity of the comment, as the man from Barclays continued:

"I've noticed in the Wall Street Journal that you've just received your US licence, very well done. You must be extremely delighted."

Trying to contain his legendary temper, John commenced his instructions.

"My bank will shortly be transferring over to you the sum of one hundred million sterling which is to be deposited in my personal account with you. It should be on your screen in the next couple of minutes. I want you to use the entire amount as security to short the US dollar in my personal capacity. I want you to establish a forward contract so that I am in and out of the market within a one week window. The dollar to fall, sterling to rise."

"I'm sorry, did I hear you correctly Sir John; can you confirm you said 'short'? Our analysts' collective view of the dollar is that it's on an upward trajectory over the next year. Let me take a quick look at the internal FX screen: yep, today we are at $1.50. The projected graphs show the dollar going from strength to strength as the US economy recovers. Unstoppable, I would say, could go well below $1.40 to the pound, even $1.30 or lower. Are you sure you want to short it, you will be going entirely against the market trend?"

"Absolutely! Now could you get on with it please? I have a very busy day!"

"As you wish, Sir John. I'll send a formal confirmation to your private email that we have executed that transaction the moment we have received cleared funds."

When his client had put the phone down, the ever-cautious banker paused to collect his thoughts. Did d'Abo know something he didn't? He decided to call the compliance department and asked them to recover the recording of the conversation and immediately send it to the bank's Chief Executive. Within five minutes he had sent an internal memo to the CEO, if for no other reason than he didn't want to be personally blamed if this all went horribly wrong, as he fully expected it to do. Equally, if the bank's entire foreign exchange experts had missed something that the exceptionally well regarded d'Abo had spotted, he wanted a share of the prize money come bonus time.

The CEO listened intently to the tape of the conversation, carefully reading the internal memo he had received moments earlier. Immediately, he called his senior $/£ trader and asked him to come to his office. They listened again to the recording and double-checked that the money had arrived with the irrevocable instruction from d'Abo's bank. It had. They were now legally obliged to execute the transaction, but both thought, impolitely, that he'd lost his marbles.

With a shrug of their collective shoulders and being exceptionally busy men, neither gave it further consideration. After all, they received and dealt with eccentric and unconventional requests on a daily basis. It was not their money being thrown away. The bank would take d'Abo's bet any day of the week. It was certainly a far from normal transaction, but they would make a handsome commission, so what was there to worry about? Both agreed that despite d'Abo's chutzpah, acknowledged financial audacity and reputation for risk-taking, there was not a chance in hell that the dollar was going to fall.

Two hours later – after ruminating further on the eccentricity of the FX order, the contrarian position being taken by d'Abo against all conventional wisdom in the market and the massive external scrutiny the bank was now under on its dollar trading desk – the CEO thought it prudent to make a quick call to his new friends at GCHQ.

At his office desk again, John opened his private email account and saw the confirmation that the 'short sell' order had gone through. Even the slightest disruption to the US FX market on Monday afternoon, when the States opened, would see the dollar tumble and he would make a fortune. "I'll make that chap Soros look like an amateur", he said out loud to no-one in particular, then added, "I'd better also make arrangements with my solicitor to buy the apartment."

★ ★ ★

The distinctive black berets of the Philippines military commandos, part of their country's 'unconventional warfare group', were now lined up on the Washington's deck, fully kitted out. They were to join forces with the detachment of US marines that had already been assembled, as they all boarded the fleet of six helicopters preparing to fly the short distance to Fiery Reef. The pre-agreed plan was to land in the middle of the new runway and fan out in both directions to secure its entire length. They had allowed thirty minutes to conclude the operation, after which a technical team would follow to establish secure communications links and to set up barracks of some sort for the men to be left behind. The tricky bit of the operation was what to do with the couple of hundred workers on the reef? Thankfully for Admiral Farley, that prospective headache had been taken away. The British contingent had graciously offered to transport them back to Manila, so they could continue their voyage back home to their base at Portsmouth.

The pilot of the lead Black Hawk helicopter was in the middle of a routine radio call to the flight controller, 'Flight' in the vernacular, nonchalantly noting that he had the landing site in view and they were now two minutes from disembarking the troops. Against all expectations and pre-briefing intelligence, his instrumentation flashed a signal that a ground-to-air missile was heading his way. In the blink of an eye, the on-board computer systems immediately engaged the helicopter's weapons and fired a stinger missile in response.

The pilot instinctively took evasive action and manoeuvred his craft away from the incoming fire. Given the proximity of the helicopter to the landing zone, the explosion when the two missiles collided resulted in a stupendous flash of light which temporarily blinded him. Despite the effect of the blast wave on the helicopter, throwing them violently around, they mercifully had not been hit or damaged. The bank of screens in front of him had instantly located the source of the inbound missile on the airfield and with one press of a button on his joystick, a second missile snaked its way towards the target, instantly destroying the ground-to-air missile installation. With the coolness befitting his years of combat experience, the pilot calmly radioed to say "inbound missile taken care of Flight, ground installation destroyed, no damage, touchdown in thirty seconds".

"Jesus, what the hell was that?" Farley stood up from his chair and grabbed the nearest binoculars to scan the horizon for the remnants of the explosion. "Why in God's name didn't we know they had missiles on the reef?"

The six helicopters made a series of hard landings in the sand only moments later and the soldiers on board, who had initially expected to saunter to their allocated positions and enjoy the sunshine, instead ran like hell to their pre-determined assembly points. It took them considerably less time than the designated thirty minutes to secure the airfield, meeting no resistance whatsoever. From what the senior commander on the ground could ascertain from the – by now – completely terrified workers, the Chinese had simply left the missile system under camouflage netting and effectively set it on autopilot. A rapid search of the entire site yielded no military personnel, nor any other defences. The commander radioed that the objective was secured, waved his own helicopters away and requested that HMS Dragon commence the evacuation of the workforce.

There then followed a torrent of signal traffic with the Pentagon and the Admiralty, informing them of the successful recapture of Fiery Cross, despite the near catastrophe with the missile attack. Admiral Farley immediately invited the two British destroyer captains to a conference in the Washington's wardroom to discuss tactics, while they awaited retaliatory action from the Liaoning. Frantic activity then ensued in the corridors of power. The diplomatic services of the UK and USA were immediately called into action at the United Nations and speeches rapidly drafted to defend this most decisive and unexpected of actions. The ship's officers and crew readied themselves for the response that would surely come soon.

★ ★ ★

Despite it being a Friday afternoon, the Prime Minister had called an emergency cabinet meeting for five o'clock, much to the intense irritation of those forced to cancel their weekend plans and return to Downing Street. Earlier, the Chancellor had provided his colleagues with a memorandum on the anticipated events in the foreign exchange markets when America opened on Monday afternoon, the conclusions of his special advisor, Sir John d'Abo, took centre-stage. However, given the dramatic events in the South China Sea earlier in the day, the Secretaries of State for Defence and the Foreign & Commonwealth Office were also asked to submit a briefing paper.

The mood around the Cabinet table was sombre and unusually grave. Many of those in attendance had considerable experience of how the government machine reacted to military engagements in faraway places…most of which you would be hard pressed to locate on a map of the world. But, today, there was an undertone of crisis in the air. If the three most senior members of the government were to present papers at the same meeting, something very serious was afoot. While everyone was taking their allocated places around the table, the Cabinet Secretary quickly circulated the remaining two papers.

The PM opened the dialogue by emphasising that, under no circumstances, must anyone discuss what they were about to hear outside the Cabinet room. Content that that was fully understood, he then asked the Minister for Defence to commence proceedings. Over the next twenty minutes, he outlined the ongoing involvement of the Royal Navy in the South China Sea, noting that they were now engaged in repatriating the construction workers to the Philippines, where they would be given free passage back to their respective countries. The two destroyers would then await further instructions from the Admiralty and, providing there was no retaliatory action from the Chinese – which required them to provide further assistance and support to the American Carrier Group – they would return to the UK forthwith. He carefully cautioned everyone around the table that, given the state of affairs they faced, this was a far-from-certain outcome. He summed up his department's position thus:

"In the light of what the Chancellor will elaborate upon

shortly, the Americans have decided to take what may be regarded by the rest of the world as a highly-confrontational course of action. Make no mistake; they have certainly kicked the proverbial hornets' nest here! You may be familiar with the logical dilemma, known as Morton's Fork: the unenviable option between 'the devil and the deep blue sea'. Militarily, we have a stark choice before us: if we do nothing, we risk a material escalation of tensions in the area; if we do something, we may end up with the same unpleasant consequences."

The Defence Secretary solemnly closed his file, knowing full well that he had a long night ahead of him at the MOD.

The Foreign Secretary then ran through a very long list of territorial provocations entered into by the Chinese in their endeavour to re-conquer the Spratly Islands, *et al*, and establishing at least two viable military airfields within the space of a few months. Clearly, he argued, this was contrary to all the signed treaties which governed the disputed islands, which (he reminded everyone) stretched over many thousands of square miles. The UK and the Americans would be robustly defending their military actions in a specially convened session of the United Nations, scheduled for a few hours hence. It goes without saying, he continued, that the Ambassador for the Philippines will emphatically protest his country's long-held territorial rights over Fiery Cross Reef and would be expected to receive the unwavering support of the other affected governments in the region. He then concluded:

"This may well be a decisive, indeed, seminal moment in Sino-British relations. From the UK's perspective, we are entering uncharted waters here; but, as on many prior occasions, we simply must stand shoulder-to-shoulder with our American cousins. By acting decisively now, we are endeavouring to forestall an even greater issue later, should these airfields ever be completed to the point where they are a direct threat to the region."

With that, the Chancellor took centre stage to speak. He began his address to cabinet in his usual measured, carefully calibrated, tones:

"I am assuming you have all read the briefing paper I circulated earlier today? So, I would just like to concentrate for the moment on what we expect to happen on Monday. For the past three weeks, we have had a multinational team of world experts endeavouring to find a solution to an audacious plan, namely: that China intends to mount an attack on the dollar. This would be similar in concept to the one Soros mounted on sterling during the ERM crisis some years ago. As you will be fully aware, such an action would have massive knock-on consequences for the UK economy, indeed all the world's economies. It has thus to be stopped at all costs. We believe we may be able to forestall this happening through the good offices of GCHQ and the equivalent agencies in America. Simply put, we intend to mount a cyber-attack on China's computer systems, which in effect will stop this before it even starts."

He paused for effect, before continuing: "However, I would be less than honest with you if I did not say that, thus far, we have not found a way to do this which is guaranteed to work. If we cannot accomplish this, then we will have to publicly confront the Chinese on Monday morning, UK time, to tell them we know what they are about to do. Our only hope then would be the resultant public humiliation across the globe. I am sure many of you here today would agree that they may well simply stick two fingers up at us and proceed anyway!"

The Prime Minister then drew the meeting to an abrupt close, without discussion.

"We have a prospective catastrophe of enormous magnitude on our hands here which the government must be seen to be in control of: come what may! I want you all to leave here and fully consider the implications of what you have heard on your respective departments. Send the Cabinet Secretary your carefully measured analysis by noon tomorrow. Next meeting, Monday morning, 9am sharp."

With that he stood up to leave, turning to the Chancellor and saying, in a voice that all could hear: "Still no bloody solutions, Charlie."

CHAPTER TWENTY ONE

Hong Kong, London & New York, D-2

Preparations had been well underway for many hours – on both sides of the political and ethical divide – as the pro-democracy supporters started to gather in the Central Business District of Hong Kong. The local TV stations, RHTV and TVB, were already *in situ* and had been broadcasting continuously since dawn. Many of the principal news agencies across the globe were showing the minute-by-minute feed of the ever-growing crowd to their stunned viewers. To a man, they were all fully anticipating a humanitarian catastrophe and considerable bloodshed. The broadcast anchors on the ground were confidently predicting that a "simply incredible two million protestors would be at the Saturday lunchtime rally: nearly 1/3rd of the population of Hong Kong."

In the many Breakfast TV shows now on air – all of which were endeavouring to set the scene for those not there – the ubiquitous 'live piece to camera' shots gave the event added realism. The ever-swelling mass of humanity took their place behind the barriers in peaceful, virtually silent, protest.

Every journalist agreed one thing: the massive numbers now assembling in the streets would unquestionably exceed the enormous gathering in 1989 - which was a direct reaction to the events in and around Tiananmen Square, where over two thousand protestors were killed. To those uninitiated viewers around the world, who were unfamiliar with the heartbeat of

Hong Kong, it was explained that the rallies were normally held on Sundays. Therefore, to hold one on a Saturday, in a city dedicated to business and commerce of every kind, was a signal of their unwavering intention to put principles above money.

The authorities, for their part, were far from complacent, and more than willing to lock horns with the protestors. They had been given ample warning of today's gathering and had taken quite extraordinary steps to prevent – what the more histrionic among them were convinced would be – full scale civil disobedience and bloody riots on the streets.

The wholesale deployment of the well-organised People's Liberation Army troops from the mainland was rapidly augmenting the ranks of the local police force; for whom all leave had been cancelled for the weekend. Judging by the body armour the fresh troops wore, the water cannons that were being strategically located in the side streets, the case upon case of tear gas canisters, rubber bullets and pepper spray now littering the ground; it was beyond doubt that Beijing was in no mood to compromise. Bizarrely, the Hong Kong police had been given countless megaphones in a valiant attempt to vocally intercede with those assembling on the streets, and somehow persuade the protestors to remain calm and peaceful. It was unconstrained brute force, versus placard-waving men, determined women and innocent children, all demanding what they professed to be their basic human right: democracy.

CJ, as their *de facto* – but unelected – leader, would address the rally at noon from a specially built stage located close to the heavily guarded Central Government Complex. He knew full well that he might be taking his life – and almost certainly his liberty – in his hands; but his supporters had braved the authority's wrath to hear him speak: so he would not let them down.

The previous evening, CJ had attended a candlelight vigil in Victoria Park. There, he was greeted by a cheering crowd of about ten thousand supporters, all simultaneously unfurling a sea of yellow umbrellas, the movement's powerful symbol of resistance. Later he held a private dinner at his house on the Peak with Colonel Sanford and the US Consul General to Hong Kong, who re-emphasised his country's unwavering support to their cause. However, they both cautioned him to be especially careful during tomorrow's rally, as they had unequivocal intelligence that China was spoiling for a fight.

By lunchtime on Saturday the city was at a virtual standstill. Connaught Road Central and Harcourt Road were overwhelmed with people, banners held proudly aloft, all marching determinedly towards the Government Complex and the inevitable clash with the authorities. The main protagonists on such rallies were usually the Hong Kong Federation of Students, but today it seemed as if every resident of the metropolis were there *en masse*, determined to support the protestors.

At the fringes of the parade it was already clear that the police were behaving with hostile intent; aggressively pushing and jostling with the crowd, in an almost pointless endeavour to stop them spilling into government buildings. By the time CJ and his entourage had made their way to the stage to speak the atmosphere was electric.

Speaking without notes, CJ reminded the multitude of fervent supporters in front of him, that – contrary to China's oft stated contention – their flawed policy towards Hong Kong did not have an "unshakable legal status and effect": especially if the people deemed it to be undemocratic. The crowd roared their approval as he demanded an "equal and just" Hong Kong, one that would "no longer bend to the whim of Beijing". This was not civil disobedience he said, but a protest over the very future and status of an independent Hong Kong. Before he could get another word out the atmosphere escalated dramatically. Wave after wave of tear gas was catapulted into the midst of the hundreds of thousands of protestors assembled to hear the speeches. The TV broadcasters were caught in the middle of the *mêlée*; their commentaries by now being made in choking and spluttering tones, as they endeavoured to flee the hail of rubber bullets now raining down on them. Around the world, viewers were seeing a level of hostility never before witnessed on the island. It was not long before the fearsomely equipped riot troops marched forward from their assembly points in the nearby side streets, aggressively banging their truncheons on their shields. The heavy-handed confrontation that followed was horrendous. Terrible injuries were inflicted on the protestors as CJ was rapidly bundled away by his supporters before he too was badly hurt or worse.

Two hours later, the state-run Chinese media went over the heads of the local politicians and judiciary and declared a curfew from midnight until nine the following morning: ominously adding that the troops would enforce 'martial law' if this was not adhered to.

Governments across the globe reacted in unison to condemn the violence they were witnessing and the unilateral proclamations of the police and army to 'lockdown' the city. It was clear for all to see that many lives would be lost in the bloodbath that was now unfolding. Their condemnations were echoed in every parliamentary chamber and legislature in the East and the West, irrespective of their political colours; a massive shift in the political tectonic plates of Asia had just occurred.

Only a select few realised this was all part of a carefully calibrated plot to deliberately destabilise the region, wreck the financial markets and put China where it belonged - ahead of a fatally weakened United States.

★ ★ ★

Despite the Prime Minister's previous request not to be disturbed while he went through the briefing notes for an upcoming EU summit, the highly efficient switchboard at Number 10 immediately put the call through to his private office.

"C is on the line Sir. He says it's very urgent." The PM placed the paper he was totally absorbed in carefully back on his desk, simply annotating where he had got to with a cross. "Put him through."

The head of the UK's Secret Intelligence Service – as he preferred MI6 to be referred to – was on the line. Unlike his fictional counterpart M, the appellation "C" was real and in everyday use, even today. It was derived from the service's first incumbent, Sir George Mansfield Cumming-Smith, whose staff simply abbreviated his name to save time in the typing pool.

"Prime Minister, I need to see you on a matter of the gravest concern. I'm available at the earliest opportunity you have in your diary. Very briefly, for the past couple of weeks I have been receiving a series of increasingly disconcerting intelligence reports on your man d'Abo which we need to discuss. We need to act. I would recommend we also include the Chancellor in the meeting, if you could be so kind."

"Just a minute C, I'll check with my private secretary." He called through on the intercom and asked if the Chancellor could be available in an hour's time. On being eventually told that he was, he confirmed the meeting.

Given the absence of traffic hold-ups, the drive from 85 Albert Embankment to Number 10 generally took no more than a few minutes. But on this occasion there was, yet again, some 'blasted trades union rally or other' in Parliament Square, which caused C to be fractionally late: a cardinal sin in his eyes, necessitating starting the meeting with an apology. His car was one of the very few allowed to pass through the gates at the entrance to Downing Street, with only the cursory salute from the police team on duty and not the normal top-to-toe body search.

"Prime Minister, Chancellor. Thank you for seeing me at such short notice."

He took a seat opposite them. "I have a somewhat complex story to impart, which you may on occasions find difficult to believe. It is important for me to say at the outset of this briefing to you, that what I have to disclose has been verified from multiple sources, including the DCRI in France, the equivalent of our MI5. It concerns Sir John d'Abo and his secretary, one Miss Anne-Sophie Moreau. You quite possibly may know the Moreaus, Chancellor; he is a prominent French industrialist with fingers in many pies, especially weapons manufacturing. We hold a modest-sized dossier on him: background only. Our colleagues in France have confirmed that he is clean and his business interests legitimate, although they carefully monitor his corporate tax records since he moved to Monaco."

He produced two large files and two sealed padded envelopes, all marked Top Secret and handed them across the coffee table in the Prime Minister's private quarters.

"So, gentlemen, firstly some background. Miss Moreau studied politics at the Sorbonne, graduating some eight years ago. Her tutors describe her as very bright, but strong-willed; even wayward. They ascribed this to her being the wealthiest person at the university by a country mile. She didn't spend much time either studying or completing her work, but somehow she passed. There is an unsubstantiated rumour that money changed hands. I'm told that she then became infatuated with another student, who was apparently Chinese in origin and with whom she then spent the next three years in Hong Kong. To all intents and purposes, she then goes off the radar at this point, only to re-emerge eighteen months ago.

A subsequent investigation of her passport reveals that she

made several long-stay trips to mainland China, where we now assume she was radicalised."

The two men opposite C sat in silence, carefully absorbing his every word, which as yet did not contain anything untoward.

"On her return to Europe, she becomes embroiled in a blazing public row with her parents in some swish restaurant in Nice. It's not clear about what exactly, other than that the paparazzi caught the whole matter on camera, including her slapping her father across the face and storming out. Needless to say, the very next day the picture was on the pages of most of the national newspapers. The French security services tell me that her parents have not spoken to her since and have formally disinherited her. The police have tried to get the truth from her father about what really happened that day, but he refuses to discuss the matter and they can't compel him. She then enters the UK some two months ago."

"And where does d'Abo fit into all this, apart from the disclosure that his secretary has a colourful past?"

"I'll come to that in a moment Prime Minister. For someone who is used to living the high life, but is now financially cut off and jobless, speculation and tittle-tattle mounts that, if you'll excuse the phrase, 'she's on the game'. Your distinguished counterparts in France, anxious to avoid any unwelcome publicity about a very high-visibility family, had her formally investigated, very guardedly naturally. They quickly discovered that she is in regular receipt of a large sum of money, paid every month from some chap in Hong Kong. Being French, they naturally assume that it's coming from some rich sugar daddy, paying handsomely for her services. The authorities concluded that they cannot detain her for this, so the matter is dropped."

Putting his half-moon glasses on and clearing his throat, C then slowly turned the pages of his report, which they all had in front of them, in order to find a specific entry.

"If I can now draw your attention to the transcript of a series of conversations shown on pages 26 through to 42." Dutifully they both opened the sealed envelopes and found the relevant starting page.

"As you are aware, the cyber-monitoring unit at GCHQ became involved with another matter regarding d'Abo on August 1st last, when the Chancellor asked them to increase their surveillance of the foreign exchange markets. You will both readily appreciate that when they engage in such a task, endless people get drawn into their ever-widening net, including those at its very centre. Within a week their attention was drawn to a series of emails from the UK to China. These have been 'red flagged' as a direct consequence of GCHQ's electronic surveillance systems which ceaselessly track certain key words and phrases, such as 'catastrophic collapse of the dollar' and so forth.

Astoundingly, they were amazed to see correspondence containing this and similar phrases sent from Miss Moreau to some contact in China. She was relaying a series of position papers prepared for the Chancellor by Sir John d'Abo. They were forwarded verbatim. No analysis or adumbration, just simple copies. There is also the transmission of a string of in-house notes on the takeover his bank is involved in and the full details of d'Abo's trips to America. Finally, there are regular updates of where Sebastian Fortes is and what he's doing in Hong Kong."

Somewhat flustered, the PM asked C to take a moment's reflection while he carefully read the series of entries. When he had finished he simply said, "Almost beyond belief! Verbatim transcripts! Have you got to the bottom of who her counterparty in China is?"

"Before I turn to that and the contents of the second envelope I have left with you, I need you now to look at pages 50 onwards. You will be well aware that over the past three weeks, GCHQ has been crawling all over the major banks here in London.

As you may well imagine, this exercise has caused alarm and consternation amongst the boards of these institutions. The chaps in Cheltenham have recently received a call from the Chief Executive of Barclays asking if they could take a close look at a transaction that had just crossed his desk. When they did so, they were completely dumbfounded. Following an audit trail of the money transfers involved, it transpires that d'Abo has taken the money that you made available to him Chancellor and bet the entire amount on the dollar falling in value on Monday."

The Prime Minister exploded, "Bloody hell, what in God's name is going on here, Charlie?"

"I'm as shocked as you are! This is all utterly unconscionable, deplorable!"

C persisted: "This latter event, the FX business, was the clincher. I immediately authorised my agents to surreptitiously take a look inside d'Abo's and Moreau's apartments. We've yet to search his country estate, but my chaps are going to do a thorough sweep of the place on Monday when he's in the London office." He paused as silence filled the room.

"If you could kindly open the padded envelope, you will see it contains a DVD. I can show it to you on my laptop here if at any point you wish to see its contents. It's been carefully analysed and would appear to be copy number 3 of 3. Where the other two are we as yet do not know. The edited twenty minute film contains a series of graphic sexual encounters between the two parties and a series of recorded conversations where d'Abo, willingly, or more possibly imprudently, talks about the currency investigation he is engaged in. It does not take a genius to predict that this film is to be used to blackmail him when the time comes. For what exact purpose and when, is as yet unclear."

The Chancellor was first to react: "I'm completely and utterly staggered C, you've knocked the wind entirely out of my sails with your disclosure. This implies not only that John is a traitor to his country, but is engaged in brazen theft and the duplicitous and deceitful use of Treasury funds. We've been taken for absolute bloody idiots!"

"My thoughts exactly, Chancellor. That's why I thought you should know about this immediately. The question, as always, is what to do about it? We have been very carefully tailing them both for the past few days and monitoring literally every form of communication they undertake. We have also bugged their apartments and their offices. I gather he thinks her mother owns the girl's apartment. In fact, it's rented for her by the same person from Hong Kong who sends the monthly pay-cheque."

C adjusted his position on the sofa before continuing.

"My recommendation, Prime Minister, is to do nothing for the time being. We may discover something to our advantage, especially as we are only two days away from the time when we think the Chinese may strike. The only thing that is out of our hands here is the timing of any blackmail threat. If it arrives by letter, fax, email, or text, then we will probably see it before d'Abo does; if it is to be by phone, then we get notice of their intentions the moment he does."

The Prime Minister leaned back in his chair in silence, closed his eyes and put his hands together next to his lips as if in prayer. Once more there was a deathly hush in the room. When he eventually returned to the meeting from his inner-most thoughts, his mind had only one thing on it: the political consequences of this most unwelcome of revelations.

"We will invite d'Abo here on some pretext or other on Monday morning when you can arrest him. You can place her in custody whenever you like. We cannot be accused by the media of being dilatory in this matter. I expect your team to take a very large brush to all of this C and ensure the metaphorical carpet covers all the traces. Is that clear? We've enough presumably to deport her to France, assuming they want her?"

"Yes, Prime Minister, I'm absolutely sure of that. I can make suitable arrangements with the French authorities to that end later today. If they say yes, I'll have her extradited immediately. This action would, however, almost certainly tip the Chinese off. So if I may, could I just ruminate on this before doing anything?"

"Thank you for bringing this to our attention C; it's an unwanted distraction amidst all the geo-political issues in play right now, but we may yet have time to reduce the effect of this particular threat. I commend you and your team for their usual thorough and timely involvement. If you don't mind, there is something I would just like to discuss with the Chancellor in private."

With that, the head of MI6 left to do his master's bidding, which, as usual, was to clear up the unholy mess they were now embroiled in.

"Charlie, how could we miss this? How could *you*, of all people, miss this? I thought John was completely trustworthy, totally dependable and unflinchingly loyal. One of us. I gave him a bloody knighthood for God's sake. I'm not going to have my legacy ruined by a grubby, salacious scandal because he can't keep it in his pants: if the press get one whiff of this we are finished. It will be the Profumo affair mark 2 and we all know what happened to the government then. I don't want to lose you so close to an election Charlie, but be prepared to resign on Tuesday if this is not resolved and completely, entirely, utterly hushed up. No 'ifs or buts' old chap, you will be duty-bound to take one for the team."

"Perhaps there is another way to resolve this problem, Prime Minister."

★ ★ ★

Alison Fletcher had assembled 'her boys' (as she now referred to Lewis, Mac and Alex) for a Saturday afternoon, much-needed, pep talk. Time was slipping through their collective fingers and she wanted to ascertain whether they would have resolved the technical issues they faced before the opening bell on Monday. The topic had now reached the very epicentre of the White House. The President, no less, wanted to meet her at 5pm tomorrow to make a final decision on what course of action to take.

The 'boys' told her that they now had the full and unconditional cooperation of the UK and US agencies and by the end of the evening they would be able to seamlessly link their computers into what would be one cohesive whole. They could now match the opposition for speed and, just possibly, out-gun them by the merest fraction of a second. The single obstacle to progress lay outside their control: the new operators of China's Milky-Way 2 computer were installing progressively more and more security measures as the time grew nearer. This, if nothing else, was as clear an indication of their guilt as you could find: computer-driven weather forecasting never requires this much protection.

Their counterparts in Guangzhou were putting up obstacles quicker than they could find a way around them. Every day it got progressively harder to penetrate their defences. Despite this they were completely confident that – should they ever be able to do so – they could infiltrate the destructive coding immediately. This, they were completely convinced, would stop the opposition executing the transaction. However, the problem they faced was that the programme files they wanted to introduce were larger than the figurative hole they had to drive them through. It reminded Alex, a keen film buff, of Apollo 13, where the astronauts had to fit a round tube into a square aperture, using only the bits and pieces scattered around the spacecraft; or face utter calamity! The parallel had not escaped them: the problem was, as Lewis frequently reminded them, they couldn't find the requisite equivalent of a tube, square, oblong or any damn shape anywhere they looked on the Chinese computer.

The Chairman of the Federal Reserve was not prone to defeatism; her unshakable faith that they would resolve this was however beginning to wane. If they had not got a solution by the time she met the President tomorrow, she felt certain that her only course of action was to let the world know this catastrophe was about to occur. The only problem with this approach, she readily acknowledged, was that the Chinese would simply say it was an American fabrication from start to finish: they had no such intention. Then there would be a stupendous political bust-up, the Chinese might well achieve their objective by default, and the Fed's reputation would be left in tatters.

"Come on, guys! We need your Churchillian spirit here: the darkest hour is just before dawn, and all that. One more push for me please. I hate to say it, but it's in your hands now!"

CHAPTER TWENTY TWO

London, New York, Hong Kong & South China Sea, D-1

The Sabbath, for many dyed-in-the-wool traditionalists in England, still revolved around the well-established routine of church and pious entreaties to the Almighty. If sufficient penitence had been exercised at the pews that morning, this would normally be followed by a convivial three pint lunch at the local pub, and hours of mindless TV; lasting well into the night. The dog days of summer had been especially delightful this year: warm evenings in the garden tending the roses, cricket matches to watch on the village green, and long country walks past babbling brooks; while listening intently to delightful birdsong.

The Prime Minister had sought refuge at Chequers; his weekend country retreat, following the revelations of yesterday. Under normal circumstances he too would be fully engaged in such autumnal pursuits, in much the same way as his fellow countrymen were undoubtedly currently doing, blissfully unaware of the events unfolding across the globe. However, his diary today had degenerated into a stream of endless meetings following the debacle in Hong Kong overnight, and the brewing conflict in the South China Sea. He was more than ever convinced that this was an orchestrated series of events.

Monday's emergency cabinet meeting at nine would precede an anxious few hours, while they all waited for the American markets to open later in the afternoon. The Governor of the Bank of England and his advisers had just left, leaving him feeling extremely disconsolate: his synopsis that the country would be left in "economic tatters" if the dollar collapsed, merely adding to his elevated blood pressure. The recurring phrases "dramatic repercussions", and "total ruination", would stay with him for hours.

He also concluded that he must initiate a COBRA emergency committee for some time after cabinet, and before the US markets opened. He had little choice: the world was possibly in mortal danger of imminent financial implosion and super-power conflict. The only problem was that calling such a meeting was highly visible to the press pack and, inevitably, led to awkward questions being asked as to why it had been arranged.

Perhaps if he asked the relevant senior ministers and security officials somehow to mysteriously find themselves in 'Cabinet Office briefing room A', like the old days before such meetings somehow acquired a sexy name, he could then avoid the inevitable media assumption that this was a life-or-death emergency. He pondered the matter for no more than ten seconds, after which he decided to hold off making that particular call until he had been fully briefed by the various Ministers of State that he had requested to speak at cabinet: hopefully this would clarify his decision.

Inevitably, he would also have to speak to the President later in the day, and almost certainly – given events in Hong Kong – the Chinese. It could quite possibly turn out to be a momentous set of conversations – one which, erudite university professors might later conclude, signalled the dawn of a new Great Depression and a repeat of 1929.

★ ★ ★

Despite the simply incredible amount of surveillance equipment and satellite feeds flowing into the USS Washington (which were now focused entirely on the carrier fleet advancing towards him), Admiral Farley could not comprehend why the Chinese had failed to react in any meaningful way to the recapture of Fiery Cross Reef. Their flagship, the Liaoning, had effectively retained electronic silence for the past couple of hours: perhaps, he conjectured, they were unaware of what had happened, although that was extremely unlikely.

Looking at the screens in front of him, it was clear that they had now decided to split their forces, and – judging by their compass-bearing – were sending a handful of ships to, presumably, confront the Japanese at the Senkaku Islands. But apart from the predicted zigzag pattern they were deploying, they appeared to be slowing down. When he requested their revised ETA at the Reef, it became immediately apparent that they were proceeding with the intention to rendezvous with his task force some time during Monday afternoon: at exactly the same time that the other Chinese ships would encounter the Japanese fleet. 'Ominously coordinated', was his immediate reaction. As yet, the Washington had detected no high-altitude aircraft cover for the Chinese fleet, nor any unusual patterns of helicopter movements. They seemed in no hurry to engage in an immediate conflict and, if anything, he instinctively felt they were almost teasing him to make the first move.

★ ★ ★

The Chancellor had been in a truculent mood all day. Unlike his boss, who, he felt sure, was languishing idly in the countryside while Rome burned; his own career was unquestionably on the line. Unless a miracle occurred in very short order he was toast; all hope of being the next Prime Minister would be gone. He had little alternative but to beaver away in the office in what, he increasingly felt, might well be a vain attempt to deal with the mounting series of crises he was expecting on Monday. His officials were run ragged with what they regarded as never-ending, highly unreasonable demands for information; as well as insistent, but futile, requests for solutions. There had been no news from Mackenzie Gore at the Federal Reserve, and no bright ideas from the Bank of England or GCHQ. Not to put too fine a point on it, he knew he was screwed.

However, Charlie Sheer was, if nothing else, a combative, deeply cunning and at times belligerent politician. He was damned if he was going down with this particular ship. Seismic events in the financial markets were one thing – however unpleasant; they could be shrugged off as beyond anyone's control, let alone his – but the revelations about d'Abo had shaken him to his very core. After all, he had known the man for years, appointed him to endless government committees and international enquiries, submitted the initial idea to the PM to have him knighted, and – God help him – had signed the bloody loan documents that transferred the funds into d'Abo's hands.

After a late, indigestion-inducing lunch, of over-ripe fruit and 'British Rail' cheese sandwiches at his desk, his scheming mind began to put flesh on the bones of an idea he had been ruminating over since his meeting with the PM and C yesterday. He ill-temperedly requested the Treasury switchboard to locate the Chief Executive of Barclays and put his call through. Ten minutes later he was on the line.

"Regarding this loan and short selling matter we are reviewing with your organisation. Did I understand you correctly the other day when you said that your bank would be the counterparty to the d'Abo transaction? So no third party was involved?"

"Indeed, Chancellor."

"Good, now I want you to do the following, without fail. Firstly, completely and totally unwind the FX operation. Make it disappear from your books entirely: I don't care how you do it, it never happened. Secondly, immediately return the monies that d'Abo has deposited in your bank to the Treasury. Without fail these funds must be back in HMG's account no later than 8am on Monday. Thirdly, I want you to assemble absolutely everyone who knows anything whatsoever about this within the bank first thing tomorrow. Instruct them to destroy every trace of this episode ever happening from your bank's computer and written records."

"I'm sure that can all be done, Chancellor."

Sheer continued in decidedly menacing tones:

"I don't want sure, I want certainty! A group of particularly unsympathetic men from GCHQ and MI6 will be visiting your offices by 9.30 to ensure this task has been completed. I want you to make it abundantly clear to those members of your staff with any knowledge of this affair that their liberty is at immediate risk if they say anything, at any time, to anyone about this matter. Is that completely clear?"

He put the phone down, and said to the switchboard, "Get me d'Abo."

★ ★ ★

A bleary-eyed and exhausted Alex Cadbury very reluctantly took a late night call from Hong Kong, massively disrupting his concentration and making him lose his train of thought. As usual, he was hunched in his customary pose, staring intently at the computer in the office which he shared with Mackenzie Gore. Given the absence of any real progress, it seemed to them both that they were now occupying a bunker under siege.

A couple of hours earlier the 'bloody opposition' had massively enhanced their security protocols, making it well nigh impossible to transfer anything, other than the bare minimum of data, into their computer. A modern day 'Great Wall of China', as Mac had tactlessly put it; before quickly being reminded that Genghis Khan had successfully managed to get around the old one, so they would too.

They now both deeply, deeply, regretted not sending their adversary's computer the malicious STUXNET malware – which the programming teams at the NSA had painstakingly prepared – when they had the chance. But that particular window had passed and they now faced an unimaginable set of hurdles, with precious little time to resolve any of them. The only positive, in a decidedly bleak scenario, was that they could now prove the Chinese were intent on flooding the market with 'sell orders' for the dollar. That, at least, was a modest piece of ammunition available to the President in whatever action he decided to take.

The sheer quantity of data they wanted to send to the Chinese computer in order to block the millions of 'sell orders' they anticipated, simply could not now be transferred. That door had effectively closed, with only the merest chink of light still showing. Try as they might, they both knew that this was far too small a window to get anything suitably damaging through. Time had almost expired, and they both felt they had been beaten. It was two in the morning, Daylight Saving Time, on Sunday, August 22nd.

"Alex, my dear friend, it's Seb here, I trust you are well? Can you put me on speaker with Mac please?"

"Sure, although we are awfully busy here right now Seb, as you can probably imagine: up to our collective asses in alligators, as Lewis keeps tactfully reminding us. We've still not found a way to get the malware through their security cordon."

"I'll bet you are." He paused briefly for maximum dramatic effect: "Mac, are you familiar with Ockham's Razor?"

"My dear laddie, the Razor is a credo I have followed my entire career. I'm a great proponent of it: *lex parsimoniae,* and all that, if my Latin is correct." He turned to his colleague, who was looking suitably bewildered and utterly disinterested:

"If you're not familiar with the concept Alex, it's a term

ascribed to the Franciscan friar William of Ockham in Surrey, a 14th century logician and philosopher, if my memory serves me well. Why the hell do you bring up something as obscure as this, Seb? It's the middle of the bloody night here."

"As always you're quite correct, Mac. I'd expect nothing less from a very distinguished fellow of Magdalen College. Anyway, I digress from the point in hand. While I was being repeatedly knocked senseless in China, my mind returned again and again to something an old professor of mine kept repeating. I paraphrase his erudition, but the gist of it was, 'always select the simplest and most elegant solution to a problem'."

"It's a mathematician's and computer programmer's first instinct Seb. Where is this leading us?"

"Well, I have an idea."

★ ★ ★

CJ felt he had managed to escape the carnage at the rally by the skin of his teeth, his eyes by now streaming with excruciatingly painful tears. With the screams of his followers still ringing in his ears, Sapphire had unceremoniously bundled him into a nearby office until the worst of the commotion was over and the tear gas cloud had dissipated. She phoned through to Sanford and made a request to bring CJ to his offices until some form of order had returned to the streets and a decision made as to what to do next. He acquiesced immediately and asked everyone to prepare for their imminent arrival. The threatened curfew had created utter chaos in the city, rendering such a threat utterly unenforceable. If anything, the crowd by now were emboldened to the point of outright civil disobedience and reciprocated hostility.

By four-thirty, feeling exhausted and desperately anxious for the supporters left behind in the increasing violence, he had made his way across town to the security of the CIA's offices,

Sapphire by his side. Armed guards had now been posted immediately inside the doors and on the various corridors. It would be inconceivable that the authorities would endeavour to retrieve CJ from here; but Sanford reasoned that anything was possible, given the bloodshed being shown on the monitors in his office. CJ, determined not to be cowed by such brutality, asked if arrangements could be made for him to speak directly to the pro-democracy movement supporters, via the local TV networks.

"I'll try CJ, but they may not be able to make it here in the midst of all this chaos. What we could do however, is tape a message here and bounce it over to CNN. They are bound to want to broadcast it."

Sanford picked up the phone, spoke for no more than a minute, and came back: "OK, they will do it. Let's go to the situation room; I suggest you start drafting your speech."

★ ★ ★

"Ah, John, glad I caught you, it's Charlie here. There have been a few developments and I was wondering if you could make an early supper tonight. Been at my desk all day and, quite frankly, I am famished. Need to bring you up to speed and all that. Shall I book a table at your club, Whites, for seven o'clock? Jolly good, see you then."

★ ★ ★

The Chairman of the Federal Reserve had grown accustomed to her monthly hour-long meetings with the President. These were typically business-like and exceedingly cordial: she was in her element, always firmly in charge, and her viewpoint never, or rarely, questioned by those in attendance. But a private get-together on a late Sunday afternoon was most definitely out of the ordinary. She had little doubt that today was also going to be an especially uncomfortable appointment. Lewis had nobly asked to accompany her and, being the gentleman he was, take whatever flak was going to come the Fed's way together.

They were directed through the ultimate corridors of power into the opulence of the Oval Office to meet their Commander in Chief. Normally, they would be armed to the teeth with statistics, graphs, economist's outlooks, and they would be unfaltering in the opinions they gave him. On this occasion however, they were stepping into the lion's den almost empty-handed. The only scintilla of hope being the lines of coding Alex and Mac had extracted from the Chinese computer which demonstrated beyond all doubt what they intended to do tomorrow. They both knew, however, that this evidence, in and of itself, was not compelling enough to stand up in the court of world opinion: much more would be required.

In preparation for the turmoil they were now anticipating, the Fed had made available an enormous quantity of money to the two hedge funds they had been working with on this project. Their job was to buy any dollars the Chinese were intending to sell: but if it got to this stage, the FX predators – scenting blood in the market – would unquestionably complete China's job for it. Such matters were, after all, a zero sum game; for every loser there was always an equal and opposite winner. Wall Street would always chase a buck, no matter how unpatriotic.

President R. J. O. Chessington, (the "IV" as he liked to be known as, in homage to his many antecedents), was chiselled from the same granite rock as another maverick politician of a bygone era: Spiro T. Agnew. They were both from similar Southern stock and had a commonality of approach to anyone who had the temerity and impudence to cross swords with America. Chessington had a reputation as an enthusiastic proponent of his predecessor's school of politics, which were loosely fashioned on the phrase: "let's bomb them back to the

Stone Age". 'Them' would often be replaced by a choice Anglo-Saxon phrase or two. In his eyes the world was divided down a new Mason-Dixon Line: those for, and those against, his interests. Woe betide you if you found yourself on the wrong side of the divide.

He had surrounded himself by a coterie of hawks in the military and on Capitol Hill, whose collective dander was now up. Hong Kong and some spat on a desert island in the middle of nowhere were now centre stage in a struggle for global supremacy. American hegemony, his one and only foreign policy doctrine, was without question the cornerstone of a safe, prosperous and peaceful world. The suspicion that China was now about to let loose a foreign exchange war directed at his beloved country was the last straw.

The briefing did not last long, largely because Chessington had already made up his mind on what to do. The Liaoning would be the first to feel his wrath.

Alison Fletcher was at pains to point out that every avenue was still being explored and they still had twenty hours to find a solution; but she was making little progress. They would return tomorrow with the section of the speech he would give to Congress, explaining the financial background to the crisis, and why he had no option but to take the action he was now contemplating.

★ ★ ★

As the Chancellor briskly entered Whites, Sir John d'Abo was already inside; serenely passing the time until his guest arrived, reading the newspapers, whilst enjoying a glass of the very acceptable house claret, all in amiable silence. The dining room was almost empty, as was often the case this early in the evening. Members tended to eat around 8.30 or 9.00 at the weekends, so there was little likelihood of them being overheard, or even seen, if grave matters of state were to be discussed. He'd not been able to reach Anne-Sophie all day and presumed she had gone shopping again without her phone. He regretted not making firmer arrangements with her for later that evening, but he would try again to reach her after dinner.

"Shall we go through Charlie; I'm told the lamb chops are highly recommended tonight; but don't have the soup, it's some foreign muck."

The waiter arrived almost instantly and took their order, with the Chancellor – entirely and conspicuously out of character – ordering a particularly expensive bottle of the 2007 Pomerol.

"John, do you mind if we eat before I get to the substance of our meeting. All hell is breaking loose in Hong Kong as you've probably seen. I gather your chap, Sebastian, is safely holed up and taking refuge in the CIA's offices. I'm afraid this is going to get worse before it gets better. Ah, excellent, the wine's here: do try some of this excellent vintage."

The talking meandered for the next hour without structure or purpose, and a second bottle was enthusiastically consumed. It was all getting rather hearty when Charlie abruptly changed the conversation.

"John, the Prime Minister and I had a visit from MI6 on Saturday. He brought with him a couple of files and some exceedingly disturbing news."

He paused to finish his glass and raised his finger to suggest yet another bottle be delivered. "It relates to you, I'm afraid, and to your secretary. I'm sorry to tell you John, but you've been played for a complete idiot. Miss Moreau is not at all what she seems. Indeed, we now have incontrovertible proof that she is working for the Chinese. How do I know this, you may ask? Well, she has been passing every item of correspondence between you and me, to her contacts in Hong Kong – everything John, without exception. Every memo;

every position paper; details of every trip you take or Sebastian takes; absolutely everything."

"Dear God! That can't be true! I had no idea."

"It gets worse John, much worse. MI6 also left with the PM and me, a film of your bedroom antics and unguarded conversation, which relates to the work you are engaged in, and which is – I don't need to remind you – 'Top Secret' and of grave national importance. The security boys are convinced the film will be used to blackmail you, and probably attempt to bend the will of the government, keen to avoid a sensational scandal with its principal financial advisor."

John sat there in open-mouthed horror at what he had just heard. He didn't need to be told that he was completely cornered and, almost certainly, totally ruined.

"The PM reckons we could just about have concealed this in the midst of the present turmoil in Asia. To coin a well-worn phrase, this would be 'a good time to bury bad news'; but, deeply regrettably, John, there was one more revelation which takes this matter into a whole new dimension."

The waiter arrived with the next, and final, bottle, which was poured but not touched.

"The Chief Executive of Barclays and I have been chatting about your little scheme, and I'm afraid the moment this was revealed to the PM he instantly changed his position. It's blatant theft John, for which you will probably get twenty-five years hard labour in Pentonville prison. This girl has got you by the balls, so much so that you, your family, your bank, are going to pay an enormous price for your indiscretion."

"What the hell can I do Charlie? Help me here, for pity's sake!"

"The only thing I am prepared to do for you John, is give you time to sort out your business and family affairs. Go back to Buckinghamshire immediately, tonight, literally right now, and put your house in order. I doubt we will see each other again after this evening. Oh, and don't call anyone, especially Anne-Sophie, as your phone is bugged, obviously. You will get a visit tomorrow morning from the local constabulary who will arrest you for fraud and misuse of public funds. I'm trying to stop them charging you with treason, but the CPS are already dusting off their files."

With that, the Chancellor got up and left the table; pausing only momentarily to say over his shoulder: "A strumpet's fool, John, a strumpet's fool."

d'Abo slumped to the table with his head in his hands and, with a quiet voice almost choking with anguish, asked for the bill to be put on his account and for his chauffeur to be summoned.

"Buckinghamshire, George! There is something I have to do."

CHAPTER TWENTY THREE

New York, Washington, Whitehall & Hong Kong, D

August 22nd had arrived inauspiciously and with undue, almost ominous, haste. For an unfortunate few, sitting in their palatial offices at the Federal Reserve or the UK Treasury, it felt like the sands of time were slipping inexorably and rapidly through the hour glass, and out of their normally resolute control.

As is the immutable nature of things in the international financial marketplace, events unfolded across the globe in their preordained sequence: starting at daybreak in the east and progressing relentlessly westwards as the sun rose and fell. Trading floors would automatically open and close in a never-ending sequence, like a slow-motion relay race. Countless participants in the key financial centres around the world would ceaselessly pass their winning-or-losing positions to delighted-or-hapless colleagues along the monetary daisy-chain; day in, day out, irrespective of the prevailing circumstances. This heart never missed a beat.

Given the nature of the world's international clock, it would be 9.30pm in the evening in Hong Kong by the time 9.30am arrived in New York, when their stock market was formally opened to the traditional sounds of a ringing bell, heartily clanged by some business tycoon or screen idol. While Stock Exchanges merrily adhered to a strict timetable for when they commenced their daily activities and each knew precisely when they finished; the currency markets were in perpetual motion.

A problem that might initially be described as a mere ripple in Tokyo, could eventually become a tsunami by the time it had passed through London and eventually swamped Wall Street. Today, many in high office were bracing themselves for this inevitability.

For the past fifteen minutes Sebastian had been deeply engrossed in a very late-night conversation with his New York-based colleagues, Alex and Mac, who, by this stage, were contemplating the preparation of their resignation letters; rather than have to face the wrath of the President later in the day. Pleasantries having been duly exchanged, and a technical updating completed, Seb began to outline the basis of his idea.

"Do I understand you correctly, Alex?" he said. "If you are to surreptitiously place any new software into the Chinese computer, we are restricted to only a few lines of code at the most?"

"That's spot on, my friend; we're utterly screwed I'm afraid," interjected Mac. "I fear that we've been checkmated. So, if you have any brilliant ideas, now would be a good time to share them."

"OK guys; and I'd be grateful if you two geniuses could bear with me as I take this very slowly, step by step? If I may, I'm going to make the following assumptions: firstly, they will be selling their dollars through their own currency 'Dark Pool' which we know they have at China's central bank. Presumably they will do so by flooding the FX market with gazillions of very small sell orders so as to overwhelm and engulf the system, which they hope will then crash and implode."

"Correct", concurred Alex.

"Secondly, I assume that they have one overriding instruction to do this, rather than millions of the damn things for each specific trade?"

"Right again. We have previously identified that particular

section of their computer code, so we know precisely where it is and can quickly get access to it."

"Finally, I take it for granted that to achieve their plans, they will want to sell dollars and buy their own currency. If the market behaves rationally this would automatically push their currency up in value, while simultaneously pulling the dollar's value down. In all probability they will keep selling their dollars until they have exhausted their reserves; all $1.3 trillion of them?"

"Yep, we'll go with that," yawned Alex.

"However – and this is the key bit guys, so get the very cold towels out if you can – to put a firm order into the market they will have to establish a price at which they are prepared to sell their dollars. For example, today the yuan / dollar exchange rate is approximately 6 to 1. Put in plain language, it takes 16.6 cents to buy 1 yuan. Suppose it only took 1.66 cents, or even 0.166 cents to buy the same yuan. As I see it, all we need to do is move the decimal point a few places in their 'sell' instructions, so that we end up being able to buy all the dollars they possess, for just a handful of yuan. Instead of 6 to 1, let's say we surreptitiously move it to…let's pick an exchange rate of say, 0.006 to 1. By doing that we could acquire their entire reserves at a minuscule cost: in the scheme of things, a pittance."

"You know, that may just work," responded Alex, feeling for the first time in weeks like they might just have alighted upon a viable solution. "I'm very confident we can get such a simple instruction into their software without detection; and it would be a small enough piece of coding to get through the barriers they have recently erected to stop any new malware."

Sebastian persisted with his list of market technicalities: "It's also absolutely critical Alex, that you also specify in the revised 'sell' instructions that the FX settlement is instantaneous and not the more normal next day: we don't want the Chinese having the slightest chance to refuse to settle these trades."

Mac pushed his way into the conversation, somewhat over-excitedly, his heart racing in a caffeine-induced high; "Assuming that our resident boffin here can accomplish this, then, as I see it Seb, the key to success is to be able instantly to scoop up the barrage of orders they intend to produce and buy absolutely everything they are selling. All in that micro-second before the rest of the market even sees it on their screens. That way, no one but us will see these trades. Please tell me Alex, that we now have the computer processing power to do that?"

"One hundred percent for sure Mac. We can set up our new mainframe linkages with the agencies to capture every dime they sell."

Sebastian continued, "You're probably aware that the Fed doesn't hold any yuan to make these purchases, but by glorious coincidence our good friends in the central banks of Brazil, Japan and Singapore do. Can you get Lewis to speak to these people? I'm sure they would be delighted to help, especially as they think they are about to get screwed on the currency exchange markets later in the day if our intelligence is correct. Once you have decided on how far to move the decimal point, do the calculations as to how many yuan we need and get it transferred to the Fed immediately. Is that feasible in the time we have left Alex?"

"I think so. I'll speak to Lewis and Alison the moment they arrive in the office, hopefully in a couple of hours' time, and get their approval to proceed. Oh and Seb, be prepared to have your ass kissed by a very grateful President; we might even get the Chairman involved as well!"

"Great, that will be a first. I'll leave you gentlemen to get some well-deserved rest. Let me know what the powers that be decided please." With that Seb put the phone receiver down and went next door to chat further with Lyn who was having a very early breakfast.

★ ★ ★

235

An hour earlier CJ had concluded a rousing thirty-minute TV interview for CNN which would go out on the early morning news in Hong Kong. His intention was simple: to put a stop to the carnage currently being endured by his loyal supporters in the pro-democracy movement and those innocent citizens caught up in the struggle. Confidence was high that it would be simultaneously broadcast by a hundred plus TV stations across the world, all of whom – judging by the phone calls of support now being received – seemed equally anxious to put pressure on the PRC to relent and change its approach.

CJ was heartened to hear from Colonel Sanford that the United States, Japan and Britain had jointly tabled a censure motion at the United Nations, condemning the violence in Hong Kong and calling for a cessation of hostilities and an immediate withdrawal of the riot troops back to mainland China. The US Department of State had also taken the unusual, indeed highly provocative, step of summoning the Chinese Ambassador to issue him with a *démarche* making its displeasure very clear. It also intimated, in far from diplomatic terms, that there would be grave consequences if the events in Hong Kong were not brought to a swift end.

In Washington DC, a Congressional debate on the matter had been scheduled for Monday afternoon, which judging by the vast numbers already registered to speak could last several days. Anger and utter dismay were the predominant moods on Capitol Hill, but those on the hawkish Right were now agitating for a much more robust response. The President, they said, must be seen by the Free World to act decisively. The political classes across the House were demanding answers to the disturbing question on every commentator's lips: 'Are we witnessing a new and unsettling military blueprint emerging in the East?'

Everyone agreed: martial law in Hong Kong was inconceivable in such a bastion of capitalism and free market thinking, especially as it followed so closely on the heels of a similar state of emergency being imposed by Chinese troops in Myanmar. It was an affront to human dignity, and – they argued vociferously – 'the pro-democracy movement must know it could count on the unwavering support of the United States, politically and, if necessary, militarily'.

There were also murmurings amongst the more senior members of the Senate that things were not well in the South China Sea, although detailed news had not reached them as yet on the specifics. It would only be a matter of time before the savvier politicos amongst them put two and two together.

If, into this already boiling pot was poured the imminent currency debacle, all hell would break loose, and the President would be backed into a corner. Many of his supporters felt that he would secretly enjoy getting embroiled in such a confrontation: after all, there were lots of unresolved scores to be settled; vital American interests were at stake; it was time to up the ante.

★ ★ ★

Alex, having spent half an hour pacing the tiny office he shared with Mac and brooding over the conversation with Seb, decided it was too important an issue to sit upon until office hours prevailed, and put in a call to Lewis. Despite being some ungodly hour in the morning, he took the call. Once he had understood the basic concept of what the pair of them intended to do, he immediately approved the "Decimal Point Plan", as it was now being called. Lewis said he would make the requisite calls to his fellow central bankers to assemble the required quantity of yuan; square away the technicalities and legalities with Alison in a couple of hours' time; and confidently predicted they would get presidential approval during their 7.30am conference call with the White House. "Make it happen guys!"

★ ★ ★

Admiral Farley was casually pacing the bridge as the early morning sea fog was beginning to lift, when he received confirmation that the nuclear submarine, Corpus Christie, (which he had deployed earlier) was now on-station. It was currently tailing the main Chinese flotilla at a distance of twenty nautical miles and appeared to be undetected. The sub's sealed orders were to be opened only when the USS Washington sent the code word, 'Intrepid Guard': the commander knew full well however, that it could contain only one instruction: "Sink the Liaoning".

Intercepted signals from the naval chiefs of staff in Beijing to their carrier fleet clearly indicated that they were being ordered to retake 'their reef' under cover of darkness later that day. The instruction was quite explicit: 'such an engagement was to be deliberately timed to take maximum advantage of the turmoil expected in the financial markets.' It pointedly continued, 'on absolutely no account should you proceed into combat before 10pm, Monday, August 22nd, China Standard Time'.

Farley immediately forwarded the signal to the Pentagon, with the suggestion that the President be immediately informed: it was yet one more piece of compelling evidence that this was a co-ordinated show of aggression.

★ ★ ★

The streets of Hong Kong were starting to fill up once more with banner-waving, and by now increasingly quarrelsome, student demonstrators. The working week had commenced in what could justifiably be described as a state of grave foreboding on both sides of the concrete barriers. The roads were overflowing with litter, torn placards and detritus of every kind; while the hospitals were filling up with the walking wounded. Worse still, there were now countless bodies in the mortuary.

Last night's curfew had been strictly and brutally enforced at those locations where the riot troops had gathered in sufficient numbers. Carnage ensued in several places near the most important government building which were by now heavily fortified. But in other locations, several of the local police force turned a hope-filled blind eye to most transgressors. There was still hope and, amongst the more single-minded freedom-fighters, cause for modest optimism.

By eight-thirty in the morning, cars, delivery trucks and motorbikes were once more buzzing hither and thither in pursuit of commerce of every kind; while the trams had cautiously restarted an hour or so before. Sanford and Lyn, meanwhile, decided it was sufficiently safe for CJ to return to his house on the Peak – if only temporarily – in order to collect fresh clothes and enable him to more readily contact his supporters.

The TV broadcast had been well received by the local community and a semblance of organisation was gradually and purposefully creeping back into the activities of the pro-democracy movement. CJ had previously circulated plans for another rally in the evening, starting at 9pm. He calculated that this was either foolhardy in the extreme, or would reach a crescendo by the time the markets opened in New York half an hour later. The question, as always, was 'how would the Beijing authorities react this time'?

★ ★ ★

The Cabinet Room at Number 10 was gradually filling up for the 9am meeting, when the Cabinet Secretary took Charles Sheer to one side and asked to have a private word with him. "I'm afraid the PM is not feeling too well Chancellor, bit faint apparently. Hardly surprising: I think he had about twenty quite intense meetings over the weekend and didn't get much sleep. He asked if you could chair the meeting as well as giving your own briefing. The medics have been and gone; but have told him to rest today."

"OK, please tell him that I will of course do that. Can you get me a synopsis of those meetings, please? Oh, and add that I hope he recovers soon; we need him at the helm."

Inside, however, he was fuming: 'I'll lay odds this is a smoke screen and the slippery bastard is trying to avoid the flak that's undoubtedly going to explode in my face later today'. He picked up his papers and wearily went back to meet his colleagues, with Lord Tennyson's "Into the Valley of Death" ringing in his head.

"Ladies and gentlemen, apparently the PM has regrettably had to take to his sickbed and can't be with us today. I'm told it's nothing serious. I know many of you have a very busy day ahead, as do I. So let's try and make this brief and finish no later than ten o'clock. I want also to make it absolutely clear that no one will speak to the press on financial matters, other than me. We are expecting a very tricky day for the pound, and I don't want to have to make a 'the markets have been especially turbulent today' Lamont speech, while pretending I love singing in the bath."

Deep inside, however, he knew this was completely unjustified bravado. Black Monday would once more be centre stage in the political lexicon. The only bright light, if one could express it as such, was that the currency rollovers for Singapore, Japan and Brazil would be handled by the London banks without undue drama in the next hour or two. Thanks to the Fed's self-interested largesse, the American hedge fund buyers were in place and ready to immediately buy the swaps if China decided to play hard-ball. But, as yet, the infinitely more troublesome dollar raid was the proverbial 'paddle-less canoe' heading straight over the waterfall. As the emergency cabinet meeting started, news of a possible solution had yet to reach him from the team in New York and he hadn't spoken to Sebastian for at least two days. He now had little choice but to seek approval from his colleagues to defend the pound and deplete the country's already strained reserves. The cabinet, of course, had little meaningful choice but to acquiesce. However, as this was utterly unexpected news to many of those around the table, the mood was sombre and the situation facing the country, they all agreed, was decidedly bleak.

The presentations by the Foreign Secretary and the Secretary of State for Defence were equally stark: while the geopolitical significance of the new landing strips being built in the Spratly Islands went over the heads of most of those present, Hong Kong was another matter altogether. 'Fat Pang' had never really been forgiven for handing back the former colony in 1997 – not that he had a choice – and now it looked like all their worries and fears for its future were about to be fulfilled. At least we had a couple of gunboats in the area, but precious little influence, other than a well drafted 'tut-tut' at the UN.

The Chancellor drew the meeting to an abrupt close as he was passed a note that the Governor of the Bank of England was patiently waiting in the adjacent room and needed to have confirmation of the cabinet's decision before preparing for the onslaught. "COBRA meeting at twelve noon please."

★ ★ ★

The bespectacled, completely bald, White House Chief of Staff was quite frankly the very last person on earth you would wish to encounter first thing on a Monday morning. He was regarded by everyone who had the misfortune to meet him as ill-mannered, uncouth and far too impertinent for his own good. It would take a team of the very best clinical psychologists in DC to pinpoint where his perpetual state of aggravation had come from....concluding, no doubt, he was still suffering from maternal deprivation and trauma during early childhood.

There was never a moment in his "exceptionally busy day"

when he was not publicly 'raging against the storm' caused by some, quite probably unintended slight, perpetrated against his beloved country; or the injustices resulting from some defamatory press statement; or when his ferocious temper was being directed at some junior member of his staff, for some as yet undisclosed misdemeanour, who was by now being flayed alive in some dark corner of the West Wing. Megalomania and staggering power in one person's hands are often cruel bedfellows. Others felt he had simply grown, over time, to imitate the behaviour and tactics of his boss.

His was always the first face to pop up on the conference screen, in this case punctually at exactly 7.30am, with a prepared blizzard of questions for the Chairman of the Federal Reserve and her unflappable deputy. The President, he informed them, was apparently delayed in another conversation with the Pentagon where there was an urgent need to clarify the battle orders to the USS Washington in the event that 'things kicked off'.

Alison Fletcher was, however, having none of his impudence. At her unflinching insistence they waited ten minutes in total silence until the President came on line. It was made perfectly clear that on such occasions she would only be dealing with the organ grinder.

"Mr President, I have two items of good news to impart. Firstly, you will recall that the sovereign currency swap contracts for Singapore, Brazil and Japan are to be rolled over today; these have now been completed in the London banking market without any drama and they are now under our direct control. It's not at all clear to me, however, that the Chinese leadership have actually appreciated, as yet, that we have taken this action. About twenty minutes after we had executed the numerous deals involved, they contacted each of the three central banks involved to say they were going to materially revise the terms – apparently oblivious that the deals had been cancelled.

Needless to say, I have asked them to stall their replies for a couple of hours, as you, or we, contemplate how best to use this information as leverage against the Chinese. There is just one curiosity to add. The person suggesting these revisions was not, as we would normally expect on such occasions, a communiqué from a director of the PBOC – instead it was from someone in the Politburo itself. That's never happened before.

Secondly, we have at last found a way to breach the security of the computer system which they will use to attack the dollar in a couple of hours time. It is our considered view that we should let them proceed with their plan and, with a little sprinkling of genius, acquire their entire US dollar reserves at the merest fraction of their value. They won't even know what hit them in the nano-second after they make the fatal mistake to proceed with their plan. It will be like shooting fish in a barrel, as my Texan colleague here so eloquently describes it."

Unlike many of his less illustrious predecessors, President Chessington was renowned as a lightning-fast decision maker; his critics would often, and rightly, say he was too quick for his own good at times. But, on this occasion he immediately knew he had the Chinese on the ropes. They would pay dearly for their temerity.

"OK, Madam Chairman, do it with my blessing. Call me at 9.31 and tell me the good news that they have initiated this heinous act against America and we have them by the balls. What time would it then be in Beijing?"

"Same time, but in the evening, Mr President."

"Perfect, I'll call their Premier at 9.32. No, on second thoughts, shall we let them stew until 10pm? Just tell me one more time this will not go wrong."

"You have my word on it, Sir," interjected Lewis.

With that the computer screens went blank, and an ominous silence filled the room. Alison turned to her colleague and quietly said:

"Very brave, Lewis. Very brave indeed. I hope you will grow to like the sea views from your suite at Alcatraz or somewhere equally unsavoury. If this goes wrong I can see us both being incarcerated behind bars for quite some time to come."

★ ★ ★

The Chancellor was making his way through the Cabinet Office corridors to chair the mid-day COBRA meeting when an aide handed him a brief note. In the stark, dispassionate, language of a civil service memo, it simply read: 'We have been informed by the Aylesbury police that they have been in attendance at the home of Sir John d'Abo in Haddenham and found a body, believed to be his. More details to follow from the Chief Constable." Charlie Sheer carefully placed the note in his jacket breast pocket. 'One problem dealt with', he thought. Now for the rest.

★ ★ ★

Having finished his conference call with the Chairman of the Federal Reserve, the President of the United States immediately placed a priority call to Admiral Farley.

"So, Jim, at precisely 9.31pm local time, unless you hear directly from me to the contrary, you are to let the bastards have it. Is that clear?"

"Perfectly clear Mr President."

★ ★ ★

Alex and Mac were now in their element, playing the ball on the front foot, confident of a home run, controlling the game. The complex computer linkages between the Fed, the NSA and GCHQ were now in place and following the necessary testing procedures, were fully functional. They had very carefully inserted the revised 'sell instructions' into the Chinese computer code without any alarm bells going off, to great sighs of relief. There was now about an hour to go before the markets opened: only then would they know for sure whether everything was going to work as anticipated.

Lewis, meanwhile, had made all the arrangements for the yuan to be transferred to New York and to be put under the control of Alex's company in Connecticut. SQT were now on stand-by to make the purchase of the dollars in exchange for Chinese currency. A collective decision had been made to move the decimal point three places to the left, thereby instantly rendering the value of China's dollar reserves to only one thousandth of its original value. This was going to hurt. In one press of a computer button, China would undo years of economic toil, commercial effort and the hard work of its citizens.

"Alex, my dear friend, I think I can sum up our position thus: as we are often heard to say down at my local pub, just before closing time, as the boys happily head off home to either the fury, or embrace, of their wives and sweethearts after having had more than one drink too many: 'the die is cast laddie'… our personal River Rubicon awaits."

"Never a truer word spoken, Mac. However, I prefer Lewis's more down-to-earth phrase, 'got them by the cojones', myself."

It was now simply a question of pacing the room, making futile gestures to tidy the office, filling the coffee pot, lighting a metaphorical candle to the gods; and silently letting the remaining minutes tick away.

★ ★ ★

On board the flight deck of the USS Washington, two F-22 Raptor stealth fighters were being readied for take-off. The lights on the carrier's airstrip turned green; the after-burners roared into action; the jets' brakes were released, and within seconds they were soaring at incredible speed, majestically borne aloft high into the night sky. Admiral Farley was dutifully following the explicit orders of his Commander in Chief, which he hoped would be the final act of the 'Intrepid Guard' mission.

The two pilots were tasked to fly due North on a bearing taking them directly over the enemy fleet and thereafter onto Guangzhou, into decidedly hostile territory. Their laser-guided weapons systems had already been programmed, the target's co-ordinates now irrevocably set. The most advanced airplane in the world was now entirely reliant on its unique stealth capabilities to evade detection; if they failed, they knew that the US Carrier Task Force faced instant retaliation. They had absolutely zero intention of failing.

★ ★ ★

All afternoon the half dozen Chinese programmers had been putting the final touches to their masterpiece. They had done exactly what their paymasters had demanded of them, and were by now basking in the glowing praise being heaped upon them by their grateful superiors. The time had at last come to leave the grime and the clutter they had endured for the past month, and enthusiastically await their promised enormous recompense. The programmes they had painstakingly created were then ceremonially switched on to automatic transmission, with the instructions to proceed being irreversible. Neither man nor machine could now change this particular course of history. They collected their meagre belongings; said fond goodbyes to each other, knowing full well they would never meet again; locked the warehouse door behind them; and stepped into the waiting fleet of cars.

★ ★ ★

Sebastian had decided at the last moment to accompany Lyn and Sanford through the crowded streets of the city to hear CJ's speech. It was being billed by the local TV stations as a pivotal moment for the democratic process. The numerous social media sites of Facebook and Twitter were almost overwhelmed with activity, first anticipating and then confidently predicting the outcome of the rally. Everyone was playing their part in identifying imminent trouble spots and vociferously encouraging support. There was no way he could possibly miss this, despite the dangers involved and the insistence of his colleagues that if he got kidnapped again, the cavalry might be otherwise engaged.

All who were there that balmy summer's evening later recalled it as a truly bravura, indeed virtuoso, performance by CJ; who spoke eloquently and movingly of the absolute need for autonomous governance in Hong Kong and the inherent justice of the cause they all subscribed to. By now, the immense crowd was boisterous and rowdy in the extreme, cheering each and every word uttered by him. They left the greatest roar of the evening for the rallying cry, "Now is the time to seize our electoral freedom from the oppressive clutches of Beijing". To a man, woman and child, everyone symbolically linked arms, waved their pro-democracy banner or held aloft an item of yellow clothing. Every moment of the spectacle was being beamed across the world to an audience transfixed by the images on their televisions.

The crowd surged forward towards the stage where CJ was addressing the assembly, everyone noisily shouting their approval, making it impossible for Sanford to catch the detail of the incoming message on his earpiece which was linked directly to the Pentagon. He did, however, look at his watch: 9.20pm. He gathered Lyn and Sebastian together and told them they must immediately go back to the CIA office and get clarification of what precisely had been said. They left a note with Sapphire, asking her to swing by the situation room with CJ, assuming that was feasible, when the rally had finished. Above the nonstop hullabaloo, Sanford could only decipher one clear message: that he should anticipate an important announcement some time towards midnight.

★ ★ ★

The countdown to 9.30am was approaching far too rapidly as 'the boys' nervously gathered in their tiny office. Each was ready to humbly embrace their moment of triumph, or face the unthinkable financial apocalypse that would surely await them if their plan failed. All the detailed systems checks had been positive; everyone and everything was in its place; the ultra-precise atomic clock, blinking unfailingly on their wall, registered a few more seconds to D-Day. They had at their disposal the most amazing array of computer power ever assembled, all carefully aligned to take the fight to the enemy at the speed of light. All hoped and prayed that they were now ready to play whatever curved-ball was to be thrown at them.

As if by some 'divine magic', privy only to those in the inner sanctum of the citadel, the row after row of computer monitors directly in front of Lewis, Alex and Mac flickered into life. It was as if they had been taken back in time to Coney Island, circa 1905, when a million new-fangled electric lights at Luna Park illuminated the night sky for miles around. The simply staggering amount of 'sell orders' cascading down the rolling screen were stupendous to behold; it was matched only by the activities on the other monitor, where every 'sell' instruction was met by an equal and opposite 'buy' instruction. In less than the blink of an eye it was all over. The screens went blank once more. The deed had at last been done. They stared at each other in utter awe. Alex's colleagues at SQT were now the proud owners of $1.3 trillion, bought for a song. The normal yuan-dollar exchange rate had not moved at all, not one iota, indicating that the 'normal' FX traders at their desks that Monday morning had not even noticed it had happened. They had scooped the jackpot completely and utterly off the radar: the treasure pick pocketed from the very vaults of China's very own 'Dark Pool'. Best of all, as yet, no one had the slightest idea it had happened. All hell had been prevented; now to tell the President.

★ ★ ★

The Oval Office was full to overflowing with White House officials, all seven members of the Joint Chiefs of Staff, and a representative collection of Senators, Congressmen and various House Committee Chairmen. Not surprisingly they were all anxious to know why they had been summoned to this particular meeting, furtively described as being 'of strategic national importance'.

At 9.45 the President entered the Oval Office from one of the private side rooms, clearly in high spirits, accompanied by the Chairman of the Federal Reserve. If there had been a fanfare of trumpets, it would not have been out of place.

"Ladies and gentlemen please be seated. I've called you here today because I wanted you to listen in while I make a call to President Liú-Sūn of China."

The phone on the historic and deeply symbolic Resolute partners desk – a gift from Queen Victoria and the setting for endless photo opportunities throughout the years – buzzed once.

"The President of the People's Republic of China is on the line, Sir."

"Mr President, I need to speak with you urgently on a matter of grave importance. Thank you for making yourself available. Earlier this morning we had a rather interesting couple of minutes on the foreign exchange markets here in New York, which we need to discuss and, if possible, resolve. It appears that one of our larger, more nimble-footed, hedge funds has acquired your entire dollar foreign exchange reserves for a fraction of their real value. I'm sure it was some unintended, easily explainable mistake on your central bank's part. Regrettably, however, this action seems to have upset some of my Generals here, who think it was a deliberate act designed to sabotage the United States and destabilise the world financial markets to your country's advantage. Would you care to comment on that before we decide what to do about this potentially grave matter?"

President Chessington looked up to the assembled onlookers and slowly raised his right hand to indicate he was tightly squeezing the balls of his counterpart in China.

"I can categorically assure you Mr President, that I know absolutely nothing about this incident. How could our dollar reserves have been sold like this? That's preposterous!"

"All true, I'm afraid. I'm also sending you copies of various messages we have intercepted over the past month, and some very interesting computer gobble-de-gook which I'm sure the world will conclude demonstrates beyond all doubt, that your government initiated a deliberate act of financial sabotage against my country."

By now the President was flamboyantly waving two squeezed hands in the air. He had every intention of making this very painful indeed.

"But this has never been discussed, considered, approved, permitted or indeed initiated by any of my staff, or the Politburo. I can assure you that I have personally no knowledge of this incident whatsoever. Could you just repeat again please: one of your hedge fund companies has somehow acquired our entire dollar reserves?"

You could sense the incredulity and disbelief in the

Premier's voice, as he issued a hurried volley of instructions at some hapless secretary who was scrambling to reach the head of the PRC's central bank.

"Sorry to spring this upon you over dinner, but the proof is incontrovertible. As we say here, you've been caught red-handed. If I were you, I'd check with your Minister of Finance. The question is, Mr President, what are we going to do about it? I've asked the rating agencies to swing on by the White House later to clarify what happens to your country's financial standing when it's discovered you have no dollars in the vault any more. I gather that's not going to go down well. I think the phrase used was 'a blood bath'. So, the time has come to address what we require by way of concessions to get you out of this mess, which I should add for emphasis, is entirely of your own making."

"Just one minute please Mr. President, I have the Chairman of our central bank on the other line. May I put you on hold for two minutes while I endeavour to clarify what is going on here?"

The line went dead. Silence evocatively filled the room, reminding everyone present of those eerie voids so often to be found in a play by Samuel Beckett. When the Premier eventually came back onto the line, his tone of voice had changed markedly.

"Mr. President, it would appear you are correct, although once again I reiterate that this must be the action of some rogue elements working without my approval or permission. Nonetheless, I've been informed that we intend to cancel the transaction immediately and declare it null and void."

"I wish it were that easy; but it's all gone through the clearing system fifteen minutes ago and been – I think the technical term is – 'settled' in the normal course of events on the foreign exchange markets. The Chairman of the Federal Reserve is here with me in the Oval Office and she assures me that the transaction is irreversible by you; but as a magnanimous gesture of goodwill on our part, we could agree to describe the whole unsavoury business as…what was the term you used Alison… ah yes, the infamous 'Fat Finger Syndrome'. Funny language these guys use, don't you think."

If ever a presidential smile could define a moment in a person's destiny, the silent click of the official White House photographer's camera had managed to capture it perfectly.

"So once again, here are our immutable terms to get you out of this mess. We will keep quiet about this unpleasant business for twenty-four hours while you ratify our demands with the Politburo and make a public announcement outlining the actions you will now take. Our requirements are simple and very straightforward. One, you declare free, unconditional, and immediate elections in Hong Kong. Set a date for a month hence. Two, you formally abandon the newly constructed airstrip in the Spratly Islands that you have built on Fiery Cross Reef. You will officially hand it back to the Philippines, and renounce all territorial rights over this area of the South China Sea. Perhaps you could also move your carrier group out of the area as well; they are making an awful nuisance of themselves right now and I'm sure you would like to ensure they all return safely to their loved-ones. Three, you immediately make peace with Japan over the Senkaku Islands."

He paused momentarily to let the list of demands be fully absorbed by the Chinese Premier before continuing:

"There, not so bad really; I'm sure you've had worse at the dentist. In return, I guarantee you will have your funds back by noon tomorrow and you can demonstrate to the world what an incredibly farsighted and magnanimous politician you are."

"I will be back to you with my answer in one hour Mr President."

"Make that thirty minutes, we are awfully busy here." With that he clicked the phone dead and looked up from the desk to behold a sea of frozen faces almost dumbstruck with what they had just heard.

"OK guys, get off to work. I'm taking bets they will be back within twenty minutes. Any takers? Alison, a moment of your time, please."

When the room had finally cleared, he said: "I'm assuming they will begrudgingly agree to all of my demands. Money always talks, although you can bet your bottom dollar – sorry, inappropriate phrase in the circumstances – that they will put all of these matters straight back on the political agenda in a couple of years' time. But, today's near-disaster buys us some diplomatic space to find a permanent solution to these issues. You may also be interested to know that I've already taken definitive steps to totally incapacitate their ability to do this again; so when we reverse the transaction can you conduct it central bank to central bank. I'm sure you can manage to prise the money out of Diddly-Squat's sticky mitts somehow. You can tell Bill and Dwight that I said they are rich enough already."

"Certainly, Mr President, I'm sure that's not going to be a problem."

"Oh, Alison, can you get your team round here in a couple of days' time, for a photo call and a congratulatory drink. Praise and honours for all I think."

"I'm willing to bet my number two has already drunk the bar dry, Sir."

"I'll bet he has: Texan, what more can you say! Plus, see if you can persuade the UK Chancellor to attend, it would be a fine gesture on our behalf to sprinkle some fairy dust on his party's election chances, and thank him for his invaluable contribution to the Special Relationship and so forth. Oh, and could you also arrange for 'Decimal Point Man' to come along as well; I'd like to meet him."

★ ★ ★

Towards midnight, the totally unexpected news of China's inevitable capitulation to all the terms demanded earlier by the United States was greeted with unrestrained jubilation: Beijing had made a complete and unconditional *volte-face* on the Hong Kong elections. Everyone had assembled – champagne glasses in hand – at Sanford's temporary office deep within CIA headquarters in Central. They had gathered to hear him relay the details and finer points of the US-China settlement, but frankly they could hardly believe what they were hearing.

The President had called personally to let him be one of the first to know the momentous change his team had masterminded. Despite the hour, the streets were still heaving with vociferous protestors still waving their yellow umbrellas in defiance. To the relief of all, the level of violence had subsided significantly and the riot troops, thankfully, had by now melted into the dark.

As yet, the crowds were largely unaware of the historic outcome of the presidential phone call; the bare bones of which the TV stations were only just beginning to stream on the ticker-tape news displayed at the bottom of the screens.

CJ, who had arrived about thirty minutes earlier, was totally emotionally drained having managed this time to conclude his speech, receiving a rapturous ovation. On hearing the proposed changes in the election process, he was already engrossed in making detailed plans for the forthcoming elections. They all agreed it was time to have a serious all-night celebration before the team was dispersed back to their other less dramatic duties; and back to a time before this whole adventure had overwhelmed them all.

Sanford had been told he was required to report later tomorrow evening on board the USS Washington, where he was to be the guest of honour at a formal ceremony to recognise his elevation to one star General. He had also been given the very agreeable duty of conferring upon Lyn Andrews the rank of Major, with a suggestion that she might wish to take a couple of weeks R&R in London.

★ ★ ★

Moments earlier, Sebastian had held a brief conversation with Charlie Sheer, who was anxious to tell him of John d'Abo's untimely death before he heard it from anyone else. As was only to be expected, this shocking news temporarily dampened the festivities, which were now in full swing in the other room. The Chancellor made it perfectly clear however, that he could expect a period of serious hero worship from the government on his return; cryptically adding, "When the details behind your boss's bereavement will be explained". In the euphoria of the moment this particular comment completely passed him by. He was anxious to return to the newly-promoted Lyn and the festivity, fully intent to make it through to dawn with any of the team still left standing.

They had flamboyantly arranged for the 'company plane' to take them back to the UK in style, and *en route* to drop Sanford off in the Philippines. Sapphire, on being asked in front of everyone, if she would graciously agree to accompany him to the ceremonies, responded enigmatically that 'she would be delighted, but only on the strict proviso that they reprise the "tu-tu-ku" rhythms of the previous night in her apartment'. Lyn beamed and winked at her in a conspiratorial, all knowing, 'women-of-the-world' way. More champagne was once more passed around; it clearly would not be too long before tables were being danced upon. 'Once more with feeling' instantly became the *cri de coeur* of this newly-established, very rarefied and elite fraternity.

They all boarded the aircraft together in a somewhat fragile state, having said farewell to CJ, Reed and Bain; the latter two of whom were made of sterner stuff and waved them goodbye from the airport bar having had a most welcome "heart reviver".

On the last leg of the journey back to London, Lyn suggested that, as they were now alone for the first time in days, and shortly to be passing over the land of the Karma Sutra, they should try the 'Indrani', which she described as 'the best position for the gentleman who is packing a little extra downstairs.'

"Quite", said Sebastian.

CHAPTER TWENTY FOUR

The Fourth Estate, D++

In the days and weeks that followed what erudite financial historians would subsequently describe, (when the, more-or-less, true story eventually filtered out into the public domain), as 'a close run thing' for the mighty US dollar, some very insightful readers across the world may well have been able to piece together a much clearer picture of what actually happened behind the scenes on that auspicious day in August. The *dramatis personae* were, for the most part, not national or international figures, presidents or prime ministers, but simply bit players hoofing away at the back of the chorus line 'doing their bit'. Many were the unfortunate victims of friendly fire, others malicious revenge; almost all had their lives altered forever. Only those who were very close to them were aware of the profound changes the events had wrought.

Within the London offices of the Times newspaper, the distinguished editor of the Register – which daily announced the alliterative, 'beginnings, betrothals and bereavements' of the great and good – was sitting quietly working on the usual Royal Family obituary updates, which he tirelessly undertook once a month. It was exceptionally unusual for the paper's illustrious Editor to ever visit his humble desk, but there he was directly in front of him. He felt sure he was about to be fired, as His Holiness was accompanied by a couple of rather thick-set types, who clearly were from 'security'. At any moment they would be giving him a black bin bag and clearing out the contents of his desk, while slinging him unceremoniously on to the street to face a life of penury.

"Miguel, these rather threatening chaps here are from MI6 and they have an entry they would like us to make in tomorrow's paper. Sorry, let me politely rephrase that: not like, but categorically insist. Whatever you were doing on the d'Abo matter, I want you to stop it immediately. These bastions of law and order insist you withdraw, and permanently destroy, anything regarding d'Abo that you've sent to the printers or have on your computer. Apparently, the invisible 'powers that be' want us to print the following text in tomorrow's edition: matter of national importance and all that. Absolutely no changes, understood!"

Retirement can't come soon enough, thought Miguel, who took the extensive note proffered him by the paper's pin-striped, bow-tie wearing Editor. He prided himself on the exactitude of his 'obit' entries – be it for obscure punk rockers, deranged politicians or Nobel Prize winners – all were treated with the same level of respect, courtesy and meticulous precision. A lifetime of scrupulous attention to the finest of fine details was to be thrown in the bin. He read the suggested wording with a mixture of incredulity and contempt: nothing could have been further from the truth. Abandoning the principles of a lifetime in journalism, he mechanically began to typeset the obituary of Sir John d'Abo that had just been handed to him.

'... died of a sudden and unexpected heart attack at his country house in Buckinghamshire on Sunday evening having had a noble and distinguished career in the City ... the latter part of which was dedicated to unflinching public service at the behest of the Chancellor, Mr. Sheer ... immediately prior to his untimely death he was secretly leading a team of international bankers and officials to resolve the dispute with China over the US dollar ... however, it would appear that the future of d'Abo's Merchant Bank is now uncertain ... the Prime Minister issued an effusive statement from Number 10 Downing Street thanking him and his colleagues for their valiant efforts ... pouring praise on Sir John's unstinting hard work for the nation .... who would be forever grateful for his patriotic dedication to his country .... a man who would be sorely missed ... he leaves a wife, but no children.'

With the men from the security services looking intently and menacingly over his shoulder, Miguel carefully deleted (or as he preferred to call it, 'spiked') the previous draft text he had carefully written. Perhaps, he thought, the 'great and the good' in their wisdom don't want to despoil the reputation of the man who – he knew full well – had in fact died of, what his unimpeachable sources told him, were self-inflicted gunshot wounds. He had not yet managed to complete his own paragraph dealing with the question of d'Abo's demise, or indeed murder. The real truth, such as it was, would undoubtedly be buried with him.

★ ★ ★

'Le Figaro' devoted one solitary column inch to a report that the daughter of a prominent industrialist, Miss Anne-Sophie Moreau, had been arrested at the *Gare du Nord* in Paris, having earlier caught the Eurostar from London. It inferred that she was now in custody facing 'very serious', undisclosed, charges. She would never be seen, or heard of, again.

★ ★ ★

By contrast, the prospects for d'Abo's wife, according to the glossy magazine 'Hello', were decidedly looking up. In a somewhat salacious piece – featuring a considerable photo montage of décolleté-filled silk tops, tight jodhpurs and riding crops – they had printed a four-page spread of Lady Isobel basking in the arms of one of the world's most famous polo players, just days after the death of her husband. It reported that she was at the Palace of Versailles, attending some swish equestrian event or other, when the news was announced of her husband's untimely death; but, the article impertinently implied, she was "taking the grief in her stride".

Friends commented that she had never looked more radiant draped on the arm of Argentina's multi-millionaire team captain, who had a very impressive polo handicap of 10 and bulges in all the right places. It continued with the authoritative throwaway line that she had been having a secret liaison with the bounder for years. There was growing speculation that she would be leaving shortly for a new life in South America, just as soon as she had sorted out the ownership and future management of the family bank.

★ ★ ★

The Financial Times, in a related and lengthy editorial, wondered if Sebastian Fortes – now accorded super-star status for his role in the 'dollar affair', and who had recently been appointed a CBE for his efforts – would take the helm at the bank. Lady Isobel's recently-acquired penchant for new blood had led her to publicly indicate that Sebastian would be her preferred choice to succeed her husband, although a decision was some way off. There had been speculation within earlier editions of the FT that she would sell the bank, but this rumour had now dampened down and the City was once again expecting a new era to dawn at d'Abos under the newly invigorated management team. There was even strong gossip in the US market, fuelled by a piece in the Wall Street Journal, that d'Abos Merchant Bank would link up with Saturn Quantum Trading in Connecticut, thereby bring together the "dynamic duo" of

Sebastian Fortes and Dr Alex Cadbury to create the ultimate financial powerhouse. All involved refused to comment on press tittle-tattle and speculation… "for the time being."

★ ★ ★

On the faded notice board of the Hong Kong Ladies' Recreation Club hardly a soul noticed or cared that the two Ians, always Bain and Reed to their friends, were now 'joint first' on the club's squash ladder. They had enjoyed a particularly arduous game earlier in the day, but by now had totally forgotten who had won: such is the effect on their camaraderie that a second pitcher of Bloody Marys induces. Their conversation was very animated, as was often the case when together, on the topic of the forthcoming elections and their newly acquired friend CJ's chances of success. The drinks were being heartily consumed, as per normal, on the balcony overlooking the tennis courts. The sense of occasion emboldened Reed to suggest they undertake the Iron Man challenge together next year; when, he modestly suggested, the recovery to his gammy leg would make him invincible. Or possibly they should take up golf, or hang gliding. They ordered another pitcher of bloodies in order to give the matter the consideration it duly deserved.

★ ★ ★

The South China Post had dedicated literally thousands of column inches to the events in Hong Kong, where CJ had now formally declared his intention to run for the presidency of the Legislative Council. Under enormous international political pressure, Beijing had at last relented and formally relaxed its grip on who could participate in the process; much to the welcome applause of liberally-minded commentators from across the free world. The consensus of opinion was that CJ would be swept to victory following his 'heroic interventions' to pacify the riots and bring calm back to the streets. Under his leadership – the paper's front page headline blazed in size 30 fonts – the pro-democracy movement was now planning to contest every one of the seventy seats in the Council, where major changes were now inevitable. There was even a rumour in Hong Kong that Sebastian Fortes had been secretly offered the role of Financial Secretary by CJ, should he win the forthcoming election.

★ ★ ★

The China Daily, and that other organ of state control, China Central Television, were ferocious in their venom, bile and vitriol for the humiliation inflicted upon the country by America. Treachery and political plotting, naturally, were never far from the surface in China; even if very few people outside those at the top table were aware of it. In this case however, the press and TV had publicly directed their incandescent rage at the seven maverick members of the Politburo who the leadership were blaming for dragging China into conflict with the United States and possible economic ruin. The two ring-leaders were to be expelled from the party and immediately executed for treason following a rapid and entirely sham trial. The five other miscreant 'capitalist lap-dogs', 'flies and tigers', who were accused of abandoning their country for political gain and personal enrichment, would spend the rest of their miserable lives in prison chains, as close to the Arctic circle as they could be forcibly dragged.

More prosaically, page six of the local newspaper in Guangzhou reported a mysterious and exceptionally violent explosion, which it attributed to a dangerously leaking gas main. No one would ever have thought to link this event – which, the paper noted, took place around 9.45 on the evening of August 22nd at a disused warehouse on some obscure industrial estate on the outskirts of the city - with the demise of the "gang of seven", or some meaningless petty squabble over a reef thousands of miles away.

In this insignificant vignette of provincial Chinese life, there appeared to be no report of any deaths, although the building in question was completely flattened by the mysterious blast. The paper was therefore dutifully encouraging all other tenants on the estate to carefully check their own gas supplies for further leaks. It reported that several local officials were being questioned by the police in respect of a failure to follow the approved inspection routines, which apparently – despite there being substantial payments made to cover such things – had not taken place as required for the past three years. Accusations of petty corruption and dilatory practices were being vigorously investigated, and further actions against the people concerned could not be ruled out. Few people gave a fig.

★ ★ ★

No one, outside North Korea's ruling elite and the Central News Agency, paid a moment's attention to an equally obscure piece in the leading party newspaper *Rodong Sinmun*. In an article entitled 'Our Strong and Prosperous Nation', casual mention was made of the imminent closure of Bureau 39; (naturally there was no explanation forthcoming about exactly what it did, or why it did it); and its replacement by a newly-invigorated agency, dedicated to the spread of communist zeal, North Korean style, throughout the world. Central Command, it faithfully reported, would be dedicating considerable resources to this endeavour and entreating its new officers and staff to complete their Glorious Leader's work. It conspicuously failed to mention the countless arrests that followed the disclosure of those names who had been the beneficiaries of the Bureau's previous largesse. Prison cells across the globe were gradually filling up with dishonest politicians, industrial magnates and government officials all caught in the headlights of the CIA's disclosure of who exactly received what, by way of crooked and shady payments.

Press barons in the affected countries who, somehow, by the grace of God, managed to escape being tainted by the corruption themselves, delighted in their close scrape with the authorities. They seemed almost overjoyed to describe such munificent back-hander's and staggeringly extravagant bribes, as more akin to wheelbarrows full of folding notes than the usual insignificant daily production of welcome brown envelopes.

Meanwhile, in a tiny provincial newspaper in Casper, Wyoming, the real estate pages of the 'Star Tribune' took great pleasure in announcing the sale of yet another delightful rural property. It didn't disclose that the purchaser was Mr. Chang Jin-soo and his lovely wife and daughter; primarily because the authorities had taken great care to conceal their identity. A life of pleasant domestic obscurity now awaited the newly-arrived family as they unpacked their belongings and gratefully raised the Stars and Stripes on the flagpole in their new back garden.

★ ★ ★

The UK press – having satiated themselves on the brilliant role played by those "Plucky Brits in the City of London" who had saved the world from those ghastly Johnny-Foreigners – were now engrossed in the forthcoming general election. The opinion polls were neck and neck, when the Prime Minister suffered the first of what turned out to be a series of heart murmurs; eventually diagnosed as aortic sclerosis. Given the resultant "highly-elevated cardiac risk", the papers reported that the PM felt he had little option but to resign on health grounds and hand over the mantle of power to his Chancellor. Charlie Sheer was still riding high on a wave of goodwill following the publicity he had received, and glowing words of tribute garlanded upon him from the President of the United States, for his role in saving the dollar. His deputy and increasingly popular protégée, Amanda Price, was immediately promoted to be the new Chancellor. The leadership change was warmly welcomed by the press ("the new dream team") and described as an opportunity for a clean sweep in British politics. Both of the new incumbents instinctively knew that electoral success was within their grasp. The opinion pollsters agreed.

Her first action on entering Number 11 Downing Street, however, was worthy of Machiavelli himself: she carefully placed into her personal safe two very important documents. She just happened to have kept the duplicate copy of the d'Abo loan document, embarrassingly and flamboyantly signed by Sheer, the original of which he had subsequently shredded; and the 'real', untampered with, coroner's report on Sir John d'Abo's death. These, she reasoned, were not only her insurance policy against the vagaries of power and the eventual treachery from friend and foe alike that automatically went with the territory: they would eventually prove her ticket to Number 10 itself.